Praise for Claudia Mair Burney and

Murder, Mayhem & a Fine Man

"This novel showcases Burney's talents not only in the characterization and writing departments, but also proves she can craft a sweet love story–cum–mystery and do a little psychological delving in the process."

–*Blogcritics*

"Amanda Bell Brown is a refreshing addition to the cast of today's amateur sleuths."

–*Mysterious Reviews*

"Funny as heck, very touching, climactic, and most importantly real. . . . A wonderful combination of Christian lit, romance, comedy, and mystery."

–*Romance in Color*

"Amanda Bell is one funny, sassy, intelligent package deal! Claudia Mair Burney has an infectious style that leaves her readers laughing out loud and begging for more. . . . The dialogue is fresh and funny, at times totally unexpected, but a delightful change of pace."

–*Christian Bookworm Reviews*

"Funny, smart, self-deprecating, and strong, Amanda Bell Brown is the best private psychologist-sleuth to emerge in religious fiction in decades."

–Phyllis Tickle, author of the Divine Hours series

"A sassy, intelligent, church-girl-whodunit romance! Get out the Godivas, wiggle into your fuzzy slippers, and enjoy this hold-your-breath read! Way cool!"

–Sharon Ewell Foster, author of
The Resurrection of Nat Turner

"Claudia Mair Burney does a great job of blending mystery, romance, humor, and Christian truth to create a story that is hard to put down. I laughed out loud and I teared up, but I never stopped turning the pages."

–Angela Benson, author of *The Amen Sisters*

"Seamlessly combines sass, smarts, and spirituality. Burney draws characters you love, and her page-turning story line integrates faith beautifully into the plot. Sign me up for the fan club!"

–Lisa Samson, author of *Quaker Summer*

Books by Claudia Mair Burney

AMANDA BELL BROWN MYSTERY SERIES

Deadly Charm
Death, Deceit & Some Smooth Jazz
Murder, Mayhem & a Fine Man

EXORSISTAH SERIES

The Exorsistah
The Exorsistah: X Restored
The Exorsistah: X Returns

OTHER TITLES

God Alone Is Enough: A Spirited Journey with Teresa of Avila
Zora and Nicky: A Novel in Black and White
Wounded: A Love Story

Murder, Mayhem & a fine man

an amanda bell brown mystery

Claudia Mair
Burney

POCKET BOOKS

New York   London   Toronto   Sydney   New Delhi

Pocket Books
A Division of Simon & Schuster, Inc.
1230 Avenue of the Americas
New York, NY 10020

This book is a work of fiction. Any references to historical events, real people, or real places are used fictitiously. Other names, characters, places, and events are products of the author's imagination, and any resemblance to actual events or places or persons, living or dead, is entirely coincidental.

First Pocket Books paperback edition July 2013

POCKET and colophon are registered trademarks of Simon & Schuster, Inc.

For information about special discounts for bulk purchases, please contact Simon & Schuster Special Sales at 1-866-506-1949 or business@simonandschuster.com.

The Simon & Schuster Speakers Bureau can bring authors to your live event. For more information or to book an event contact the Simon & Schuster Speakers Bureau at 1-866-248-3049 or visit our website at www.simonspeakers.com.

Manufactured in the United States of America

10 9 8 7 6 5 4 3 2 1

ISBN 978-1-4767-2710-3
ISBN 978-1-4165-6504-8 (ebook)

In remembrance of a saint, my great-grandmother,
Amanda Bell Brown
1886–1975
Memory Eternal

acknowledgments

M ANY, MANY THANKS TO:
Philis Boultinghouse, for unwavering belief in me.

Chip MacGregor, for being an extraordinary agent and ferocious beast on my behalf, and a very fine man and friend.

Beth Jusino, Tiger Girl, for earning your stripes on this one.

Lissa Halls Johnson, for dancing with me once again.

Friends who supported me through both joyous and difficult seasons: you know who you are. But I have to call the names of a few of you: Lisa Samson, Marilynn Griffith, and Don Pape, I wouldn't be here without you. Terry, Heather, Paula, Lori, Dee, Stacia, Mark, Sam and Bethany, Alison, Ginger, Kim, and Jeff, you're my stretcher-bearers, and you're the best! Gail Burwell and Evette Drouilliard, you're always in my "amen" corner.

Family, you are my inspiration, especially: my amaz-

x   acknowledgments

ing husband, Ken, Mama, Latrecia Stone, Mom, Rutha
Burney, and my "Carly," Carlean Smith. I'm waving at
you up there in heaven, Daddy; James Hawthorne. Uncle
Jasper McLaurin, thanks for the medical advice.

Joe, thanks for all that Jazz.

Amanda Bell Brown mystery fans, thanks for waiting for my change to come.

Burney/Bandeles, I don't know how you put up
with me. I love you.

Thank you, Lord Jesus Christ, Son of the living God;
have mercy on me, a sinner.

The Lord's Prayer

Our Father which art in heaven, Hallowed be thy name.
Thy kingdom come, Thy will be done
in earth as it is in heaven.
Give us this day our daily bread.
And forgive us our debts, as we forgive our debtors.
And lead us not into temptation, but deliver us from evil:
For thine is the kingdom, and the power,
and the glory, for ever.
Amen.

Matthew 6:9–13 KJV

Murder,
Mayhem &
a fine man

chapter
one

I HAD EVERY REASON to be peeved, and I told Carly so.

"Why didn't you just get me a T-shirt that says, 'I turned thirty-five today, and all I got was the chance to poke around at a crime scene'?"

" 'And this lousy T-shirt.' Don't forget that part," Carly added with a grin.

"And I'll bet that lousy T-shirt would be small enough to fit a toddler."

"It's okay. I'd have given you a Wonderbra to go with it. Happy birthday, sis!"

Honestly, she's just like our mother.

Carly, unlike our mother, is a medical examiner and happened to be on call that night. I knew I shouldn't have gone out to dinner with her, but frankly, I didn't have anything more compelling to do than watch a boxed set of the newly released season of *CSI: Crime Scene*

Investigation—my birthday present to myself. Carly had offered to buy me a Cajun dinner at Fishbones instead. She'd already purchased a saucy little dress and matching shoes for me from one of the high-end boutiques she can afford but I can't. Still, I would rather have watched *Crime Scene Investigation* on TV than be involved in one.

I shot her the evil eye.

Carly had insisted she take me out because, being Carly, she couldn't imagine my choice of how to spend my birthday evening. "C'mon, Bell. You can't spend your thirty-fifth birthday holed up in your apartment watching television."

"It's not television. It's a DVD," I told her, but she was talking right over me—as usual.

"And how can a psychologist be depressed? What's up with that?" To her, the idea of a depressed psychologist bordered on heresy.

"Why can't I be depressed?" I paused to give her my best sassy glare. "Don't medical examiners die? What's up with *that*?"

She sighed and said, "DVD or not, *CSI* is a TV show." She poked her lips out in the mock outrage I'd seen her play many times before. "And pathologists do not die."

I looked at her.

"They expire," she said, followed by a wicked grin. I smiled in spite of myself.

"Then I'm not really depressed. I'm having an *episode*."

I'd spoken the gospel truth about that. Even if I *had* been mowed down by a full-blown clinical depression, there would be good reasons for it. I'd never married. I'd just turned *thirty-five*. I was halfway to seventy! And I had a raging case of endometriosis, which, according to my doctor, meant I shouldn't wait a whole lot longer before trying to make a baby. Only problem was—I lacked a man. I had no significant other, husband, boyfriend, main squeeze, or any other variation of that theme. No knight in shining armor had appeared, magnanimously holding a test tube full of his little soldiers, mine for the taking.

We continued the argument all the way from Greek Town, stopping only when we pulled up in front of the house surrounded by bolts of yellow crime-scene tape.

Carly stopped her black Escalade next to two police cruisers, their light bars splashing colors against the house and trees. Groups of people—some still in their nightclothes—huddled on the sidewalk. The yellow crime-scene tape halted any looky-loos from getting too curious or too close for their own good. I glanced out the passenger window at the house. It looked awfully familiar. Number 2345—a small white house nestled in a ghetto upgrade neighborhood. Nothing about the nondescript ranch stood out. So why did a nagging uneasiness tug at me the moment I set eyes on it?

Number 2345—the one that sits a little farther back than the others.

I vaguely recalled, at some time or another, actually writing down directions to this very house. *I've been here before.*

A blue unmarked Crown Victoria pulled up beside us.

Carly thrust her gearshift into park and turned off the ignition. She fluffed her long black hair and wagged her eyebrows at me. "Honey, God is smiling on you. A yummy birthday treat has just arrived." With no other explanation, she jumped out of the SUV. About three seconds later, I understood why.

He was stunning. Tall, but not too tall, and lightly tanned. He sported the classic boys-in-the-hood do—impeccably groomed brown curls, a little high on the top, with a fade on the sides—and he wore it well.

This white guy has been hanging around the brothers.

Wait.

I took another lingering look.

Is this white guy a brother? Or isn't he?

He possessed the kind of exotic good looks that appeared to be an ambiguous blend of races—at least black, white, and Latino. He must have pulled all the fine out of that multicultural gene pool. Mr. United Nations had on a gray lightweight wool suit, tailored to perfection. His white button-down shirt had been starched to military attention. His artsy tie, knotted charmingly askew at his neck, looked like an expressionist painting. I sensed a little wildness there, and it looked good and natural on him—like wildness looks good on mountains and waterfalls.

He walked up to Carly with a hand extended. She ignored it and managed to entice him into a hug.

"Carly Brown," he said, nearly humming her name with a voice as smooth and rich as a cup of Godiva hot chocolate. When he released her, I stole another look at his face.

He smiled, and one word came to mind: *Wow*. But this wasn't the time to be ogling some blue suit, even if he was in plainclothes. Dead folks were in the house, for goodness' sake, and CSI stuff needed to be done. Shoot. I wanted to see Gil Grissom or that fine Warrick Brown— or at least a reasonable facsimile. Then again, this plainclothes cop would do just fine as the on-site hottie.

"How are you, Jazzy?" Carly asked after she squeezed him. Knowing her, she had also given him a strategic but subtle brush.

He grinned at her. Laughed even. "How's the most gorgeous medical examiner in the county?"

"County?" she complained, with mock hurt in her eyes. She batted her lashes as though she might be going blind. "Last time you said *state*."

"Aw, sistah, my bad," he said.

I stole another look at him.

He's black and a hood rat at that.

He continued oozing charm in Carly's general direction. "You already know you're the most gorgeous medical examiner in the United States."

"And Canada."

I groaned. Great birthday. I get to sit in an SUV on an unseasonably hot September night—at a crime scene—listening to Carly flirt. I spent my adolescence doing that—minus the dead bodies, thank goodness.

Could it get any worse?

I shouldn't have wondered. If I've learned anything in thirty-five years, it's that one should never pose the question, "Could it get any worse?" As it happens, one's situation can almost always get worse, and mine promptly proceeded to do so.

"Get out the truck, birthday girl," my sister said, "and let me introduce you to Jazzy."

Wonderful. Another opportunity to be negatively compared to my beautiful, intelligent sister. I stepped out of the SUV. Jazzy appraised me from head to toe with one quick, sweeping glance. *Okay, handsome. Go ahead—I dare you to ask me how old I am.*

"Birthday girl," he said, "how old are you?"

I started to answer like my great-grandmother and namesake would. I could picture Mama Amanda Bell Brown rolling her shoulders back, standing erect, and cutting her eyes at him. Then her stern retort, "Old enough to eat corn bread without getting choked." I would have said it just like Ma Brown, but the guy smiled at me, and darn it if my heart didn't start to flutter. I lost the nerve to be so sassy. "Classified information," I muttered with a fake smile to return his generous one.

"She's thirty-five," Carly said.

I mentally plotted my sister's destruction.

"Happy birthday," he said.

Honestly, he could have been a toothpaste model. I felt disoriented just looking at him.

"Nice dress."

Nice dress? He had that right. Thank you kindly, big sis. The brassy red number defied my own personality. I would never have ventured to buy it—not even for my birthday, not even if I could afford it. The soft, crimson silk turned more heads than a chiropractor. I'd have to do some business with God about the plunging halter neckline. The A-line skirt made my legs in the red stiletto sandals look—quite frankly—devastating. I finished the look with a shawl embroidered with African-inspired designs. It alone tempered the heat my hookup sent out into the atmosphere.

Mr. Colgate Smile stood there looking a little stunned, trying to stop checking out my rarely seen gams. I said a quick prayer that it wasn't lust, but merely a strong appreciation for the beauty of God's creation the man was enjoying. As birthday fun goes, his thinly veiled delight in my appearance had become the highlight of my now-dismal night. When I put on that dress,

I'd had no idea I'd meet someone who looked like a fashion model. But since it happened to be *my* big day, and since I'd already been upstaged by the dearly departed, I'd ask Jesus to forgive me for enjoying the whole thing. Heck, I wasn't getting any younger. Compliments like the ones in his eyes don't come down the pike too much anymore, and I let myself enjoy the moment.

Finally, he found his manners and said, "Another lovely Brown woman, whose name is . . ." He held out his hand to shake mine. Unlike Carly, I had sense enough to actually shake the man's hand instead of sexually assaulting him.

"Dr. Amanda Brown," I said, using my cool, professional psychologist voice. I reserve my nickname for my closest family and friends.

"Everyone who loves her calls her Bell," my sister chimed in.

"Nice to meet you, *Bell*."

No *Doctor*, no *Miss* Brown. Went straight to *Bell* like he was entitled.

"I'm Jazz Brown." He flashed me that megawatt grin. "No relation."

"Like we wouldn't have noticed you at family reunions," Carly said.

"On the bright side," he said, nearly charming the two-hundred-dollar strappy sandals off my feet, "if I were to marry one of you, you wouldn't have to change your name."

"I'll be darned if I'm not already engaged, Mr. Brown," Carly said. "But, my baby sis here . . ."

As soon as I got the chance, I would kick my big sister with the enthusiasm of Billy Blanks in a Tae Bo infomercial. I gave both of them an exaggerated sigh. "Aren't there dead people in that house?"

"All work and no play, Bell?" Jazz teased.

I pointed at the house. "The dead are crying out like the blood of Abel in there."

"She's only tripping like that because she doesn't do this for a living. So what have we got, Sugar?"

Sugar! She called him Sugar as if it were his name. Why can't I be that confident around gorgeous men?

"Report I got said it's two males. No visible cause of death."

"A double suicide or something?"

"No note, and probably more like 'something,' but you're the ME. You can tell me." He flashed me a look me that said "You stay back."

"My baby sis here is a forensic psychologist . . . and a theologian." Carly nodded toward me. "Maybe she can help or, at the very least, say a prayer for you." Although serious, she said it in a teasing way so that if he said no, she'd save me face.

"A praying theologian slash forensic psychologist at a crime scene," Jazz said. "Interesting."

Interesting? He had to be kidding. I sounded like the bomb, if I must say, and apparently I must.

But I didn't. I denied it like Peter on Good Friday. "I'm not actually a theologian."

I hate it when women dumb down for a man, and yet . . .

"I did most of my training at Great Lakes Theological Seminary, but in *psychology*," I said, appalled at myself.

A seminary degree automatically made me a theologian in most people's minds. Still, did I have to act as if I didn't know there are sixty-six books in the Bible?

"In fact," I added, like an even bigger idiot, "calling me a *forensic* psychologist is a stretch."

"Are you or are you not a forensic psychologist?" He had a challenging gleam in his eyes.

"I am, but . . ." I tried to decide if he would consider me a forensic psychologist based on whatever nebulous definition he may have. I spent my workdays administering tests to inmates at the county jail, writing reports, and testifying in court. I'd studied crime-scene photos but had never been on-site. I hated that I felt defensive, standing there sweating and discrediting my own hard-earned skills. All because he was prettier than me.

He cocked his head to the side and regarded me with teasing eyes. "I consult with forensic psychologists on occasion. You're welcome to join us," he said. "Or not."

With that he seemed to dismiss me, and I could tell he had read me like the Bible on Easter. He might as well have called me 'fraidy cat to my face. I didn't appreciate his attitude.

"I'll have a look," I said, trying to sound cool. Frankly, I'd rather have him extract my molars than go into that house of horrors. My fascination with true crime was one thing. It even extended to taking a few postgraduate criminology classes. But being knee-deep in the dead? I'd just as soon leave that to Carly. Yet I wouldn't let him see me punk out. I'm tough. I'm Bell Brown. If Carly could be cool in there, so could I. We came from good stock. Strong black women.

"I'm going in," Carly said, sounding bored. She went to her SUV and grabbed her kit out of the rear of the car, punctuating the quiet evening with a soft thud as she closed the hatchback. She walked to the front door of the house without us, where a uniformed officer nodded a greeting. He moved a piece of yellow crime-scene tape so she could enter.

Detective Jazz Brown sized me up for a few more moments and smiled like a sated cat. He stretched out his arm, but his eyes still mocked. When I moved to his side he placed a hand at the small of my back, guiding me to the front porch. I felt a tingle at his touch. He leaned in and whispered to me, "You have five minutes, *Dr.* Bell Brown. And don't contaminate my crime scene."

What have I gotten myself into?

I should have stayed home and washed down a few chili dogs with a diet cola, *watching* the bad guys get caught in the privacy of my bedroom. Now I was about to walk into a *real* crime scene with a gorgeous, arrogant detective who had a slight attitude that both annoyed and attracted me. And I had to prove myself.

Fine. I knew all about suicides. How hard could it be? I'd give the man one competent, professional insight. Five minutes. Show him what I'm made of, then get the heck out of there and never see those delicious brown eyes of his again.

I said a silent prayer. *Lord, let me help in some way, however small.*

With that simple prayer, the trouble began.

chapter
two

ON THE PORCH I could smell death lurking. Rotting flesh is a stench you can almost feel. It claws like a predator, violating the senses. My eyes watered. I swallowed hard, trying not to gag. I began to sweat, as if my pores wanted to throw off the foulness that covered me like a shroud.

Only five minutes. One useful insight.

Jazz turned to me.

"You know that Scripture that says, 'We are fearfully and wonderfully made'?"

I nodded.

"That smell is the 'fearfully' part."

My mouth tried to make all the appropriate movements for a smile, but it didn't quite succeed. My feet refused to go forward. We hadn't stepped inside the house yet, and I could tell he'd already counted me among the carnage.

Jazz reached into his pocket and pulled out a small, circular tin. He unscrewed the lid, revealing an ointment of some kind. He swiped some of the mixture onto his index finger and smeared it under his nose. In that swift motion, I caught the scent of peppermint, eucalyptus, and rosemary. I'd smelled this on Carly before. He held the tin out to me, and I dabbed a bit of the aromatic blend under my nose. It felt cool and stung a little.

"It helps," he said. "Some people use Vicks Vapo-Rub, but I like this better. It's also great on dry skin." He flashed his childlike grin, and the kindness in his face soothed my jangled nerves. "I turned Carly on to this stuff."

That had better be all he turned her on to.

I chastised myself for the stab of jealousy.

"You don't have to go in," he said, probably having seen my expression change. Thank goodness he didn't know the real reason.

"It's okay." I could do this.

A uniformed officer manning the door greeted us. He looked about twelve years old.

"Officer Daniels, this is Dr. Amanda Brown."

The young, ruddy blond had the chunky build of a football player who doesn't play much ball anymore. He seemed weary, yet eager to please Jazz. He looked at us, and I could almost see him drawing an inaccurate conclusion. "Lieutenant Brown, I'm sorry to interrupt you enjoying an evening with your wife."

Jazz smiled—another slow, easy dazzler—directed at me first and then at Officer Daniels. He removed his hand from my back. "Dr. Brown is not my wife."

Hmmph. I felt oddly disappointed. For one psychotic moment I really wanted to be his wife. I had to wonder if turning thirty-five made me vulnerable to some temporary midlife, no-man mental illness not yet classified in the *DSM-IV.*

Daniels blanched, reddened, then swore. "Sorry, sir. When you said Brown . . . and the two of you look so nice together and all . . . I mean you look nice, not particularly together, but . . ."

"It's okay, Daniels," Jazz said. "Dr. Brown is a forensic psychologist. She's going to have a look at the scene."

"It's bad in there; the heat made 'em ripen fast," he said, his embarrassment faded by the sobering reality just inside the door. "Other than me and the ME who just went in, it's all clear. Richards has the back of the house covered, and the Crime Scene Unit should be here to process the joint in a sec."

Jazz thanked the officer and then moved closer to the door. He stopped just outside it, reached into his suit-jacket pocket, removed a pair of latex gloves, and pulled them on. He looked at me. "Are you ready?"

I went momentarily mute and nodded.

"Usually I'm a gentleman, but I'd better go in first."

He stepped inside, and I followed.

I'd had fantasies about what I would be like at a crime scene: My sharp, clinical eyes would take in every detail, my dazzling brain cataloging and calculating. Everyone would grow quiet, awaiting my brilliant assessment, and I would deliver—solving the crime, saving the day.

Only that's not how it happened. First, the entire extent of my criminology knowledge took a leave of absence. I felt like a woman who had been the perfect Lamaze student, then forgot all the breathing exercises the moment the first contraction hit.

Once inside I processed the images before me as square pixels of random information. It was as if my mind were down-loading digital photos without a high-speed connection. Shoe. Man's shoe. Foot in shoe. Another. A thin leg in black trousers. Another. Broad, bony chest in red polo shirt. Arm. Arm. Skin color wrong. Bluish. Back locked in an arch.

Carly crouched over the man on the floor. She ran her glove-sheathed hand down his rounded spine. "The bowed back is opisthotonus. Poor guy had spasms that caused the large muscles of his back to contract. In a case like this, rigor mortis sets in immediately. They've been dead about twenty-four hours." She coughed and wrinkled her nose.

"Seizure?" Jazz asked.

"Spasms like a violent reaction to strychnine would cause. Look at the blue coloring and the face," she said, nearly touching his lips.

I looked at the young man's face. Lord, have mercy— his mouth was stretched into a broad, teeth-baring grin. "He looks like he's smiling," I said, stating the obvious. The image etched itself into my memory. His eyes were wide milky protrusions with a swirl of blue in the center. Dark brown hair fell carelessly across his forehead.

"Risus sardonicus. The death smile."

I imagined the spasms Carly had described and could almost feel his suffering. My heart pounded so hard I thought it would explode. In that moment I knew what the psalmist meant when he spoke of the valley of the shadow of death. I stood there now, and it scared me.

Carly lifted the man's arm. The part closest to the ground had purpled. "Lividity," she said to Jazz. "Doesn't look like he's been moved." She turned her attention back to her exam.

I took a deep breath. Only one more body to see. This one lay on the couch, bent into the same unnatural pose. His face frozen in the same deathly grimace. This time everything processed faster in my head. Like the first man, he appeared to be in his late twenties to early thirties. He was somebody's child, somebody's friend, a person Jesus loved. I shut my eyes. Prayer came fast, and tumbled out of my mouth unbidden: "Our Father which art in heaven, Hallowed be thy name. Thy kingdom come, Thy will be done in earth, as it is in heaven. Give us this day our daily bread. And forgive us our debts, as we forgive our debtors. And lead us not into temptation . . ."

Rote memory. A prayer I'd learned as a child at my great-grandmother's knee, emerging like unexpected grace. I guess Jazz liked the idea of a praying psychologist more than I'd realized. Before I could finish my prayer, he stood in front of me. His hands cradled my elbows. We prayed in unison: ". . . but deliver us from evil: For thine is the kingdom, and the power, and the glory, for ever. Amen."

His voice caressed me. "Let me take you outside, Bell. You can come back a little later if you want to. The Crime Scene Unit just arrived. They'll need to start collecting evidence."

"Uh." My arms flailed about as I searched my mind for something sensible to say. Speech had abandoned me, but apparently crime scenes inspired my finest gesticulations. My left leg began to shake uncontrollably. I started blinking hard, and tears spilled from my eyes. I couldn't think past the prayer. I couldn't breathe for the suffocating smell.

What happened here?

I had a gnawing sense that we'd stumbled upon something more than a willing suicide. I could feel Death crouching nearby, having snatched *two*. The room felt all wrong. Something bad—not just suicide bad—had gone down. It sickened me in a wave of cold and nausea.

I became vaguely aware of the small group of men and women wandering into the room—real crime-scene investigators—unglamorous and preoccupied. Two men with camera equipment began to take photographs of the scene from every angle imaginable.

My body trembled. I tightened the red shawl around my arms. Jazz's strong arms enveloped me.

"You're getting cold."

I rested my head on his chest.

Carly ignored me while she worked, as if she saw me hugged up with a strange man at a crime scene every day. Activity buzzed around us, but he didn't let me go. He tried to avert my attention. "Talk to me." When he spoke, I felt the rumble of his voice against my face. "What's your favorite color?"

"Purple. At least, it was before I saw that guy's arm."

He drew away from me and took a long look at my red dress. "You should consider changing it to red." He pulled me back into his arms. "What's your favorite Scripture?"

Another welcome diversion.

"The Ninety-first Psalm. In *The Message*."

He rubbed my back, and, my goodness, it would have felt rather cozy if I could have just shaken the horror threatening to engulf me. The sound of his voice became my anchor. "I like that one, too. What does it say in *The Message*?"

"Verse fourteen says, '"If you'll hold on to me for dear life," says God, "I'll get you out of any trouble."'"

"Do you do that?"

"Most of the time."

"You hold on to God like you're holding on to me?"

"I try to."

His chuckle rumbled in my ear.

We stood that way until my heart beat in sync with the steady thump of his, drumming against my ear.

Camera lights flashed in a small storm around us.

"Are you okay?"

"Um-hmm."

I couldn't very well stay in his arms all night—well, I could, but he had work to do. Besides, the time had come for me to show him what I'm made of.

I reluctantly pulled away from his warmth. For a moment I watched my sister across the room, now examining the victim on the couch and dictating notes into a digital voice recorder. Her image mirrored something solid and reliable to me. I thought of Ma Brown, daughter of Aimee, a slave woman, who gifted her child with stories—of beatings, of rape, of being greased and sold on an auction block, and also of finding freedom by following the North Star. I tried to take courage from the praying matriarch of my family, long gone home to her Jesus. Her likeness remained in my sister and me.

I'm not as strong as you, Ma. I'm not even as strong as Carly.

Then the small still voice inside me whispered, *Yes you are.*

The voice surged through my body, and I knew, as I know the back of my freckled hand, that if Ma Brown could hear me from heaven, she'd say, "Call on Jesus."

So I bowed my head in reverence and called, *Jesus. Oh, dear God, sweet Jesus.*

I felt my great-grandmother's strength surge within me, and I pulled it around me like a quilt. Jazz lifted my face with his hand. In his gesture I felt my great-grandmother's Jesus comfort me, stilling my quaking body with a touch from this beautiful man who had stopped working to pray with me.

"Lieutenant," I said, "I've been in this house before."

chapter
three

LIEUTENANT JAZZ BROWN raised an eyebrow. "You've been here? Do tell."

"Just a sec."

I stood rooted to the spot, taking in the room. The plain décor had a stripped-down, ascetic feel to it.

It didn't look like this before.

White walls, old paint. Nail punctures pocked the surface. The pictures or posters once adorning the walls were now gone. A simple, flat basket—nearly as wide as an end table—lay on the floor in the center of the living room near the dead man. Big, plain floor pillows—the kind that one would get for a dorm room—rested on the worn green shag carpet.

I turned my attention to the area just beyond the bodies. A small bookcase with three shelves held a few books. I tiptoed over to it and crouched. A worn Gideon's Bible leaned against a paperback Webster's student dictionary. Next to them stood a thin, black three-ring binder with the name "Gabriel" labeled on the one-inch spine. Six spiral-bound notebooks were stacked in a neat pile next to it.

I called out to my sister, who was now thoroughly engaged in examining the second victim. "Carly, you said something about strychnine, right? You're sure they were poisoned?"

"Can't say for certain till we get them back to the morgue and do a tox screen, but it looks like it to me."

"A suicide?"

She shrugged. "It's possible."

I looked at Jazz. "What's your first impression?"

"I've been a detective for too long to trust impressions. I'm like Joe Friday. Just the facts, ma'am."

"And what are the facts?"

Jazz prowled the room like a stealth lion, careful not to disturb evidence. "No cups or glasses by the bodies or in the sink," he said. "No syringes. No pill bottles. No suicide note." He stopped his perpetual motion and closed his eyes briefly. "Johnson," he said to one of the CSIs, a woman hovering over the body on the floor, "make sure they scour this house for poison. Anything these guys could have ingested."

When he finished barking orders, he came back over to me, reached out a hand, and helped me up from my crouching position. Again, I felt sparks. He briefly locked eyes with me and his fair skin betrayed him; a blush spread across his cheek.

Jazz looked relieved when another brother—six feet two inches of dreadlocked, cocoa brown fineness—walked up to us. Jazz shifted his attention, thank God, to the man wearing a navy blue Windbreaker that said "CSU Forensics." Where does the city of Detroit get these guys? I wondered if the Wayne County Jail was hiring. I needed to work with cute guys.

Cocoa Brown Hottie greeted Jazz with a complicated hand-shake that black men do effortlessly. Women would have to take Soul Handshake 101 to master it.

"Hook me up, Souldier. I'm looking for strychnine. Be ruthless," Jazz said to his comrade.

"No doubt, Lieutenant," he said. They finished with another variation of the handshake, and the man he called Souldier turned to face me.

Jazz introduced us. "This is my boy, Souldier, with an S-O-U-L. He's the shift supervisor for our crime-scene investigators. You'd like him, Bell. He's a dedicated Christian."

"Blame my mother," Souldier said. "That old Pentecostal song 'I'm a Soldier in the Army of the Lord' got to me when I was knee-high to a grasshopper."

Jazz was right. I did like him. Then again, what woman with eyes wouldn't? I thrust out my hand to shake his.

"I'm Amanda Brown."

"Brown?" Souldier shot a quizzical look at Jazz.

"She's Carly's sister, a forensic psychologist."

Souldier laughed. "Oh, okay. I have to keep an eye on Jazzy. He'd pull a fast one on a brother."

"But enough about me," Jazz said, silencing any more commentary that would clarify what the handsome CSI supervisor meant. They'd piqued my curiosity, but the two of them created such a pretty distraction that I didn't bother to ask for details. Besides, I needed to spill my guts about why I'd been in this house before I spilled them in another, less productive way.

"I think I came to a Bible study here."

Souldier excused himself and joined his team, now busy setting numbered markers by the bodies and taking more pictures. A woman working with a portable ultraviolet light illuminated fibers on the floor pillows barely noticeable to the naked eye. They worked with solemn efficiency.

Jazz Brown studied me with greater interest. "Do you recognize the deceased?"

"No. It had to be years ago that I visited, and the people I met were *alive*."

He gave me a half smile. "Your five minutes are up, Dr. Brown. Any other observations?"

"While I wouldn't rule out suicide just yet, I'd consider the possibility that they may have had assistance."

"Go on," he said, without a hint of his former mockery.

"I'd do a psychological autopsy. Find out everything I can about their last days—what they did and what their state of mind was leading up to"—I paused and sighed—"their demise. I'm sure that's your standard procedure anyway, Lieutenant."

Jazz nodded.

Sadness settled over me. I felt so sorry for the dead men. "Do you have their identities?"

"I do."

"Is one of them named Gabriel?"

"No."

"I'd start with the notebooks. Since these guys have so few possessions here and neither of them is named Gabriel, it's probably significant. I'd also look closely at all their relationships—or lack of relationships."

"Do you have any specific relationships in mind?" Jazz asked, taking another quick glance at the two bodies.

"This could have been more than a suicide pact between two close friends."

He looked impressed. "Tell me more, Dr. Brown."

"It may be something religious."

He paused for a few moments, and his eyes swept the room while the CSI team labored, dusting for prints. Souldier gave directions to a man holding a digital video camera.

Jazz turned his attention back to me. "Why religious?"

"Look at the room. It's fit for a monk. There's a Bible, but no other reference materials that would illuminate the scriptures. Just a Gideon's Bible, probably lifted from a motel room."

He nodded. "Keep talking, Doctor."

The odious smell of decaying flesh and escaped bodily fluids assaulted me again. Jazz seemed only mildly fazed by it. I blew a quick breath out of my lungs and steeled myself to continue. "I don't see many creature comforts here, so maybe the absence of décor is less about feng shui and more about control. If this is some kind of religious thing, I'd bet whoever the leader is keeps a tight rein on what gets into the heads of the followers. Look, if it was a Bible study I attended here years ago, that wasn't a good thing." I wished I had a drink of water. I wished I were somewhere else—a place where the odor wasn't about to make me lose consciousness.

"What do you mean?"

"I mean I used to investigate cults and toxic churches."

Jazz laughed. "A praying forensic psychologist slash theologian slash *private investigator*. You're full of surprises, Bell."

Then, I did it again. "I'm not a private investigator. I used to . . ." I decided *not* to get into my complicated past. Not here.

Carly had finally finished and needed to supervise the transporting of the bodies to the morgue. She removed her gloves, came over to me, and started kneading my shoulders. "Are you feeling all right, Bell? You look a little queasy. I'm heading out, why don't you come with me?"

"Go ahead, Carly. I want to tell the lieutenant something else."

She narrowed her eyes. "Are you sure you don't want to come outside *now*?"

I nodded, and she squeezed my shoulder. "See you outside, then."

I turned my attention back to Jazz. "Lieutenant . . ." My gag reflex reacted. I swallowed hard, trying to pull myself together, and pointed to the spiral-bound notebooks on the shelf. "Hopefully those belong to a copious notetaker. Find out who Gabriel is. He may just be your killer." I gulped again, my stomach clenching into a tight knot. "That's my take, Detective." I imagined myself turning an unflattering shade of green.

For a moment he said nothing, his expression somber. "I'd better get you outside," he said finally, and cupped my elbow. I felt that spark once again. My stomach flip-flopped. I wondered if it was my attraction to him that was affecting me, or if I was about to be sick.

"Is there anything else, Dr. Brown?"

"Just one more thing." I didn't realize in my queasy state that I'd uttered the most famous line of my favorite television sleuth, but Jazz noticed.

"What's that, Columbo?"

I answered by throwing up on his charcoal gray alligator shoes. I hoped they were fake but knew they weren't. The pain in my gut stopped me from caring. I had a fleeting mental image of myself as the next corpse Carly would examine. Thankfully, I was wearing clean underwear and had a fresh pedicure.

Jazz sighed, moving back from my mess. "I knew you'd contaminate my crime scene."

He stepped out of his shoes, peeled off his socks, and stuck them in his ruined shoes. It didn't seem to bother him that his team of professionals could barely contain their snickers. He walked me to the door, careful to disturb as little as possible. I slithered through it, feeling every bit the slug, and moved into the yard, grateful to be outside, even though the wretched smell of death still clung to my clothing.

To my amazement Jazz asked, "May I take you home?" He was still barefoot, looking perfectly at ease, walking to his car.

Wild.

"Carly will drop me off," I said, trying to keep up with him. My cheeks burned from embarrassment. "I'm so sorry about your shoes."

"I keep a spare pair of kicks in my trunk."

He leaned against the Crown Vic, and his gaze swept over me again. "Carly will probably be busy tonight at the morgue. She got two for the price of one. Where do you live?"

"Ann Arbor."

He raised an eyebrow. "What brings you to the *beast* side of Detroit?"

I smiled at his nickname for the eastern part of the city. "Carly and I were having dinner, and then she got the call."

"You finish your dinner?"

"No, but uh, I'm not hungry anymore."

"You will be soon," he said. He smiled a little. Already I missed seeing his pretty teeth when he smiled as wide as the sky.

"I'll take you home, if you can hang on until I'm done here." He folded his arms across his chest in a classic defensive posture.

I didn't know what to make of his change in body language. After all, I didn't *ask* him to take me home. Truthfully, I'd have gone with him if I had to crawl to Ann Arbor while he rode my back. So why the protective armor all of a sudden? I decided to give him a gentle reminder of whose idea it was.

"I'll wait for you if that's what you want."

"You'd give me what I want?" He gave me a red-hot gaze.

That sounded pretty enthusiastic for a person just giving me a ride.

"Are we still talking about you giving me a ride home?"

He paused, opened his mouth to say something, and then thought better of it. We stood there staring at each other until he crossed his legs, his body language shouting, *Don't get too close.* Finally, he broke the silence. "I have no idea what made me say that."

I knew what made him say it. Shoot. I had high hopes for the night myself.

Where did that *thought come from?*

Sometimes I hate my inner voice that reveals all kinds of unsavory motivations.

Fatigue settled on me, though I tried to rub it out of my eyes. I thought about Jazz and his heat-seeking eyes—but closed body language—and realized my own arms had crossed. For a professional people-reader, I wasn't altogether sure what was going on between us.

We couldn't very well stand there all night emotionally shielding ourselves. Jazz moved first, guiding me to where Carly stood by her SUV. I tried to relax as he placed his hand at the small of my back, but honestly, the man made me tingle all over. I could read my sister's smirk as she spotted him leading me. She might as well have given me a high five and shouted, "You go, girl!" She eyed the detective. "Those guys might be dead, but chivalry is not, is it, Jazzy?"

"Not tonight."

Carly grasped my hand. "Sorry for the sucky birthday, sis."

"It's okay. You owe me. By the way, Jazz offered to take me home."

She looked at us and smiled broadly. "Then, you owe *me* one." She released my hand and gave Jazz a playful nudge. "She could stand a good bodice ripping tonight."

"Is that what she's wearing?" he asked innocently.

Carly laughed in that sultry way of hers. "No, so it should be easy."

"Can we keep things professional here?" I said, louder than I intended.

"Tell that to your sister," Jazz said.

She leaned over so she could whisper in my ear, "Look at him. Haven't I taught you anything?" With that she kissed my cheek and glided away.

I looked at the handsome man in front of me. Maybe I *should* borrow a few truths from the gospel according to Carly: Thou shalt have a good birthday. No matter who is dead.

I didn't know if I should say, "Amen, sister," or pray for divine protection.

chapter four

I DEFINITELY SHOULD HAVE PRAYED for divine protection.

Actually, Jazz needed the heavenly bodyguard, not me.

I have to give it to the brother. His mama must have raised him right. Despite my daring banter and freshened breath, Jazz was a perfect gentleman. When we got to my place, he parked in the lot behind my apartment building, stepped out of the Crown Vic, and whisked the door open for me. I felt like a princess in my fancy red gown, taking the hand of the prince.

Only, in fairy tales you don't trip on your high-heeled sandals when you step out of the carriage or crash your head into the prince's chest with the kind of force that could cause heart failure.

Jazz definitely needed protection and maybe a chest

X-ray. He laughed a robust boy-next-door kind of laugh. "You don't get out much do you?" he said after he'd caught his breath.

I didn't answer. Did I really need to proclaim my utter nerdiness? Of course I didn't get out much, but did he *have* to notice?

He walked me to the main entrance.

When I could look at him again, I managed to say, "Thank you for an interesting evening, Lieutenant Brown."

"Thank you for your input—before you hurled on my feet."

He thanked me. I liked him a little more for that.

"I'll pay for your shoes," I said. As if I could.

"No need. I'm just sorry you had to see that scene on your special night."

"I'm sorry for those poor men. I can't stop thinking about them."

"Me, too. But you're a nice diversion."

"Uh. Thanks." So now he's brazenly flirting?

"Don't worry. I'll find the bad guy and put him away. It's what I do."

"That's a tough job. I'll say some prayers for you."

"You do that, Bell." He shoved a hand toward me.

I stuck out my hand to shake his and realized the top of my head was still stinging from my forceful plunge into his chest. I wondered if I hadn't given myself a concussion and hoped I hadn't broken a few of his ribs. His left hand still rested on the spot where I'd slammed into him.

"My mother would never forgive me if I didn't see you to your door," he said. "Besides . . ." He gave me that full, amazing smile again. "You seem to be having a hard time with shoes tonight. May I?"

"May you what?"

"Help you?"

"Sure," I said, not knowing how he intended to help.

He scooped me into his arms as if I were a bride about to be carried over the threshold. "Where to?" he asked. Those brown eyes of his held such a playful twinkle that I laughed.

For the second time that night, words escaped me. *Lord, have mercy on my man-deprived soul.* His arms felt so good around me I forgot to protest. I forgot everything. "What did you just ask me?"

"I asked where I could deposit you."

"Apartment 3B. That's the third floor, Hercules."

"Relax and enjoy the ride."

So I did.

Hercules did just fine carting my size-ten rear end up the stairs. What a perfect finish to the night's trauma, even if he did start to strain a bit by the time he got to the second floor. I didn't begrudge him that.

I wasn't mad at myself for enjoying his attention,

either. Being held by him felt like a little bit of magic, and magic had been missing in action for a long time. I closed my eyes and felt the acrobatics in my stomach rival a Ringling Bros. Circus act. Inside me trapeze artists flew, feathers floated, and animals roared. A beautiful woman in a red dress grinned. She must have been the clown. It didn't matter. A heady rush of adrenaline whooshed through me, and I opened my eyes to take a good look at the man causing all the commotion.

Perspiration beaded on his forehead. Both of us still smelled like death, but I'd never, ever, seen a more beautiful man.

When we got to 3B he set me down.

"Happy thirty-fifth birthday." He looked at me with his soft, wonderfully kind eyes, and I decided right then and there to fall in love with him.

"How old are you?" I asked, feeling flirtatious and bold.

"I'm thirty-seven."

"Do you believe in magic?"

"I'm a homicide detective."

"It's a yes-or-no question."

He gave me one of those sexy Denzel Washington glances. "Most of the time, no. Right at this moment, yes."

"What's different about this moment?"

"You."

I did what any woman in the throes of magic would. I kissed him.

I think I surprised him. His hands found mine, and we entwined them as if they belonged together. We kissed and kissed—standing at my door—acting like a couple of kids. God knows, in that moment my heart bloomed like the last rose of summer. I wished it would never end.

He pulled himself away and stared at me for a moment. The sadness in his eyes nearly toppled me over. I shouldn't have kissed him.

I cleared my throat. "I'm sorry about that, Lieutenant Brown."

He nodded but didn't speak.

"I just wanted to be in love—if only for a minute." A flood of embarrassment washed over me, and I covered my face with my hands. "I can't believe I said that to you." I peeked at him through my splayed fingers.

He took my hands in his again. "Don't cover your face. I wanted to be in love for a minute, too." He rubbed circles with his thumbs on the back of my hands. "I'm the one who should apologize, Bell."

This kind of thing had happened before. I knew what would come next. "We're not going to see each other again, are we?"

"No, beautiful. We're not."

"You're not wearing a ring. Are you married?"

"No more questions, Ms. Detective," he said, releasing my hands. "Let's just enjoy the rest of our minute."

I shrugged and thought I'd tease him. "Since that's all we have, I love you."

He surprised me. "I love you, too."

"How much time do we have left?"

He checked his watch. "About ten seconds."

"I have endometriosis. Wanna get married and have a baby right quick?"

"Can we accomplish that in seven seconds?"

We could, but we shouldn't. That didn't stop me from talking trash. "The doctor says I need to do it fast."

He laughed. "If it's doctor's orders . . ." He pulled me into a tight hug, then sighed. His warm breath tickled my hair. "Our time is up."

I tried to pull away, but the man was strong. "Are you going to let me go?" I mumbled to his chest.

"When I have to." He held me, resting his head on top of mine and rubbing my back. We embraced each other for a long time. Finally, he pulled away from me. He touched my sassy, close-cropped hair. "Sexy haircut."

"My mother hates it. She said I look like a truck driver."

"My mother would like it."

We stood there, looking at our shoes, at the wall,

at anything but each other. Finally, I put us out of our misery. "Good-bye, Jazz." Again, I held out my hand to shake his. This time he shook it.

"Good-bye, Bell. Tell Carly I respect you too much to go with her bodice-ripping suggestion."

"You know what? It would have been a wasted effort, anyway. I've never owned a bodice. I'm not even sure I know what that is."

"You should find out."

My inner circus packed up and left town. I felt drained and just wanted to get inside. "Tell you what, Jazz. Maybe by the time I do, you'll actually be available to rip it."

Did I say that?

I did. Worse yet, I meant it.

"Touché."

"Thanks for the minute."

"If it's any consolation, we took longer than a minute."

"That's not a consolation at all." I fished in my handbag for my keys. When I found them, I turned to put my key in the door.

"Bell."

I turned around to face him.

He reached into the pocket of his jacket and pulled out an amazing string of prayer beads. There must have been a hundred luminous red garnet stones on it, with tiny crystal seed beads as spacers. An ornate, white gold cross, as gorgeous as he was, dangled at the bottom of the strand. I could feel the weight of the cross when he placed the beads around my neck.

"Try adding a tactile sensation to your prayers. I find it helpful to have something I can feel."

"But I'm not Catholic."

"Don't worry. It's not a rosary. It's along the lines of an Orthodox prayer rope, only made out of beads. The artist is my mother—and she's a Church of God in Christ Pentecostal. My father is an Irish Catholic." He touched the beads, still hanging on my neck.

"You can say the Jesus prayer, the Lord's prayer, the prayer of Jabez, the Psalms—whatever you like. I don't even think God would mind if you used thoughtful quotes from *The Purpose-Driven Life*."

I liked that he knew these prayers, and *The Purpose-Driven Life* would give him bonus points in my circle of friends. But still . . .

"I can't take this; it's too beautiful."

"Please. It's yours. Don't forget me, Bell; when you pray, that is."

"I won't forget you, Jazz."

I hurried into my apartment and closed the door behind me. I took a deep, cleansing breath and actually thanked the Lord. It could have been worse. At another time in my life, it *would* have been worse, and I'd have found myself on the altar repenting.

We'd only had a few impulsive kisses and some silly talk about being in love for one minute—a whimsical game we'd stumbled upon. Perhaps it was like Carly said: God had smiled on me, sending a little male attention my way to show me I wasn't completely hopeless.

Psychologist, heal thyself. One more look, and I'll let him go.

The image of Jazz permeated my mind, and in that vision he flashed his wide, wonderful, "too much teeth for his lovely mouth" smile. Clenching my fist as hard as I could, I stored him in a secret place in my heart. I let a fragment of scripture, Song of Solomon 6:3, seal what I felt: "I am my beloved's."

Slowly I uncurled my hand, willing myself to release Jazz Brown, while the image of his face faded away. It's a technique I'd used in therapy sessions many times. An effective, physical symbol of letting go of something one held fast to. It was a tactile, sensory exercise. Jazz was right. Sometimes it helps to have something you can feel.

I whispered good-bye to him, to my birthday, and to the twisted bodies demanding justice.

Yeah, right.

It's amazing the lies we tell ourselves just to get a good night's sleep.

chapter
five

MORNING CAME TOO SOON, and I woke up foul tempered. Dreams of Jazz and the dead men tortured me all night. Upon waking I did two things I never do: I called in sick at the jail, and I went to the morgue to see Carly.

If I thought the Washtenaw County Jail provided a dismal work environment, I only had to see the morgue to change my opinion. My heart went out to my big sister. One look and I understood her fanatical home-improvement impulses. The morgue looked every inch like what you'd see on television. The air had a stale coolness about it. The harsh fluorescent lighting would lead the majority of my clients suffering from Seasonal Affective Disorder to their deaths. Someone had made a lame attempt to make the corridor more inviting by painting it a nauseating shade of green. Tacky, framed prints of outdoor scenes—designed to inspire serenity—completed the insult.

After several security checks and my insistence that I was Dr. Carly Brown's sister and there for personal reasons, I was granted access. When I arrived at "the freezer," I found my sister amid a wall of stainless steel drawers that served as temporary homes to the newly departed. Steel tables stood in the room, topped with suspiciously human-looking mounds that were completely covered by sheets. Carly stood by one such mound.

That whole wobbly thing in my knees started. "Sissy," I said weakly, using my favorite Southern sisterly endearment for her.

Carly turned, startled by my voice. She rushed over to me and gathered me into one of her generous hugs. "What are you doing here, bunny?"

So it's "bunny" today. From day to day, I never knew what strange moniker Carly would christen me with.

"I wanted to talk to you about the guys who were found last night."

"Let me get you a chair. Please don't throw up in my workspace. It's bad enough down here."

"Okay," I said, watching the room swim.

Carly retrieved a folding metal chair, and I flopped down on it hoping I could beat the descending darkness.

"You don't look good, honey. Jazz just went to get coffee. Do you want me to ask him to get you some?"

"Jazz? Jazz Brown? He's here?" I asked, panic rising in my voice.

"I am," said that yummy voice. He seemed to materialize out of nowhere, holding two Styrofoam cups of steaming liquid. He handed one to Carly and took a sip from the other.

Okay, maybe I hadn't been paying attention, and he had come through the door like a normal person, not an apparition. I'd been focused on not passing out and all, but, Lord, could you warn a sistah about these things? Pulling together my cool would be impossible. I didn't even try. "Hello," I murmured weakly.

"Hello," he said, followed by the now predictable but still heart-stopping smile. "I thought finding you at my crime scene was odd, and now here you are at the morgue."

"My sister works here."

Carly piped up, "She's never come here before. Imagine that, the two of you here at the same time. Coincidence or destiny?"

I glared at her. Who tries to do matchmaking in a morgue?

"In case the two of you haven't noticed, I don't seem to handle death as well as you do. At least not this part. I don't happen to enjoy hanging out at the morgue."

"So why are you here?" Jazz asked, with that maddening half smile.

"I'm not here for you, nosy."

"I'm not nosy. I'm a detective."

"I'm a sister. Visiting."

He nodded, but he cocked his head to the side and gave me a sly smile. "Why do I have the feeling you're trying to get all up in my investigation?"

"Look, all night I dreamed about you—uh—your victims. I just want to know what happened to them. Simple cause of death."

He bent closer to me. "Funny, I dreamed about you, too," he whispered, probably hoping Carly wouldn't hear. My bones turned to liquid.

Of course she heard. Nothing gets past her.

"Y'all dreaming about one another, now? Whatever happened last night must have been *good*."

"He took me home. Period."

"I only stayed a minute." The look on his face resembled a sweet little lamb's, instead of the lion I saw at the crime scene. He gave me the subtlest wink.

I tried to ignore him. "Some theories suggest that dreams are an amalgam of one's day. Mere fragments and impressions of what has happened."

Carly would have none of it. "Some theories," she said, "suggest that you dream about a person because subconsciously you think he"—she gave Jazz an indulgent look—"or *she*, is hot. I believe that was Freud." Her gaze bore into Jazz. "What do you think, Jazzy?"

"I think I have a new respect for Freud. But I'm here to talk about what killed these men, not to analyze dreams."

"Right." She moved to the body on the table nearest her. Jazz followed and waited while she removed the sheet with a dramatic flourish.

I wobbled in my chair. She'd already done her autopsy, and let's just say things did not look good. The dead man on the table had a huge Y-shaped incision that went from shoulder to shoulder then headed *way* down south. God only knows where his organs were. "Can you pull that sheet back up?" I squeaked.

Carly shot me a look and, upon seeing my face, took pity. She covered him up from the neck down. "Mr. Jonathan Vogel. Age twenty-eight. Cause of death: asphyxia."

That name sounds familiar. I started sifting through middle-aged brain fog trying to find the name Jonathan Vogel.

"He suffocated?" Jazz asked.

"Asphyxia caused by strychnine poisoning. We don't usually check for it in routine tox screens, but as I'd told you, I had my suspicions. Results came back positive."

I peered around to look at Jonathan Vogel's face again. "He's not smiling anymore."

"No. Strychnine poisoning is a trip. It works fast, like you and Jazzy. It attacks the central nervous system like a good neurological toxin should, giving a beat down to the nerves that enervate the muscles. The victim—in this case our Mr. Vogel—would have gotten stiffness in his neck and face about ten minutes after consumption. After that he'd go spastic, contracting and contorting."

"Which is why his back was arched and he had the death smile," Jazz added.

"Finally, he wouldn't be able to breathe, and bye-bye cruel world. Because the contractions forced his muscles to consume the intramuscular enzymes, the poor baby froze up with rigor mortis right away. As the body decomposes, the contractions loosen up, like Bell did last night. That's why his face is relaxed now, dear sister—unlike yours."

"Maybe my face would relax if you'd stop comparing me to a dead body."

"I'm assuming the other vic," Jazz interjected, "Damon Crawford, died from the same cause."

"Your assumption is correct, Lieutenant."

"Any other drugs in their systems?"

"None that we found. Why do you ask?"

He sighed a heavy I-hate-police-work kind of sigh. "We got a tip that they were involved in the street pharmaceutical business—selling crank."

Crank, a street name for methamphetamines, had taken over as the most insidious drug in Wayne and Washtenaw counties. Its high could last for up to sixteen hours.

Carly shrugged. "All I know is what the toxicology report says. Even if they were selling it, they weren't using it. At least not when they died. Look at their adorable faces."

Their faces were so *not* adorable.

"Could've been a *crank* call," Jazz said. He laughed. I just shook my head at his awful pun. "What do you think, Dr. Amanda Brown?"

"Their place certainly didn't have the markings of a dope house or a meth lab. Did your team find any crank on the premises?"

"Nope."

"Did they find evidence of strychnine anywhere? In a pesticide hanging around the yard?"

"According to Souldier, nary a trace."

"Then I think you've got your work cut out for you. There's a murderer on the loose." I tried to struggle through the fog in my brain. But the synapses weren't firing. "The name Jonathan Vogel sounds very familiar. I can't seem to place it, though." I rested a protective hand on my tummy. "I also think I need to get out of here."

"Yeah. You look a little pale. May I help you?" Jazz walked over to my chair to help me up.

I stood, not as stably as I would have liked, but I stood just the same. "Will 'helping' involve my feet being unable to touch the ground?"

"I'll allow you to walk on your own. This time." He

raised his eyebrows. "Will that method involve me needing to change my shoes?"

"I'm inclined to say no—as long as I can get some fresh air within the next few minutes."

Carly came to me, stroked my hair, and kissed my forehead. "Come visit again, bunny."

"I'd rather pass kidney stones."

"Not a problem. I'm a medical doctor. I can help with that."

"But all your patients are dead."

"All *your* patients are crazy."

"I love you, Sissy," I said.

"I love you, too."

We gave each other a warm hug.

"Can a brother get some love, too?" Jazz said, stretching his arms out. I tried to ignore him, but Carly passed the buck, no pun intended, right back to me. "See Bell about that. I'm spoken for."

Shoot. I went ahead and hugged the big buck. We let each other go and left. Quickly. I didn't even throw up on his shoes. Jazz pressed his hand at the small of my back again, guiding me.

He had one thing wrong.

My feet didn't touch the ground at all.

chapter
six

FRESH AIR IS A WONDERFUL THING, especially after a hasty exit from the morgue. I drank in the scent of new September—air sweetened with leaves just beginning to turn and with a hint of the last of summer's bounty tenaciously clinging to the wind. Another delicious, manly scent wafted in my direction. Man scent. Essence of Jazz. I moved a little closer to him.

"I read the notebooks," he said.

"Um-hmm," I murmured, wondering if I should ask what kind of cologne he wore.

"What are you doing?"

I snapped to attention. "What?"

"Are you trying to smell me?"

"Pardon me?"

"You were smelling me." He grinned.

"That's ridiculous," I said in all truth. What's worse, he'd busted me. I took a step away from him and lowered my head. My mother always said I wore guilt like a neon sign on my face. Maybe he wouldn't notice.

He noticed. And liked it. "You leaned toward me, lifted your pretty little face, and very subtly flared your nostrils and inhaled. So, what did you think?"

When all else fails, deflect the attention away from the troubling focal point. "Lieutenant Brown, I think that if you're concerned about your hygiene, you should take more pains to make sure you're in order before leaving home."

"I just use soap and deodorant. I hope you're not disappointed."

"I'm relieved to know that you're familiar with the combination. What were you saying about notebooks?"

"I was saying," he eased closer to me, "I read the Gabriel notebooks."

"And?"

"They belonged to Vogel. Weird stuff using language reminiscent of Scripture, but it didn't sound like anything I'd learned in Sunday school or Catechism class. Lots of talk about somebody called 'Father,' but check this out, this 'Father' character didn't sound like the guy's dad or any local priest."

"That doesn't sound good."

"No, but it does sound like what you were suggest-

ing at the crime scene. You smell good too. Like vanilla
and . . ."

"Sweet amber. So, what are you going to do?"

"Investigate further." He took my hand in his and
held my wrist to his nose. "Ummm," he said. He stopped
smelling but kept holding.

I willed myself to speak. "I thought you were talking
about the case when you said you'd investigate further."

"I multitask."

"Why don't we just keep things professional?" I asked.

"You started it."

"Fine. Can we agree to finish it?"

He didn't answer, still holding my hand.

"Are you married, Jazz?"

He dropped my hand.

"Was that a yes?"

"That was an agreement to keep things professional." I watched his jaw tighten.

I couldn't hide my disappointment.

He touched my face. His features—especially his
eyes—softened at the contact. "Bell, it's been a long time
since I felt what I did last night. You took me by surprise."
He paused, looked toward the ground, then back to me,
as if searching for the words. "I'm not trying to play games
with you. I can't give you what you deserve. I don't want
to get into why. You just have to trust me on that."

I looked into his eyes. He was telling the truth, or

he was a sociopath. I hoped for the former. "Why can't we—"

"We just can't, baby. I wish we could." He brushed his hand across my cheek.

I turned away from him. The gray and uninspired city buildings surrounding me were in sharp contrast with the vivid beauty of the day, and there stood Jazz in the center, looking like the finest man God ever made. He'd made it clear that we weren't going to get together. It was my cue to exit. "I'd better get going, Jazz. Goodbye." I took a deep breath and a step toward my sunshine yellow Volkswagen Beetle parked in the front row of the lot, as I removed the keys from my purse.

Jazz jerked to a stop and gaped at me. "Tell me this isn't your car."

"It's my Love Bug."

"I asked you not to tell me that."

I grinned. "Does it make a difference?"

"It should," he said, voice serious but eyes alight with a spark of mischief. "Bell, no one drives Beetles anymore."

"I do." I ignored his teasing, pretended to be offended, and jammed the key into the car door. I might be desperate for male attention, but *nobody* talks smack about my Love Bug.

"Wait."

I had the nerve to stop.

"Can you tell me a little more about the investigating you used to do?"

Just a simple question. I answer. Then leave. No problem, right?

"About seven years ago I worked as an assistant for my mentor, Dr. Mason May. I used to covertly attend Bible studies or group meetings and report my findings. I barely remember, but I can't think of any other reason I would have been in that house."

"At the crime scene you said it was bad if you were there."

"People—concerned relatives and loved ones—hire Dr. May to look discreetly into cults and toxic churches. Bad stuff."

"Is he still around?"

I smiled. "He is. Dr. May is like a father to me. He's on staff at Great Lakes Seminary."

"Can you arrange a meeting with him?"

"I'll give you his contact information. You can tell him I sent you. He's usually in his office and available for such meetings."

"Come with me."

I started using pop psychology affirmations on myself.

You are in control. You own this situation.

"I shouldn't."

"Why not?"

"It's not my business. You don't want me, quote, 'all up in your investigation,' end quote."

You are strong. You are assertive. You are in control.

"That's not exactly what I said."

"It's what you meant."

"I just don't want you investigating on your own. Two people are dead."

"Don't worry, Jazz. I'm through with you and your investigation."

Ha! Triumph!

"No, you're not."

I didn't expect him to say that. I stammered, and my control slipped. "I—I . . . um. I just wanted to know how those men died. Honestly."

Oh, no. Now I'm confessing. This is bad.

He looked into my eyes, and the inadequate façade I'd erected started to crack. He hypnotized me with those rich, cacao eyes. "Just go see May with me."

Crack, crack, crumble.

"You can see your mentor," Jazz said. "And I'll buy you lunch. I'll even pay you for your time. Then you never have to see me—or smell me—again."

Good-bye, façade. Hello, trouble.

I sighed. "I'll go with you; but after that it's over."

"Okay, Bell."

"And don't call me Bell. It's reserved for people who love me."

"Doesn't a minute of love count?"

It did count. Way too much. "Are we driving in our own cars or going together?"

The grin and the twinkle in his eyes returned. "Will you go with me?" He laughed. "I haven't asked anybody that since I was sixteen."

"Could you please stop that, Lieutenant Brown?"

"Fine. I'll be a perfect gentleman from now on."

I glared at him. "You mean it?"

"I do. Are you ready? I'll drop you off here at your little yellow thing when we're done."

"It's a Love Bug, not a 'thing.' My great-grandmother used to say, 'Don't start no stuff, and it won't be none.' "

"Then she'd be proud of us, because it 'won't be none.' Ready?" He moved his arm toward me to guide my back.

"No touching."

"No problem," he said, but the smirk on his face told me he thought the whole thing was funny.

He led me to the Crown Vic and opened the door like a gentleman. "Buckle up. I wouldn't want your great-grandmother to think you're not safe with me."

"She wouldn't trust you as far as she could throw you."

"She would love me. I've got a gold badge. 'Protect and serve' is what I do."

"That's not even enough to convince *me* to trust you. And I'm a marshmallow by comparison."

"Then I'd tell her I was born to take care of you. And because great-grandmothers know these things, she would know I'm serious, *Bell*." Then he closed the car door like he'd only said "Watch your arm."

My heart did another little flip. Mason May's office suddenly seemed very far away.

chapter
seven

FORGET PARIS; give me the office of Dr. Mason May any day. I walk into his domain and salivate like one of Pavlov's dogs upon hearing a bell ring. Two walls are lined with books, and two are adorned with African art. A massive, antique oak desk sits near the center of the room. More books are piled on the desk and stacked on the floor. In front of the desk are two contemporary, overstuffed red chairs with mud-cloth pillows that invite you to lounge. The room is earth and fire—a marriage of passion and intellect in one sacred space. Mason's luscious "big papa" leather chair—as soft as a newborn baby—sits as stately as a throne behind his desk.

But oh, my goodness, the *books*!

Dr. May's secretary invited us to sit and wait for Dr.

May, who would join us shortly. I could tell Jazz was impressed.

"Nice digs."

"If I ever marry, I'm going to spend my honeymoon here."

"Where's the bed?"

"Don't start no stuff . . ."

"And it won't be none. Thank you, Great-Grandmother Brown. Hey, tell her to make you stop saying provocative things to me."

Just then my spiritual papa walked into the room.

"Provocative?" Dr. May's deep baritone voice thundered. The sound cheered me. "Little Bella, are you leading this nice young man into temptation?"

Jazz laughed. "Since the first moment I saw her, sir."

Pop laughed, a big booming sound.

I love that guy. He is a tall and sun-loved brown man, with springy white hair and compassionate eyes as black as crows. He could be a black angel. He's got a brilliant, theological mind to boot.

"He's not nice, Pop. He's . . ."

"I can see what he is. I'm almost seventy years old. I see stuff folks don't think I see. Stuff folks don't even know is there sometimes."

Jazz extended his hand to shake it. "I'm Jazz Brown, sir. It's a pleasure to meet you."

Mason gave his hand a vigorous shake. "The pleasure is mine, son. So, you're the one."

"The one, sir?"

"You be good to her. I've got a gun and a good eye."

I had to stop him before he incriminated himself, or me, any further. "I hope you've got a permit for that gun, Pop. Jazz is a detective. He's not 'the one.' Whatever that is. He wants to ask you about a case he's working on."

"Oh, he's the one, all right, and I do have a permit. I guess God hasn't let the two of you in on what He's doing yet." He walked around the desk and sat in the big leather chair. "Have a seat, and tell me about this case."

Jazz and I sat in the red chairs.

Pop looked at me and chuckled. "Honeymoon in my office. Lord, have mercy. You're gonna have your hands full with this one, Detective Brown."

"I'm starting to believe I will," Jazz said.

"You don't understand, Papa. We just met yesterday. We're not . . ."

"No *you* don't understand, pumpkin." He directed his attention to Jazz. "How can I help you?"

"Bell," Jazz said, sneaking a look at me, probably because he was unlawfully using my middle name, "said she investigated someone for you years ago. The house is on the east side of Detroit."

"East side. Round about where the Hare Krishna temple is? I've got a big file on them."

"No sir. It's a private residence near Seven Mile and Dequindre. The parents of Jonathan Vogel own it. He and his roommate, Damon Crawford, were found dead last night."

"Jonathan Vogel." Pop's hand went to his forehead. "Dear God. His father, Jonathan Vogel Senior, went to church with me years ago. He asked me to get some information on the man who was influencing his son. Ended up leaving the church, his heart was so broken." Dr. May shook his head, his eyes revealing sadness. "And now his boy is dead. Merciful Jesus."

"So you remember, Pop?"

He slowly nodded. He turned his gaze to Jazz. "Okay, young man. You're a detective. What's the first thing you ask yourself when you get to a scene?"

I was horrified. *He's going to test Jazz like he's his professor?*

Jazz seemed a little taken aback. "Uh. The first thing I ask myself is, How did it happen? The crime scene usually tells me that."

"What did the scene tell you?"

Jazz leaned closer to Mason. "No sign of forced entry into the house. Two bodies: Vogel and Crawford. Both young. Thin but healthy. One on the couch. One on the floor. Bodies indicate death by strychnine poisoning, but there's none in the house. We did find a Bible and a few notebooks full of references to 'Father.' But it's not the Father God of the Holy Trinity." He made the sign of the cross.

Mason May leaned back in his chair, his expression serious and thoughtful. "What's the next question you ask yourself, son?"

"I ask why someone would kill them. If the good Lord is with me, the answer to that question will lead me to who did it, and that's why we're here."

"So how can I help you?"

"Tell me about cults. I don't know this kind of killer."

"Tell him about cults, Bell."

"Excuse me?"

"Cults, pumpkin."

"Oh." I turned to Jazz, snapping out of my reverie. "'Cult' is a loaded word. It means different things to different people." I had to make myself focus. I'd been engrossed in trying to figure out what Pop meant about Jazz being "the one."

"How so?" Jazz asked.

It's really hard to pay attention to someone when you look at his face and start thinking about how his lips feel. "I mean what you call a 'cult,' someone else may call their 'religion' or their 'family.'"

"So how do you know what a cult is?"

"For practical purposes, let's begin by saying that a cult is an organization with some common goals and objectives. They can be large or small, and believe me, small can be just as destructive as large. Sometimes small cults are worse than large ones. And they're not always religious."

"Go on." He smiled at me like he was enjoying seeing me do my thing. He leaned in my direction.

An unfortunate hormonal surge slanted me Jazz-ward. "The organization centers around a charismatic leader, and when I say 'charismatic' I don't necessarily mean they speak in tongues and shout."

He looked a little uncomfortable when I mentioned speaking in tongues. "I get it," he said, with a curt edge in his voice. "So the people are into the leader. How is this different from any other religious organization? Your own church, even?"

I chuckled to think of my own pastor, Rocky. He was the antithesis of a cult leader, but I went on. "The leader usually claims to have access to something the group finds desirable."

"What religion doesn't?"

"They usually boast of special knowledge or revelation—some more special than others. It could be anything. The leader could promise to lead you to outer space where your soul will find peace and you'll live forever."

"And people buy it?"

"Yes. There are thousands of these groups in the United States alone."

Mason jumped in. "The problem with these aberrant groups is that they yield to only one authority—their leader."

"The dependence is pathological, baby," I said to Jazz. "Cults are totalitarian. What the leader says goes. For the most part, 'do as he says and not as he does' is the rule. You aren't allowed to ask questions. Eventually the leader is deified."

"You called me baby," Jazz said.

"No, I didn't."

"Yes, you did. Didn't she, Dr. May?"

"You did, pumpkin. Now finish telling your baby about cults."

I cleared my throat and proceeded as if I had not made a colossal Freudian slip. "What was I saying?" I asked, cheeks burning.

"You said, 'The dependence is pathological, *baaay-beeee.*'"

I glared at Jazz.

He got serious. "How do regular people become dependent on a cult leader?"

"Gradually. You're aware of battered woman's syndrome, right?"

"Of course."

"How does an ordinary woman become a battered woman?"

"Her abuser isolates her from her friends and family.

She trusts him but doubts herself. I've seen all kinds of psychological terrorism in those situations."

"Not just psychological. Batterers control everything: the money, the time, even her thoughts. Eventually, he ravishes any authentic sense of self she has. What's left is what the leader dictates."

Jazz seemed to ponder what I said.

"Think about the crime scene. It was totally different from when I was there years ago. Everything was stripped away, as if the house mirrored the mind-set of the victims. Empty."

The three of us grew quiet for a few moments. Jazz broke the silence. "Who is this Gabriel?" he asked.

"I don't know. Gabriel is totally unfamiliar to me."

Pop agreed. "Jonathan Vogel was under the leadership of a man named Michael."

"That's right," I said. It all came rushing back to my memory. "I remember him now. Michael Wright. He was a piece of work." A thought came to me, and I posed the question to Dr. May. "Could Jonathan have broken camp with Wright and gotten involved with another group?"

"It's hard to say," Pop said, running his hand through his fuzzy hair. "That kind of loyalty runs deep. I think if he were no longer involved with Wright, he'd stay clear of that type of group, period. Of course, it would depend on why they parted ways."

"Could Wright have changed his name?" Jazz asked.

Pop paused before answering. "That's possible, too. It's not much different from Saul in the Book of Acts changing his name to Paul after he'd encountered Christ on the road to Damascus. Wright may have believed that he'd progressed to another level spiritually. He could have changed his name to reflect his new identity."

"Lord, have mercy," I said, alarmed.

"What is it?" Jazz's eyes were full of concern.

"Michael Wright was obsessed with the number seven. He kept his group limited to seven adults."

Jazz chimed in. "Isn't that unusual? I thought cult leaders liked a large group of followers. I'm thinking of somebody like Jim Jones."

"Jim Jones liked hundreds of followers, but remember what I said about how some cults are small. Michael Wright could have many reasons for a small group. It all depends on what he wants. It could be he's too paranoid to let a lot of people in—not enough control. Big numbers weren't his thing before—and they still might not be.

"When I investigated, the group consisted of Wright, two men—one of them had to be Vogel—and four women. He excluded children in the count. If the two men are dead . . ."

Jazz finished the chilling thought, "Where are Wright and the women and children?"

"If we're dealing with Wright at all," Pop said.

Jazz moved to the edge of his chair to get closer to Mason's desk. "Dr. May, tell me your impression of Vogel Senior."

Mason ran a hand over his soft white hair. "He seemed to love his family. They came to church regularly, but he worked a lot."

"Would you say he was a workaholic?"

"I think I would have said that years ago. But a few years after his son got involved with Wright, the man seemed to be a mere shell of his former self. He took sick after that. Never did get better."

"How did Jonathan get involved with Wright?"

"I don't think the circumstances were unusual. Wright simply gave Jonathan what his own father didn't: attention and, most likely, discipline."

"Do you think Vogel Senior is capable of murder?"

Mason's eyes registered surprise. "Is he capable of murder?"

Jazz didn't repeat himself. We waited in a pause that seemed pregnant with the mysteries of the human heart.

Finally, Mason answered. "The heart is deceitful above all things, and desperately wicked: Who can know it?"

Jazz nodded. "I appreciate your time and insight. Both of you." He stood.

Pop rose from his leather chair, walked over to Jazz, and shook his hand.

"Let's pray."

I took my place beside the men, and the three of us clasped hands. Mason May called a little bit of heaven down with his vibrant, powerful invocations. His prayers sounded as melodic as psalms, and I felt goose bumps as the music of them rose and fell over us like waves. He prayed for us to have wisdom and favor with God and man. He prayed for protection and justice. He prayed for guidance and for us to experience perfect love.

When he finished, Papa embraced each of us, starting with me. "Godspeed, pumpkin. How does it feel to be thirty-five?"

"It feels good. Thanks for the gift. Tell Mama Genevia to save me a sweet potato pie this Thanksgiving," I said, squeezing him.

"Tell her yourself. She's expecting to see you before then."

He hugged Jazz next, with a manly slap on the back. Pop pulled away and looked at him, his expression somber. "God is not punishing you, Jazz."

Jazz opened his mouth as if he were going to speak but said nothing.

"He knows the desire of your heart. He put it there. *That* one, too, son."

"Excuse me?" Jazz said.

"You think what you asked for this morning is wrong."

Jazz looked surprised.

"It's not wrong to want to be loved."

Jazz stayed silent.

"Live as if it were done, and do not sin. God will bless you. He will enlarge your tents, and your seed will be called the Lord's own. It will surely come to pass."

He embraced Jazz again, and we said good-bye to Mason May.

On the drive back to the Love Bug, Jazz spoke to me only once, to ask me where I'd like to eat lunch. I declined.

We had just pulled up to the parking lot where I'd parked my car when I found the courage to ask about what had been bothering me since we left Mason's office. "He spoke God's heart to you, didn't he?"

"I'm not familiar with your Christian jargon. What are you asking me?"

"You're familiar with your Pentecostal mama. I think you know what I mean. Did he tell you something that only God could have revealed to him?"

"What he did was scare me."

"He said your seed would be blessed."

"I don't have kids, if that's what you're getting at. Maybe he got his wires crossed."

"Not Mason May."

"I thought you wanted to keep things professional," he said. His posture was rigid.

"I do."

"Let's stick to that."

"Just one more thing."

He sighed. "The last time you wanted to play Columbo, you tossed your cookies on my gators. You sure you wanna try that again?"

"It worked for Peter Falk. He did those Columbo movie specials until he was three hundred years old."

Jazz chuckled. "Yeah. I think I saw one a few months ago." His expression turned grim. "What difference does it make? I can't offer you what you want."

"How do you know what I want?"

"I have to understand human behavior for a living, too."

"Tell me what the deal is with you, Jazz."

"It's like you said at your apartment. I'm not available, Amanda."

It actually hurt to hear him say my name. I should have left but I didn't. "I'm Amanda now?"

"You asked me not to call you Bell."

"But you kept on. Why stop now?"

"What do you want from me?"

"I don't want anything from you, Jazz."

"Yes, you do," he said, softly.

He frustrated me. I didn't respond softly. "Of course I do. You picked me up and carried me up three flights of stairs. Don't you think you led me on a bit?"

"I wasn't trying to lead you on."

"You *literally* swept me off my feet."

"Okay, so I started something. I'm attracted to you. I kissed you—no, I responded to you kissing me. I flirted a little. I smelled vanilla and sweet amber on your skin, which, by the way, I'll never forget. Forgive me for being a man."

"Consider yourself forgiven, and consider me out of here."

"Don't go yet."

"And I'm staying for what?" Jazz didn't say anything. I started humming and tapping my foot. "I'm waiting, and you are staring at the windshield. Why have you asked me to stay?"

"You're mad at me."

"I don't have any reason to be mad at you."

He turned and grinned, wagging his finger at me. "Very good way to avoid telling me that yes, you're mad."

"Why should I be mad at you?"

"Do you do that to your clients?"

Of course I did. If he wanted to play verbal gymnastics, I'd beat him like a slave. "That doesn't answer the question," I said.

"You didn't answer *my* question."

"Yes. I do that to my patients."

He frowned. "That wasn't the question I wanted an answer to."

"You didn't ask me a question. You made a statement regarding my emotional state, which I responded to with a statement of my own. Now," I said, "answer *my* question."

He laughed, shaking his head. "I don't even remember your question. You confuse me, woman."

"I asked, 'Why should I be mad at you?'"

He turned his gaze back to the windshield and waited a few moments before answering. "Okay. We could talk about last night and about how I responded to you, and you to me, but you already know all that. I think you're mad because you want more. I want more, too, but I can't give it to you."

"Jazz, I'm not mad. I'm disappointed. Maybe a little exasperated. But I'm not going to pressure you. You've made yourself clear. You're unavailable. Good-bye."

He grabbed my hand. "Wait."

"What now?"

We sat there, staring at each other while Jazz cradled my hand. He sighed. "Would a general 'I don't want you to go yet' make you stay a little longer?"

"No."

"Sit here with me for a little while."

"Why are you unavailable, Jazz?"

"Can we just hang out without you asking that?"

"No, we can't. I deserve to know why. At least, if you want to keep hanging out and holding my hand, I do."

"Why are women so difficult?"

That did it. "Let me make this easier. Bye. Don't bother opening the door for me." I snatched my hand away and reached for the door handle.

"Wait."

"*What?* Are you going to say your mother would never forgive you if you weren't gentleman enough to open the car door for me? Pick a new strategy. That one is played."

"I don't want you to leave like this."

"You act like you don't want me to leave at all. You poor, gorgeous, *unavailable* detective. You want to kiss and make up, baby?"

"Yes I do. How's that for honest?"

"You know what's sad, Jazz? As irate as I am with you, I'd actually like to kiss you, too. Forgive me for being a woman."

"I didn't mean to hurt you."

"Who says I'm hurt?"

"I'm sorry, Bell."

"I'm Amanda. *Dr. Brown* to you. May I go?"

"Just one more thing." He offered a sheepish grin.

"Oh. It's *your* turn to play Columbo, Jazz?"

"It worked for you and Peter Falk."

"What do you want to say to me?"

"I'm not the only person Mason spoke God's heart to today, am I?"

He's the one all right.

I lifted my chin in defiance. So what if I didn't know whether I was defying God or Jazz? I could figure that out on my own time. "Good-bye, Lieutenant Brown."

"I'll see you later, Dr. Brown."

He opened the car door for me anyway.

chapter
eight

I F IT HAD BEEN MY DAY to work at the county jail, I could have gotten away with calling in sick again. Unfortunately, I couldn't get away with calling in sick to my private practice. I had made a gross error when I hired my mother's best friend, Maggie Harold, to be the office manager. If I had said I was sick and Maggie even vaguely suspected I wasn't, she and my mother would descend on my apartment like a couple of vultures. They would pick me apart until I spilled the whole sordid story and then haul my carcass to church before the presence of God could arrive.

I dragged myself into the tiny office space I'd rented on State Street. We'd made a comfortable reception area across from Maggie's desk in the front room, which gave way to a warm, inviting space with a "come and rest a spell, but don't get too comfortable, because you'll only be here a moment" feel that served as my office. The combination of Maggie's fine European taste, the cast-off furniture, and my "ethnic" flair made for a lovely, completely inoffensive space for us—a functional respite from a wearying world. We made our expensive coffee in an impossibly small kitchenette. I could have used a cup at that moment.

Maggie looked up from her desk and took in my appearance. "You look like death warmed over." She scowled. "Where on earth is your hair?"

"I had it cut. This is my TWA, or teeny-weeny Afro. It's chic and fabulous like *I'm* supposed to be."

"You look like a truck driver."

"You've been talking to Ma, haven't you?"

"Yes, I have. She wants to know who JB is."

I sat myself down in a chair opposite her desk and stared at Maggie. She is the picture of sophistication. A tiny woman, her once blond hair curled at the ends in an elegant gray bob. And she wore the best clothes. Today: a sky blue cashmere pantsuit. "JB?"

"Yes, Amanda Bell. JB of the massive floral arrangement that has wreaked havoc on my allergies all morning."

"Maggie, you don't have allergies."

"Look at that thing on your desk. It's a flower shop in a vase. I developed allergies just taking it into your office."

My cheeks flushed and my stomach did a few flips. I couldn't stop grinning. My internal Ringling Bros. Circus had returned. "Go away," I said.

Maggie stood and placed a hand on her hip. "Pardon me?"

"I was talking to the circus."

"Good heavens, you've lost your mind. You need your own services as a psychologist."

"I haven't lost my mind. I'm . . ."

Falling in love?

I sighed. "You're right, Maggie. I've lost my mind."

"Then get up and go into your office and have a peek at your flowers. Nothing like fresh flowers to perk a woman up." She walked from behind her desk as if she were going to shove me into my office.

"Maggie, I don't want to perk up. The circus is back, and I'm the clown."

She stopped still. "You're scaring me, Amanda Bell. Get in your office!"

"Do I have to?"

Honestly! Did he have to go and send flowers?

Maggie frowned at me. "Flowers are a *good* thing," she said, sitting on the edge of her desk. "The card says, 'If only . . . ' How could you not want to see the flowers such a poetic man sent you?"

"'If only' is not poetic; it's cruel and unusual punishment. And you weren't supposed to read my card."

"It wasn't sealed; I couldn't resist."

"How do you even know JB is a man?"

"Because I'm sixty-three years old. I know a few things. Believe it or not, I've had a man before."

"Please don't make me picture that, Maggie."

She perched her palms on her knees and leaned forward. "Who is he?"

"He's history, that's who."

"Do I call your mother or Carly?"

Honestly, if she wasn't such a great office manager . . .

"His name is Jazz Brown. He's a detective. I met him on my birthday, and I'm never going to see him again. He's not my type."

"And what is your type?"

"Available. Don't tell my mother."

Of course she would, and I'd get "the talk."

"On your birthday? Oh, you poor dear. He's married?"

"I don't think so."

"Girlfriend?"

"I'm not sure."

She sat back up. "The options are whittling down, dearie."

"Take your pick. He wouldn't say."

"Maybe he's one of those download guys who secretly likes men."

"*Download*? No, Maggie. It's 'downlow.' And *no*, there's no way that man is on the downlow."

"Well, how would I know? I don't get to see *Oprah* anymore. I'm working at 4 P.M."

"Maggie, you only work two days a week, and I happen to know you have a handheld television in your desk drawer."

"You know about my TV?"

"Ma told me."

Maggie huffed. "I'm going to get that woman—but this isn't about me."

The people in my life are experts at making whatever they're discussing about *me*.

In a rare tender moment Maggie said, "If he's playing games, he doesn't deserve you."

I hadn't expected her to say that. Nor had I expected what she did next. She came over and held my face in her hands. For a minute I had my Aunt Maggie back, the woman who used to kiss many boo-boos away, not my crotchety secretary. She gave me a little peck and released my face.

"'If only . . .'" she said, gliding like she was on a cloud back over to her desk. "You've got to admit it's kind of sweet." She pulled her little television out of her desk drawer and put the earbuds into her ears.

"I'll admit no such thing. I hate men this morning."

She spoke a little louder than usual. "Then I'm sorry to tell you Rocky has been phone stalking you since yesterday. Why isn't your cell phone on?"

"I forgot to charge it."

"What?" Maggie yelled.

"Take those earbuds out until I get into my office, Maggie."

She did not. More yelling: "What?"

"What about Rocky?" I yelled back.

Rocky is my pastor *and* my former boyfriend. It *sounds* worse than it actually is. We've been friends for seven years and were in love for one of them. He wanted lots of children, and I knew I'd be fortunate if I could have even one. Rocky said he loved me enough to give up his dream of having a brood of little Rocks. I said I loved him too much to allow him to do that. We parted amicably, but with sorrow.

She must have felt sympathy after my close encounter with Mr. If Only, because Maggie stopped watching *Maury* long enough to get me a cup of coffee before she called my mother. A short time later, coffee in hand, I listened to Maggie tell my mother about that cad JB, aka Jazz Brown. I smiled, daydreaming that Jazz, realizing how wrong he'd been, was begging for my hand in marriage. Just then Rocky walked in looking like he could be one of my clients.

"What in the world is the matter with you?"

Rocky ran a hand through his spiky blond hair, now in need of a haircut. Rocky is a hip, tattooed, passionate, emergent-church pastor, seven years my junior. He's got brown puppy eyes that make him look childlike. I'd learned not to let those eyes fool me. He's passionate about more than just Christ. But the eyes make him look sweet. He's actually downright adorable. Everyone loved him—the notable exceptions being my mother, Maggie, and Carly.

"I've got a problem, babe. Where have you been? I can't catch you at home, at work, or on your cell."

"I've been busy."

"When did you get too busy for me, babe?"

No matter that we haven't dated for a year. I can't break this man of calling me "babe." Not even at church. "Don't call me babe. What's the problem?"

"It's one of the women at church."

I hoped this wasn't about a love interest. Even though we aren't together, I still get jealous when someone shows an interest in him. "Who?"

"Susan Hines."

"Who?"

"If you came to church regularly, you'd know."

"I went to church recently."

"It was six weeks ago."

Had it been six *weeks?*

Maggie, still on the phone with my mother, told her I hadn't been to church in six weeks.

I stood, careful not to spill my coffee, and motioned with my head for Rocky to follow me into my office. He trudged behind me and plopped rather dramatically onto the couch.

Yes, I have a couch. Clients find it comforting.

As soon as I walked in I noticed my desk buckling under the weight of a floral arrangement the size of a Volvo. I tried to ignore it, and sat behind my desk, partially obscured by it. "So, what's going on with Susan Haynes?"

"Hines. Babe, she's freaking me out."

"Don't call me babe. Is she one of your girlfriends, Rocky?"

"You know I don't date women at church anymore. Who sent you a meadow?"

"Those?" I pointed to the burgeoning monstrosity that seemed to be growing before my eyes. "They're a birthday thing. About Susan Highland . . ."

"Hines. Are you seeing someone?"

"They're from some cop named Jazz Brown."

He stared at the flowers. "They're kinda scary. Did he get them at the Little Shop of Horrors?"

"I can remove them, Rocky."

With a forklift.

"It must be serious," he said, his brow furrowed. "Look at the size of that thing."

"It's not serious. Now, what about Susan Hayward?"

"Susan *Hines*! You've fallen in love, haven't you?"

"Don't be ridiculous." I couldn't keep from smiling.

Rocky scowled. "What a sucky day I'm having, and it's not even nine o'clock. Hey, you want some hotcakes and sausages from McDonald's?"

"No, but you do. And since you're leaving in two seconds, you'll have plenty of time to make it over there before they stop serving them. Now, tell me about Susan Holland, fast."

"You can't even remember her name, for heaven's sake. Are you in any shape to work today?"

"I can work. It's not like I'm sick. What about Susan whoever?"

"Now I know how *you* feel when you're jealous."

"Don't assume I get jealous of your women. Tell me why you're here, or I'll get you a prescription for Prozac."

"Don't get salty with me because you're in denial. What kind of name is Jazz?"

"What kind of name is Rocky?"

He narrowed his eyes at me. "Rocky is a way cool name."

"This coming from a guy who pastors a church called the Rock House."

He pouted.

I'd worn him out. I always won fights with Rocky.

"Fine," he said. "Susan Hines came to the church a few days ago—the day before your birthday. She'd left a bad situation."

"Bad situation" is code for "she left a toxic church or cult." Rocky runs something like a safe house for people in bad situations. He began it by taking a few people in and allowing them to stay in the house the church owns. Rocky lives there along with some of the Rock House's ministry leaders. We used to counsel people there together until our relationship became . . . complicated. I almost left the Rock House over it. Rocky would say that, based on attendance, I did leave. But I love my church. It's way cool. Shoot. Now I sound like Rocky.

I took a sip of coffee. "So, she's been staying at the house?"

"Yeah. Only, yesterday we're all sittin' around, watchin' the evening news, and she goes all hysterical. 'They're *dead*? They can't be *dead*.' She's screamin' it, mutterin' it, and then, totally silent. Like *totally* shocked. I guess two of the guys in the group she left got whacked in Detroit."

"You've been watching *The Sopranos* again, haven't you?"

"I'm trying to cut down, but listen, babe . . ."

"Don't call me babe."

"These two dudes, Jonathan and David some-body . . ."

I jumped up, moved around the flowers, and cleared a tiny bit of desk to sit on. "You mean Jonathan Vogel and Damon Crawford."

"Babe, you're good."

"Don't call me babe." I got excited. "I happen to know about the case."

"Well, talk to her. She's going all psycho on me."

"Can you describe 'going all psycho,' please?"

He sat up on the couch. "Now she's like," he said, and did a dead-on imitation of flat-affect catatonic behavior.

"That's bad," I said.

He kept looking catatonic.

"I said that's bad, Rocky."

He continued.

"Stop it."

He snapped out of it, reluctantly. "Whoa. That was trippy. It's like centering prayer or something."

"I think not. Does she have a history of schizophrenia?"

"How should I know? You're the shrink."

"Don't call me a shrink. I am a fully licensed psychologist."

"You gonna see her, babe?"

I didn't bother to correct him this time. "Of course I am. This is a remarkable opportunity, Rock. She could be a witness. She might know where the rest of the people in the group are."

"Yeah, only, she's catatonic."

"When did she see the news broadcast?"

"The day after your birthday—yesterday."

"And how was she before that?"

"She seemed fine. A little quiet, a little distant. Stunned, off balance—like they all are—but mostly fine. She talked."

"And now she's not?"

"I told you, she's like this." He went catatonic for the longest thirty seconds ever.

"Don't do that again, Rocky."

He laughed. "That is so freaky," he said, shuddering. "Come over to the house and at least check her out for yourself. Remember how fragile you were when you needed help? And nobody you know got killed the day after you left."

Rocky knew some painful things about my past, like the fact that I happened to have *been* a Susan some years ago.

"I'll be there."

"Really, babe?"

"Yes."

"And I don't even have to give you the full puppy-eyes arsenal?"

"Not today. Though I hope you are punished sorely for misusing such a charming facial feature."

"Are you kidding? God gave me these eyes like he gave skunks stink and porcupines . . . you know, those porcupine things that stick you."

"Quills."

"Yeah. See what a good team we make? You still want me, don't you?"

"Don't get beside yourself, Rocky."

He grinned at me, and I had to smile because he's just so darned sweet-looking.

"I'll stop by after my last client."

If he had a tail to go with those peepers, it'd be wagging with glee. We stood, and I walked him out of my office. Maggie rolled her eyes at him. Okay, she rolled them at us.

Rocky smiled at her. "Hello, Miss Maggie. Please send Mrs. Brown my warmest regards." Then he ran behind her desk and gave her a big, loud kiss on the cheek. She turned a deep shade of red and hung up on my mother.

Rocky spun a twirly, tappy, Snoopy dance out the door. When he was a safe distance from Maggie, he yelled, "Thanks, babe. You're one righteous God chick."

I laughed all the way into my office. And then my phone rang.

"Dr. Amanda Brown," I said, shifting to a crisp, professional tone.

"Did you see the flowers?" a velvet voice on the line asked.

I blushed, glad I was dark enough not to turn red like Maggie just had. The circus returned and got very busy inside my belly. "Stevie Wonder could see those flowers, Lieutenant Brown."

"Are you suggesting that I went a little overboard?"

"No. I have plenty of space in my office for the enchanted forest."

"I'm glad you think they're enchanted. I recently started believing in magic."

"Thank you for the flowers," I said, softly. The thought of him made me feel a little melancholy. *If only* . . . "Can I help you?"

"Don't be so formal, Bell."

"You're sending me flowers *and* calling me Bell again. Are you trying to tell me something?"

"I'd like to talk to you about business."

"I may have a bit of business to talk to you about, too," I said, feeling guilty that I'd agreed to see Susan Hines but was not quite ready to share that itsy-bitsy detail with Jazz. The psychologist part of me had taken over, and I didn't want to share this fascinating patient with anyone—not just yet.

"I've been looking for a consultant on this whole cult thing."

"I recommend Dr. Mason May. He is the foremost authority on cults in Michigan."

"He is also leaving for a cruise this weekend with his beloved wife, Genevia. He recommends Dr. Amanda Brown."

"Oh, come on. He's got scores of colleagues. He could recommend a number of people."

"I asked him if anyone else was available."

My defenses went up higher than the price of coffee at Starbucks. "What's wrong with me?"

"I thought you would have a problem working with me."

"Because we had a—what did we have, Jazz? A fling and a prayer?"

"A *fling*? I remember the prayer, but how did I miss the fling?"

I ignored him, and he filled the silence with a bomb-shell. "I've been celibate for three years." He sounded peeved, as if I had forced him to disclose a dirty little secret.

"Could you kindly watch your tone with me?"

"Could you kindly not torment me with the notion that we had a fling?"

"You've been celibate for three years?" That most likely eliminated a wife. A girlfriend. And everyone else. Maybe there was hope for us after all.

"You weren't supposed to comment on that. I wasn't even supposed to *say* that, and don't even think about asking about it, Bell."

Shoot.

"That's *Dr. Brown* to you."

"Whateva."

Something occurred to me. "Did Mason ask you why you wanted to know if someone else was available?"

"You know him well."

"What did you say?"

"I told him everything."

"Oh, no!" I'd rather have him tell my mother.

"Chill out. I just said that as payback for the 'fling and a prayer' comment."

"Hmmph."

"Don't you hmmph me, young lady. The way you turn a phrase is far more interesting, even when it's not quite accurate. 'Fling and a prayer.' Believe me, if we'd had a fling, there'd be no doubt about it." He went on and on in his outrage.

If I could die from impatience, I'd have been a corpse by the time I was able to ask him what I wanted to know. When he finally shut up, I went for it. "What, exactly, *did* you tell him?"

"I said I thought it best if we didn't work together, to which he promptly replied that he thought it best if we did. Anyway, he's got that whole 'God tells me your business' thing going on."

"I believe that's called a 'word of knowledge.'"

"I believe that's called creepy. It doesn't take a spiritual gift to see how I feel about you. I'm talking feelings, not a fling."

"Spare me the details."

"Are you going to act as a consultant on this case?"

"Maybe I'm *unavailable*."

"Score one for Bell. Look, I need you. Two men are dead. I work homicide in *Detroit*. It's not like people are going to stop shooting, stabbing, and bludgeoning one another so I can concentrate. I got two more cases since Wednesday, and my team is working extra hours. I'm losing time. We can keep it professional. I don't want this thing to go cold."

"Don't call me Bell."

"Did I mention it pays five grand?"

I smiled at his magic words. "I'm *so* available to work on this case with you."

He laughed, and I imagined that amazing smile. "I told you I'd see you later. I'll get back with you on the details. And thank you."

Five grand. I know the Lord can give you exactly what you need, but the exact amount? Amazing grace. I needed that money. Badly.

I also needed to get off the phone, quick.

Unfortunately, as soon as we ended the call and I hung up, I wondered if I was making a big mistake. The fling comment likely made him forget that I had said I may have some business with him. *What are you doing, Bell? You should have told him about Susan. And how on* earth *are you supposed to work with him?* I thought about those prayer beads he had given me. "It helps to feel something" *my eye*! Just talking to him made me *feel* plenty. For a moment I wondered if I'd need those beads after all.

A sinking feeling came over me. Ma Brown used to say, "You can't have too much prayer or love." I pictured my great-grandma, with her honey-colored skin and high, part-Cherokee cheekbones. In my vision her wise eyes told me all I needed to know.

chapter
nine

I SHOULD MAKE "Thou shalt not talk to Jazz if thou must work" a personal commandment. The conversation I had with him left me in a vegetative—albeit warm and fuzzy—state. He was like a big Valium. To the five unfortunate souls who appeared at my office for guidance, I ended up doing a lot of smiling, nodding, and using some variation of the prompt "tell me more." It's a good thing it was Friday; my clients are always chatty on Fridays. They didn't seem to notice that I was as high as a Georgia pine off Detroit's *finest*. Pun intended.

I lugged myself to the Rock House *house* immediately after leaving my office, having strategically chosen to make my appearance during the dinner hour. The timing would ensure maximum avoidance of human contact.

When I arrived, Rocky met me at the door. "Thanks for coming, babe." He kissed me on the cheek.

"Where is she?"

"Right this way."

He escorted me through the sprawling Victorian and into a small office reserved for counseling. The staff house has five bedrooms, each the picture of understated elegance. The colors are muted and soothing, and the furniture is minimal and classic. Three of the bedrooms are for staff, and one is used for visitors. The other is the counseling office—used for individual and group sessions.

Susan Hines stood in the far corner of the room, looking small and vulnerable. I noted my impressions of her: white female; appeared to be somewhat malnourished; gaunt but childlike face; thin, red hair in loose waves down her back. I was struck by how young she was—not much more than a teen.

She stood still, appearing to be without affect, staring blankly ahead with her head cocked slightly to the left, hands clasped in front of her. Someone's little girl. Where were her parents?

I approached her tentatively. "Susan?" I said, dragging an upholstered chair near her. I sat. I hoped it would encourage her to do the same.

She said and did nothing, only stared with blank, green eyes.

"Susan, my name is Amanda. I'm a psychologist."

Nothing.

"I'm here to see if you'd like to talk about what's bothering you. I'd like to help if I can."

She remained unresponsive.

"I'm going to touch your hands, okay? Please don't be frightened. I want to help you."

I reached out and cradled her hands. She didn't flinch. I pulled them apart, and she made no effort to stop me. As soon as I sat back in my chair, she folded her hands together. The gesture was subtle—almost defiant. Her message: leave me alone.

Schizophrenics can present as catatonic; however, catatonics are not always schizophrenic. A medical condition or other disorder could be responsible. I've worked with catatonics at the jail. Most of them were brought to me with either agitated, purposeless movements, or the appearance of being frozen in a bizarre or inappropriate position. If this had been the case with Susan, when I moved her hands, they would have remained in the position I had moved them to.

I've also treated catatonic schizophrenics who present with mutism—the refusal or inability to talk. It always reminds me of the writer Maya Angelou, who stopped speaking after she was molested. However, Maya Angelou was no catatonic schizophrenic. I doubted that Susan Hines was, either.

I thought back to when Rocky said she arrived at the church—the day before my birthday. According to

Carly, the men had been dead for about twenty-four hours when they were discovered. She likely arrived at the safe house on the day the men were murdered.

I felt a chill run through me along with the shocking realization that if Susan Hines had fled the group on the day the two men were murdered, she may have been running for her life. I feared for the other women in the group. What had happened to them? And where were the children and their leader?

I looked at Susan. I had to gain her trust. "Can you tell me why you came here?"

Silence.

I waited. If she were malingering, it would be difficult to maintain a fake catatonic state. She would get tired or hungry or need to use the bathroom. I would stay until she broke. It's not like I had anything else to do except watch *CSI* DVDs. And after my birthday experience, I wasn't inclined to do that for a while.

Susan Hines never looked at me. She refused to speak and as the hours passed, the only difference I noticed in her was the grim, flat line her mouth had become.

Five hours after I arrived, urine flowed down her legs onto the parquet floor. She stood the whole time. Though she showed no hint of discomfort at being wet, something briefly shadowed her steady gaze. The faintest flicker of . . . what was it? Shame? A memory?

My guess: She wasn't catatonic—she was scared to death—a feeling I was all too familiar with.

Even worse: Maybe the memory I imagined I saw in her eyes had nothing to do with her.

Maybe it was my own.

chapter
ten

I ARRIVED AT THE PARKING LOT of my apartment building a little after midnight and found a gorgeous detective sitting on the trunk of a now very familiar unmarked, police-issued Crown Vic.

He folded his arms across his chest in the now famous stance of protection, but his smile was characteristically open. His eyes were smiling, too.

"Lieutenant?" I unintentionally gushed.

"You're up past your bedtime, no?" Jazz drawled. He uncrossed his arms and hopped off the trunk of the car. I enjoyed the view as he swaggered over to me—too close. *Ummm.* I noticed that same delicious scent—only more so.

Heaven help me.

"You've come calling on a lady at midnight?"

"I've actually been here for three hours. I didn't take you for the type that stays out late, party girl."

"It's not *that* late, and, trust me, I'm no party girl—but I think you already knew that, didn't you?"

"Are you psychoanalyzing me?"

I shrugged. "What can I say? I've got skills."

"Oh, yeah? Well, give me your best shot."

"About what?"

"Why do you think I'm here, Doctor?"

I looked into his eyes; they were bright with mocking challenge. "Okay. You've been here for three hours because you really want to see me."

"It doesn't take a psychologist to figure that one out."

"And after about, say, ten-thirtyish, you got a little salty because I wasn't home."

He inched a little closer to me. "That was easy, too."

"But you got more salty thinking about who I may have been spending my time with."

"Go on."

"No denial, Lieutenant?"

"How can I deny anything to a psychologist? You can see right into my brain," he teased, pointing to his head while easing up to me, closing much-needed space.

I felt a little giddy, but I continued. "You chastised yourself, but you couldn't stop thinking about it. You should have left, but again, you really needed to see me."

"I needed my psychologist's consultation." He gave me one of those fine grins and grazed my hair with his fingers. "Your haircut brings out your eyes," he said. "They're beautiful, you know. Expressive. You wouldn't last a minute in my interrogation room. Your eyes tell all."

"It wouldn't be your interrogation room that I'd be worried about."

He nodded and regarded me with a gaze that made me want to pray for deliverance. "Do you always say exactly what you think?"

"I'm afraid not. Just ask my mother, sister, and secretary."

"And yet you do with me."

"There's something about you, Lieutenant."

"Why don't you call me Jazz, Bell?"

"Why don't you call me Dr. Brown, and see me during business hours?" I returned his teasing grin, and stepped away from him and the car, letting him know that I could resist his charms.

He allowed the room I created and continued the conversation. "I spend a great deal of time in interrogation rooms with nutjobs, some of whom are very talkative. Others are not so much. Tonight, I got a talkative one. Kept me at the station house longer than usual. I would have tried to call you, but Carly wouldn't give me your home phone number."

"She wouldn't?"

"Said something about you being *unavailable*. Put a strong emphasis on the word."

I shook my head. She didn't hear the "U" word from me, but the grapevine pretty much consisted of Maggie, my mother, and Carly. It was only a matter of time before my sister knew all the details in Technicolor. I'm surprised she hadn't found me already and given me "the talk"—and she's the one who got me into this mess. "I'm sure you could get my home phone number if you really wanted it, Lieutenant."

"Maybe I'd like to get it from you."

"So you came here and waited three hours to get my phone number?"

He shrugged. "What can I say? I'm dedicated."

"Dedicated yet unavailable. A bit of a paradox."

"As a psychologist you should know that women understand paradoxes so much better than us concrete men."

"Is that what you're here for? A woman's understanding?"

He laughed. "You sure are a tough interrogator, Bell."

"Dr. Brown," I said. I tried to change the subject. "You said some 'nutjob' detained you at work. Could this 'nutjob' have been talkative about the Vogel and Crawford case?"

"I wish. Which is why I'm here."

"Among other reasons," I supplied. The night possessed a sultry kind of heat that made me feel as bold and wild-hearted as the man in front of me.

"I'm here to talk about the case." He smiled like he knew I knew he was lying. "You gonna invite me inside? Or would you like for me to take you somewhere?"

"What makes you think I would go somewhere with you at this time of night?"

"The same thing that makes you think I sat here for hours being jealous of who I imagined you were spending your Friday night with."

"You can't come upstairs. Absolutely not."

"But it's for the case."

I wondered what harm there could be in us having a little chat about the case in my apartment.

Okay, so the alarms in my head went off so loud they left my ears ringing. My great-grandmother used to say, "Don't let the devil ride. If you let him ride, he's gonna want to drive, so don't let him ride." If I let that man inside my apartment, I'd be letting the devil ride in a red Mustang with a drop-top.

C'mon, Ma Brown. No fair. Can't you see he's way out of my league? I'll never get the attention of anyone like him again.

It was still awfully close to my birthday. Didn't I deserve just a little bit of kissing and hugging? Nothing more.

Really! Nothing more.

It had a harsh finality to it, this troubling "nothing more." No, what I really deserved was a good relationship, one that could lead to marriage—not a make-out session. I didn't care how good-looking the man was. Wasn't I too old to be stupid?

"I'm sorry, Jazz. It's just not a good idea."

"But I've waited hours to see you."

"Why is that?"

"You already know why."

I suddenly felt like I was boiling with frustration. "You seem to be interested in me, and then it seems like you're playing games with me."

"I *am* interested in you."

"But you're *unavailable.* No wife. No girlfriend. Maybe you aspire to be a monk. Your reasons for being alone are your business, but I have to ask: Why did you park the Garden of Eden in my office? Why did you park yourself in front of my apartment for three hours? Why are you here, Lieutenant?"

We stood there glaring at each other, the light from the streetlamp shining overhead, until he looked away.

Jazz chuckled. "It's funny that you should mention a monk. If I were trying to be one, I wouldn't be doing such a great job, would I? Sitting outside your apartment all night trying to pretend I want to work on the case." He crossed his arms over his heart again. That man might as well have been wearing a suit of armor. "I don't make myself vulnerable to women. I don't want to be here. I don't want to be spending the little bit of free time I have in your parking lot. And stay away from your neighbor."

"What neighbor?"

"Henry. From the apartment next door."

"Okay." I was too interested in what he had to say next to ask him about Henry.

He looked surprised. "You're just going to say 'Okay'? You're not even going to ask me why I said that?"

"Right now, I don't care why you don't want me around Henry, but I am going to ask you why you're here if you don't want to be." I moved closer to him. I expected him to back away, but he didn't move.

He also didn't answer me.

"Tell me why you're here. I want to hear you say it."

"We should be discussing the case," he said, fidgeting.

"Why are you here, Jazz?"

"Oh, now I'm Jazz. Not 'Lieutenant.'"

I touched his shoulder. "Jazz." My voice became a whisper, and it was a bad idea to touch him. I didn't want to stop. "Tell me."

His hand caught mine, and he rubbed circles on the back of it with his thumb, pulling me close until there was no space between us. "You know, I hate it that you're a psychologist. It's torture."

"A girl's gotta have some leverage."

"Can I tell you a story?" he asked.

"What's it about?"

"It's about a monk."

I laughed. "So, you *do* want to be a monk?"

"You gonna let me tell it or not?"

I sat on the trunk of the Crown Vic. "Okay, I'm listening."

He sighed. "There was this monk walking with some of his brothers one day in a busy marketplace when he saw this theater troupe. They were laughing and making a bunch of noise, when he looked up and saw one of the actresses. She was beautiful, you know?"

"Lots of actresses are," I said, thinking of Halle Berry, wishing her a terrible fate like premature aging.

"His brothers wouldn't so much as glance in her direction. But there was something about this actress and this monk. Her beauty did something to him."

"Is this a bad story?" I asked. "I don't know if I like the direction this thing is taking."

"You're supposed to be listening."

I shut up.

"Anyway, he saw her, and he said to his brothers, 'How can anyone see a woman so beautiful and not worship God?'"

"That sounds like a pickup line." I frowned. "Even monks have pickup lines? What kind of world is this?"

"But it wasn't a pickup line. He didn't even say it to her. She inspired him. She awakened him."

"All that to say . . ."

"Let's say there's some modern version of that story."

"I see, like *The Message* version?"

He took my hands. "Fine. *The Message* version, but with a few different details."

"Like?"

He came close to me again. "Say the monk is a cop. Maybe disillusioned about love. Maybe unwilling to try."

"And the actress?"

"Maybe she's a praying forensic psychologist slash theologian slash private investigator in an unforgettable red silk dress."

"And he sees her."

"And everything looks different after that. Even God."

I sat there for a while, pondering what he'd said. His face looked open, vulnerable, and afraid. I didn't have any wisecracks. No one had ever said anything that beautiful to me before.

He spoke softly, shoving his hands in his pants pockets. "I'm afraid to be in love, Bell. I can't—I can't . . ." Before I could talk myself out of it, I bounded off the trunk of that car and went into his arms, kissing him as if I could heal whatever ailed him. I'd become the actress, all right; acting like my love would be enough to change whatever kept us apart.

We stood there with the inky night applauding us, lost in our roles. The way he kissed me felt sacred; his touch all grace and tenderness. He treated me as if I were a gift from God, each exploration of my mouth delicate, tentative, reverent, until finally, breathlessly, he pulled away.

"We have to stop this, Bell."

"I'm sorry about that." I trembled at the loss of his warmth around me. I tried to lighten the mood. "How did you make me kiss you again, anyway?"

He chuckled, "You are a dangerously passionate woman. I'm just a victim here."

I stroked his cheek. "Who broke your heart?"

"That's not a conversation I'm willing to have right now. Maybe not ever."

I released him. Oh, Lord, I don't know how I did it. "Good night, Lieutenant. Call me during business hours, and we'll work. Okay?" I turned to go upstairs to my apartment.

"Bell, wait."

I turned again and looked back at him. The seasoned detective had gotten through my interrogation without telling me any real details, but his eyes said he wanted to tell all. *In time.* At least, I hoped so.

"I should see you to your door."

"I'm afraid you'll have to disappoint your mama tonight, Lieutenant Brown. That might be dangerous for you; might put another dent in that armor of yours."

"Then I'll be watching you from here."

"You'd better be."

I turned away and went upstairs alone.

chapter
eleven

HOURS LATER I thrashed in bed, beating up my pillows. I tried not to think about Jazz or Susan Hines.

I turned on the television. Apparently, I had programmed my television to tune in to every crime show known to man. And woman.

When did I become so morbid?

I turned to a religious network. An elderly Southern woman with an enormous, old-lady blue beehive hair don't—a far cry from a do—smiled at the camera with dentures as tall as skyscrapers. This woman frightened me more than all the forensic shows I had watched, combined. She wore a tomato-juice red, floor-length gown with ruby-colored rhinestones at the cuffs—singularly the most appalling formal I'd ever seen.

Actually, the dress—accessorized with a feather

boa—that Carly made for my junior prom holds that honor. I had wanted a classic little black dress. Carly complained that I had more black in my wardrobe than Darth Vader. She said, "Lighten up, cupcake," and proceeded to coerce me into agreeing to wear a *yellow* prom dress, one she herself would design.

The resulting yellow nightmare secured my place as an outcast during my last year of high school and was the reason the senior class nicknamed me "Big Bird." But the Kathryn Kuhlman look-alike's dress on TV gave my prom hookup a run for the money.

The woman spoke with a strong Southern drawl. For a moment I wondered if a special seminary somewhere *way* down South manufactured televangelists. With few exceptions, they all seemed to be Southern.

Sistah Reverend must have gotten a sudden surge of divine energy. She started blinking madly and waving her gnarled hands wildly in the air, spitting out a chant like she had some kind of Christian Tourette's syndrome: "Cheeses. Cheeses. Cheeses."

Make that *dairy* Tourette's syndrome.

Then she started coughing.

No, wait. My mind clicked. She'd said "Jesus," only it sounded like "cheeses" the way she kind of wheezed it. She pointed to the camera so that to viewers it looked as if she were pointing at them. "You need *cheeses* in your life."

I had missed dinner. A grilled cheese sandwich sounded good, but it required too much effort for my current level of exhaustion.

Surely this isn't what Jesus had in mind when he talked about hungering for righteousness.

Still, she'd convinced me that I needed cheeses. If I added crackers, I'd have myself a nice little snack.

"Put your hand on the television." The contemporary Reverend Kate Kuhlman said, "You need a touch from *cheeses.*"

I wholeheartedly agreed, and since I'd never made it to the kitchen and the hands of God didn't seem to be coming out of the ceiling, I headed to the television. I love these spiritual/technological advances pioneered by televangelists. Touching a TV screen equals *touches* from God.

I placed my hand on the top of the boob tube. Warmth radiated through my hands. I didn't think it was from the Lord but rather heat from the electronics busily working inside—but it felt nice just the same. And what the heck, who would it hurt? I kept my hand there a little longer, until Kate Kuhlman had another coughing fit, and I actually prayed that God would heal the lung condition that was making her television appearance problematic. I also prayed for her to get a head-to-toe makeover as well as new fashion and hair stylists. I didn't even feel hungry anymore.

Momentarily revived, I flopped back down on my bed to resume battering my bedding.

To keep from thinking about falling in love with 'fraidy cat, I thought a little more about Susan, avoiding that teensy detail about how I should have told Jazz about meeting her but didn't. I mean, what was there to tell? She hadn't said a word. Right?

The image of her wetting herself without flinching started to torment me, drawing darkness from my own inner depths. I twisted the pillows over my head as if I could block the memories with them.

————————

He told me I couldn't call myself Amanda. He didn't want me to have the name of a slave, and I hadn't revealed to him enough character to be given a Hebrew name. So he called me "wife"—the same as he called the other three. Miriam was the only one who'd earned her name.

He said all black people were descendants of the Israelites, and we were to reclaim our rightful place as God's chosen people. This is what he believed, and when I was with him, I believed it, too.

That day I'd told Miriam that my great-grandmother was a strong influence on me. I said I was named after her. Miriam told him I said my name was Amanda. He almost broke my jaw for it.

"What is your name?" he bellowed at me again and again, his rant fueled by cocaine.

"I don't have a name," I said with downcast eyes. I was not allowed to look at him directly.

"What is your name?"

"I don't have one. I don't deserve a name."

The tirade went on and on. He would not allow me to sleep. He would not allow me to tend to the tooth he'd knocked loose or my bleeding mouth. Even though I was pregnant, I knew I had better not ask to go to the bathroom. For three hours I stood there—mute, hurt, bleeding—while he yelled and cursed at me, until hot urine burned down my legs, pooling on the floor.

He laughed and pushed me to my knees. He thrust my face into my own urine. *"Your name is Dog. I want all you other wives to call her Dog. That's her name."* He turned to look at me. *"What is your name?"*

I didn't say a word, and his fists descended on my head in a flurry of blows. Tiny white lights exploded behind my eyes, and pain shot through my head with each strike.

Oh, God. Yahweh, help me. I'm going to have his baby.

"What is your name?"

"I'm not a dog," I whispered.

He lifted me to my feet and beat me mercilessly—until my eyes were swollen shut. Until every part of my body ached. Until a river of blood flowed between my legs.

"My name is Dog," I finally screamed—for the sake of the baby. I didn't want to die before I saw her.

I stopped talking then. If I opened my mouth I feared everything I felt would pour out and I would kill him.

They called me Dog after that, and for three months I didn't utter a word.

Even after that, I still loved him.

———————

It just doesn't pay to remember some things. I sat on my bed, my chest heavy with shame. I had to remind myself to breathe. I couldn't think of a coherent prayer to pray. It happened so long ago, but remembering took me right back there.

I'm okay. Right?

I didn't feel okay.

I grabbed the prayer beads that I now kept on the night table by my bed. I fingered the glowing wine-colored beads, wishing Jazz had taught me how to use them.

Our Father which art in heaven,
Hallowed be thy name.

I fumbled with the beads until they dropped from my shaking hands. I picked up the telephone. It was late, but he'd take the call.

He answered after the second ring, his voice thick with sleep. "Hullo."

"Hello, Rocky?"

"Babe, is that you?"

"It's me."

"What's the matter?"

"I'm okay, right?"

"Did that Susan Hines thing get to you?" His gentle voice soothed me.

"Yeah, Rock, it did."

"You're okay now. You really are."

I started bawling. "I'm not sure I'm okay."

He cleared his throat and waited for me to settle down. It took a long time. "You're more than okay, Bell. You're a psychologist. A doctor God-chick. Your bruises are gone; your broken bones healed. I'd still marry you in a heartbeat."

"You need to find someone your own age."

"Flower dude's going to take you away from me."

"That's unlikely."

"I don't know about that. I can tell you like him. A lot."

"I like Mexican food, but—"

He laughed. I could picture his horrified expression. "Babe, you don't have to remind me what Mexican food does to your, uh, constitution."

"I love you, Rocky."

"Not enough to marry me."

"Why do we revisit this? You're my best friend now."

"I could be your blond boy toy, only we'd be holy and stuff."

I smiled. "You're so silly."

"At least you stopped crying."

"Aha. You diverted my attention away from my existential angst."

"What can I say? I'm good, babe, but not as good as you. You got everything you lost, and more. Don't forget that."

I snuggled under the quilt my great-grandma had made. "Not everything, Rock. Not everybody."

"Not yet. But Jesus gives everything back, eventually. His kingdom come, His will be done, and all that. Some stuff you get on earth. Some stuff you get in heaven. She's in heaven. You'll get her back." He paused. "Hang on, okay?"

I heard Rocky stumble around his room, slam into something, say, "Whoa," and come back to the phone. "You there, Babe?"

"I'm here."

"Listen."

He played the Lord's Prayer on his acoustic guitar.

I love that guy. He serenaded me in musical supplication until my tears were forgotten. Peace settled on me while I nestled under Ma Brown's Star of Bethlehem quilt. Rocky played until I'd almost fallen asleep.

Thy kingdom come,
Thy will be done,
in earth as it is in heaven.

And, Jesus, give my little girl a big hug for me.

chapter
twelve

THE NEXT MORNING, an incessant pounding awakened me.

The door. I stumbled to it without bothering to put on a robe over my ratty, blue-flannel pajamas. They are shameless comfort clothes—soft, stained, with one of the top buttons missing. Why sew on another when there's a perfectly good safety pin to hold the fabric together?

"Police!" the pounder yelled.

My breath caught in my throat. *Somebody died.* It's my mother. My sister. Maggie. All of them.

I fumbled with the lock and snatched the door open, my heart thudding.

An unsmiling Jazz Brown stood there scowling at me. *Man, he looks good in a suit.* This one black and as fine as he was. He took a deep breath. So did I, but for a different reason.

"I thought something happened to you. I've been trying to call you since six A.M."

Did I say my pj's are shameless? Let me recant that. They are only shameless when a beautiful man is not looking at them. "Uh. Jazz, hi. I thought you said you didn't have my phone number."

"I got creative."

"And why were you calling me at six A.M.?"

A tiny smile played about his lips. I hoped I didn't have any lint in my hair. "What's up with the phone, Bell?"

"You're such a cop. And don't call me Bell."

"I drove at about ninety miles an hour to get to you." He ran his hand through his brown curls.

"The police didn't stop you?"

"I *am* the police."

"Would you like to come in, Lieutenant?"

He didn't say anything, but walked inside. I closed the door.

"I think my blood pressure spiked." He locked my door and put on the chain.

"Cocoa?" I asked, smiling at him with unbrushed teeth.

He looked me up and down, "Only if you take off your pajamas."

For a moment I thought Jazz found me more attractive than I realized. "Excuse me?"

"I'm not flirting. The pajamas. They're disgusting."

"And what did you sleep in last night?"

"If I tell you, I'll have to kill you."

I put a hand on my flannel-clad hip. "What gives you the right to criticize my sleepwear? Especially since you're here unannounced."

"Again, *Dr. Brown,* I've been calling you all morning. I thought you'd been murdered."

"Are you always this paranoid?"

"I'm a homicide detective. I happen to see murdered people on a regular basis, some of them as normal as you—at least, I thought you were normal until I saw those pajamas."

"These are my fuzzy pajamas. I *need* them like I need chocolate and a husband. So, back up off of me."

"Fine. I'll take the cocoa, please."

"Have a seat," I said, heading to the bedroom to put on my robe. Jazz sat on the sofa, but before I got to my room I heard someone—it had to be Carly or my mother—trying to open my door with a key. When the chain caught the door, pounding began.

Pound. Pound. Pound.

It only took a moment for Jazz to shoot over to the door, with me fast on his heels. He had his gun drawn. Instead of being concerned about my next houseguest, I let Jazz's manly and protective actions capture my attention. "What kind of gun is that?"

"It's a Sig Sauer .38, and no, you can't touch it," he said in a stage whisper.

Pound. Pound. Pound.

"Who is it?" he yelled.

I couldn't remember when I'd had so much fun at my door—not including kissing Jazz on my birthday, of course.

Pounder number two nearly knocked my door off its hinges, prompting Jazz to add a little more bass to his voice. *"Who is it?"*

"Who are *you*?" my sister yelled back.

"Carly?"

"Open this door," she demanded. "I've got a gun, Mace, the police with me, PMS, PMDD, and anything else that might make a woman vicious."

"You've got more than me. I ain't opening it." He laughed.

"How did you know my name?" Carly said, pounding again.

Jazz unchained the door, and my sister exploded inside, ready to come to blows. She softened when she saw Jazz, gun drawn and ready to protect my honor. "Aw, you're protecting my baby sister. Isn't that the sweetest thing? Now all you have to do is provide for her. When is the wedding?"

"Don't start no stuff, and it won't be none," Jazz said.

She put her hands on her hips. "Has she been telling you about our great-grandmother? She *always* does that. I don't understand how she remembers so much. Ma Brown died when she was nine."

"Ma Brown must have had a profound effect on your sister. She's got me close to wanting to offer prayers to the woman."

Carly looked at Jazz, with that gleam in her eyes. "What are *you* doing here?"

"Nothing is going on. I'm on business."

"Yeah, right, and Bell is in her—"

Then, the realization. I saw it in her face the moment it dawned on her.

"Oh, no," she said, pointing. "You're wearing those wretched pajamas?" She gave an exaggerated eye roll at my jammies. "Have you ever heard of Victoria's Secret?"

"Have you ever heard of No More Sheets?"

"What's No More Sheets?" Jazz asked.

"It's an abstinence thing," Carly said. "Bell made me watch the video with her. It didn't do much for me, but it did wonders for her."

It sure did. "I'm pleased to say that after a long and painful surrender, and the subsequent and inevitable depression that followed, I am now, blissfully, free of fornication."

"I can see why," Carly said. "You can market a line

of those pajamas and put Juanita Bynum out of business. Who'd want to make out with someone wearing those?"

"She has a point, Bell," Jazz said.

I sighed, more than ready to move our little huddle away from my door. "Lieutenant Brown is not here to make out with me."

"Are you sure about that?" Carly asked.

I looked to Jazz for help.

"Don't look at me," he said. "If I say I am, you'll get mad at me. If I say I'm not, both of you might get mad. I'm pleading the Fifth."

"Coward," I said.

"I will say you are a beautiful woman, despite your taste in lingerie."

Then Rocky appeared, sauntering through my still-open door. "What's wrong with her taste in lingerie?" He came over to me and kissed my cheek. "Hey, babe. I love it when you wear your fuzzy pajamas."

Two pairs of eyes bore into my handsome pastor. One pair, Jazz's, darted quickly to me, and then back to Rocky.

"And you are?" Jazz asked, looking more than a little annoyed.

"I'm Rocky," he said, smiling. "Don't tell me. You're the flower guy, right?"

I thought this would be a good time to introduce them. "This is Lieutenant Jazz Brown. Jazz, this is

Rocky Harrison. He's my pastor." *He's my ex-boyfriend.* I couldn't believe Rocky's timing. I hoped I could keep the two of them from squaring off and fighting.

Jazz extended his hand to give Rocky a clearly macho, bone-crushing handshake. Of course, Rock extended pure grace.

"Whoa. Firm handshake."

Jazz eyed him. "A pastor who calls his members 'babe' and has pajama parties with them. Must be a close-knit congregation."

Let the fight begin.

Despite the teensy amount of satisfaction I felt at Jazz's obvious jealousy, my instincts to protect Rocky surfaced. During the year we dated, we did nothing to be ashamed of. We'd kept our relationship honorable.

I narrowed my eyes at Jazz. "I don't have pajama parties, except for this home invasion I'm having right now; and I didn't send out an invitation for this one. You might also note that I happen to be the only one in pajamas. For your information, Lieutenant, Rocky has counseled me as a pastor and friend through one or two, uh, episodes."

"Yeah, man, fuzzy jammies are the uniform for 'episodes,' and I think she looks kinda cute with her little safety pin."

"If that pin got any bigger it'd be a concealed weapon," Jazz said.

"Only, to her shame, it's not concealed," Carly said. She breezed into the kitchen. "You got any Starbucks?"

"You know where it is, Car."

Rocky attempted to make conversation with Jazz. "The jammies always let me know how vulnerable she is, right, babe?" Rocky said, squeezing me. I smacked his arm away. I didn't want Jazz to think we had something going. Just in case.

"Rocky, why are you here? As a matter of fact, why are any of you here?"

Jazz went first. "I came because you weren't answering your house or cell phone."

Then Rocky. "So did I, babe. How many times do I have to remind you to keep your cell phone charged?"

"I couldn't reach you either," Carly called from the kitchen. I could hear her in there rooting through my cabinets. "Did you move the biscotti?"

"Yes, to the canister on the counter!" I'd had enough. I made a point of stomping into my bedroom and bringing out both my cordless and my cell phone. I made a show of placing them back on their chargers in my living room. "Now you can all call me." With that done, I pointed to Jazz. "Okay, you first, Lieutenant Brown. What do you want?"

"The cocoa you offered."

"You didn't come for my cocoa."

"No, I came to check on you, notify the medical examiner if you were dead, and investigate if you had been murdered, even though this isn't my jurisdiction."

"I *am* the medical examiner," Carly called from the kitchen, "but this isn't *my* jurisdiction. I came to see if you wanted to go shopping. We'll hit Victoria's Secret at the Briarwood Mall first."

I ignored my sister. "And having found me alive, Lieutenant Brown?"

"We have work to do today, Ms. Consultant."

Yes, but I hadn't expected him to show up first thing in the morning.

"And why are you here, Rocky?"

"I wanted to make sure you were okay after what happened at my house last night."

"What happened last night?" Jazz demanded, going into full cop mode. Before Rocky could fix his mouth to answer, Jazz glowered at me. "You were at *his* house last night."

"What's wrong with that?" Rocky asked, puzzled. "She used to live there."

Jazz's eyes darted back to me.

"Uh," I stammered. "That *sounds* a lot worse than it was."

Jazz's arms crossed again. "It's none of my business."

"He lives in a communal house with some members of his ministry team. We were on staff together right before I finished graduate school. I lived in the house—

the community house—as a staff member, and only for three months."

Rocky looked at Jazz. "You're in love with her, aren't you?"

This time Jazz stammered. "We—we're just working together. She's my consultant." He turned to me, looking annoyed. "Where's my cocoa?"

"I found the biscotti. Nice canister," Carly called again. "Is he paying you for that?"

"For the canister, or the consulting?"

"Consulting. You got any ham?"

"No. Who has ham and coffee?"

"I can't help it. I'm in the mood for ham. Is he paying you?"

"Yes, he's paying me." I looked at the men. "Would you two like to have a seat at the dinette?"

"Please," Jazz said.

I pointed at my little dining table, which suddenly looked like children's furniture in the presence of two very manly men. "Sit," I said.

Rocky went into the kitchen instead, and helped himself to the cocoa. He knew where I kept everything. From the look on Jazz's face, he found that to be disagreeable.

Carly shot out of the kitchen as if Rocky were a carrier of the Ebola virus, but managed to say to him, "Could you make me some coffee while you're at it?"

She eased into a chair at my dinette table, next to Jazz. "How much are you paying for my baby sister's consulting services?"

"That's really not your business, Carly."

I admired his forthrightness.

She ignored him, and grinned at me. "Is it five grand, Bell?"

I knew Carly to be remarkably perceptive, but goodness gracious. "How did you know that?"

" 'Cause that's how much I told him your procedure would cost."

"My procedure?"

"You know, the procedure you're going to have so you can get pregnant."

And on that note I fainted.

chapter
thirteen

THERE ARE MOMENTS when one prays for a loss of consciousness: extreme pain, terrible emotional duress, and when your sister tells the man you're falling in love with that you want to be artificially inseminated.

I imagine my guests did a lot of arguing and clamoring until I awakened a short time later to find the three of them hovering over me, a chorus of "Are you okay?" ringing in my ears.

My mouth opened, but coherent sound would not come out. Fortunately for Carly, the presence of a homicide detective in my living room curbed my urge to kill her for her indiscretion.

An uncomfortable silence shrouded us, which Rocky plowed through first. "You're having a procedure so you can get pregnant?"

I crawled toward the couch. "I'm considering—I *was* considering artificial insemination, which I can afford now, thanks to my sister who talks too much, and my generous benefactor here." I shot a hard look at Jazz.

"Whoa," Rocky said. He's such an innocent sometimes.

"So what? She wants to be artificially inseminated," Carly blurted out.

Jazz raised an eyebrow. "Is that what you're trying to do? Your sister didn't tell me *that.*"

I must make Carly suffer. Slowly.

I tried to defend myself. "Look. I got a hormonally fueled idea born of desperation. I'm over it. Mostly."

Jazz laughed. "I could donate to that cause for free."

I debated as to whether I should use my remaining strength to throttle him or continue toward the couch.

The couch won.

Having reached my destination, I used my meager amount of energy to yell at Jazz. "I thought I'd be working for the Detroit Police Department."

Jazz had the nerve to laugh. "You've got to be kidding. Five g's from the Detroit Police Department for a consulting fee?" He flopped down beside me on the couch. Carly took the chaise longue, and Rocky sat in my antique bentwood rocker.

I hadn't finished arguing with Jazz. "First of all, I decided against having it done, and second, you can't give me that kind of money."

"Sure I can. It's my money. Plus, you're going to help me find the freakazoid who killed Jonathan and Damon."

I really needed to get off this subject long enough to think through the revelation that Jazz had ulterior motives for paying me that had little to do with my superlative consulting skills. Suddenly our business had turned personal, and *did he just offer to be my donor?* I took a deep breath and focused on my pastor, now gaping at Jazz.

"Did you say Jonathan and Damon?"

"Yeah, I did. Do *you* know something about them, Rocky? Because I've got a team of detectives interviewing people and all we've managed to come up with is one anonymous tip that they were drug dealers. Everyone else said they were 'quiet and kept to themselves.'"

"Too bad you can't get information from Susan Hines."

Jazz looked impatient with Rocky. "Who is Susan Hines?"

"Bell's client."

Two pairs of eyes, from those who were not acquainted with Ms. Hines, settled on me.

"Don't look at me. She's not my client. She fled Jonathan and Damon's group the day of the murders, but that's all I know. I just went to talk to her as a favor to Rocky, and she refused to say a word."

"Yeah," Rocky said. "She's like this." And then the man went catatonic on me again. I tried to ignore him.

Jazz and Carly stared at him in obvious disbelief. After an excruciatingly long half minute, Jazz said to me, "Is he for real?"

"I'm afraid so."

I turned my attention to Rocky. "Snap out of it."

He responded immediately this time, shaking his blond, spiky-haired head. "That is *so* . . ."

"Trippy," I supplied. "Anyway, as you can see by Rocky's demonstration, Susan Hines is not currently self-reporting."

Jazz looked frustrated. "That's just great. I've got two people dead and, according to Rocky, a catatonic potential witness . . . whom I knew nothing about, thank you very much, Ms. Consultant."

"I don't think she's catatonic, and at this point there's nothing to tell."

Clearly Jazz is not known for his patience. "I need to talk to her. Now!"

"She's not talking."

"I can get her to talk."

"*You* can get her a bed in the psych ward at U of M. No way is she ready for you, Jazz."

"How long before you can get her to talk?"

I nestled into the couch cushions, nice and cozy. "It's hard to say."

"I need that woman to talk."

"My great-grandmother used to say, 'People in hell need ice water, but that don't mean they'll get it.' "

I could hear the mounting frustration in Jazz's voice. "I'm not asking for the impossible."

The man would not quit. I sat up. "You are asking for what I can't give you right now."

After that he turned flat-out rude. "Just do your job and get the woman talking."

"Do *your* job and find another lead. The woman is in no condition to talk to you right now." I probably shouldn't have said that, but I was a little salty because he pulled the "do your job" card on me.

He clenched his jaw, and I could tell I'd made him mad. Unfortunately, being humble with the opposite sex is not my strong suit. Actually, being humble with Jazz Brown is not my strong suit.

I got off the couch and dragged myself into the kitchen, feeling like a jerk. I pulled a pot out of the cabinet and poured milk into it. A few moments later, while I waited at the stove for the milk to boil, Jazz came in. I had my back to him, but he walked up behind me and yanked at my pajama sleeve.

I ignored him.

He kept yanking.

"Cut it out."

"Let's make up."

Making up sounded very positive; however, I refused to surrender—at least not until I heard him grovel. I went with denial. "I'm not mad."

"Yes, you are."

So what? "You're the one who's mad." I kept my back to him.

He stood right behind me, really close. "I spoke to you like a cop, not a friend. I'm sorry."

I didn't say anything.

He rested his head on my shoulder. "I'm sorry, Bell."

"I told you not to call me that."

His arms slid around my waist.

"Did I say you could touch me?"

"It's just a friendly hug," he said.

Goodness me, it did feel friendly. Which is why I gave him a firm rebuke. "Hug me when you're available."

Carly hollered from the living room. "Oh, yeah, what's all this unavailable nonsense?"

She and Rocky rushed into the kitchen as if they were coming to save me from a terrible fate.

"Are you toying with my baby sister?" Carly asked.

"Toying with her? She's too good for that," Rocky said.

"Would anyone like peppermint in their cocoa?" I said, turning to face them.

"No," Jazz said, slowly removing his arms from around my waist. He eyed the others, most likely calculating what he'd do in case they attacked.

"You don't want peppermint in your cocoa, Jazz? It's very festive," I said.

"It's the beginning of September. I don't do festive until November, and I was saying no to *them*."

"You're not toying with her heart?" Rocky said.

"No."

"But you are unavailable?" Carly asked.

"Listen, I told Bell that, but I have a good reason. She just repeated what I said as if it were . . ." He took a moment, probably to search for the perfect word. *"Evil."*

Okay. That was a little harsh.

Rocky said, "My girlfriend is not evil."

"Wait a minute," Jazz said. "Bell is your girlfriend?"

"No, I'm not."

"Not anymore," Carly said. "Why do you care, Jazz? Aren't you *unavailable*?"

Jazz hadn't finished with Rocky. "How long did you date her?"

"A year—until she broke my heart," Rocky said, giving Jazz the puppy eyes. Big, tough cops must be immune.

"Do you still see Bell?"

"We hang out, and I see her at church, unless you count something like last night."

Jazz shot a very ugly look at me. Then he turned his attention back to Rocky. "What, exactly, happened between you two last night?"

Rocky shrugged. Tried the puppy eyes again.

"I see," Jazz said.

"You *think* you see," I said. "I happened to have spent my evening trying to see if Susan would talk." I swiftly changed the subject. "Why don't you answer Carly about whether or not you're available, Mr. Inquisitive?"

Carly put her hands on her hips and glared at Jazz. "Yeah. I told you all that stuff about Bell."

I would have strangled Carly, but thought better of it since "big, tough cop" happened to be in the room. And now that I thought of it . . . "You asked Carly personal questions about me? And every time I turn around you're in my face, yet you refuse to tell me why you're unavailable."

"Fine," Jazz said. "I'm unavailable because I got married three and a half years ago."

Carly looked shocked. "Don't tell me I've been flirting with a married man for more than three years?"

Leave it to Carly to make this about *her*. She continued to grill him. "Are you still married?"

"No. She left me three months after we got married."

I know I should have stopped them, but, honestly, I wanted to know, too. And this way I wouldn't have to ask him again myself. I grabbed cups and cocoa-making necessities and started banging things around, trying to take some of the heat off poor Jazz, even though I'd fought with him minutes earlier.

"What did you do?" Carly asked. "Nobody would leave a man as fine as you unless he did something really bad." She drummed her fingers on the countertop to punctuate her accusation.

"She did," he said.

"She did something bad, or she left you?"

"Both."

"What did she do?" Rocky asked.

"Do I need to tell all of my business?" Jazz said, looking exasperated.

"You asked me all about Bell, and I told you all of her business," Carly said.

Oddly, the thought of that now both pleased and horrified me.

"What happened to your wife?" Rocky asked.

"She fell in love with my partner."

Rocky got quiet. My sister did not. "Which partner?"

"Chris."

"She fell in love with Chris?"

"Yes. They live together now, somewhere in Royal Oak. Happily ever after."

Carly started laughing.

Jazz frowned. "It's not funny."

I now had two cups of briskly stirred hot chocolate,

complete with peppermint sticks for the guys. "Can we take this roasting back to the dinette?" Honestly, they kept following me around like rats following the Pied Piper.

The gang followed me to the dinette table. I sat, waiting for Carly's coffee to brew. She hadn't finished snickering about Chris.

"I don't think his wife's affair with another man is funny," I said.

"Chris is not a man," Jazz said.

"Pardon me?" I said, politely.

"Chris is short for Christine. She's a woman."

"Whoa," Rocky said. "And now you and Bell are in love, but you're not trusting your heart to anyone." He nodded, his puppy eyes filled with compassion.

"Who said we're in love?" I said, hoping I wouldn't have to admit it.

"You did, in your office."

"I never said I was in love."

"But you are. Aren't you?" Carly said. No doubt the truth showed all over my face.

"What is this—some kind of Bell's Pathetic Love Life small-group study?"

My humble pastor said, "If it *were* a small group— like the ones we have at *church*—you wouldn't be here."

Ouch. Did I say I always won arguments with Rocky? I stand corrected.

"So she divorced you?" Carly asked.

"No," Jazz said, his jaw tightening like it does when he gets irritated. "I divorced her. Fast. I know you people might find this hard to believe, but sometimes I wonder if I did the right thing." He pressed his hands on the table and looked at each of us in turn. "Don't even think about asking me to elaborate, because I think people's values and beliefs are personal. The bottom line is this: I ain't getting married again, and I don't date."

"Wow," Rocky said. "Since we're all disclosing so much—"

Rocky's accurate assessment of my lack of small-group attendance still stung. I cut him off. "What exactly have you or Carly disclosed this morning?" I accused, hoping that would silence them.

No chance.

Carly jumped right in with her sharing. "My ex-husband died under mysterious circumstances, but I was cleared, and no charges were brought against me."

Jazz laughed. "There's still speculation about that."

"I didn't kill him," Carly protested. "I know how," she added with a wink, "but that doesn't mean I did it. Your turn, Rocky."

"Okay. I'm still in love with Bell, but she won't marry me because she thinks I'm too young for her, and because she can't give me lots of babies."

"Are you sure it isn't because you're white and goofy?" Carly asked.

"Bell is goofy, and isn't Jazz white?"

The room went silent as a tomb, and not because Rocky said I was goofy. Silent, that is, until Carly started laughing so hard she almost hyperventilated. "I'm not white," Jazz said.

I needed to educate my poor pastor. "That was a bit of a faux pas, Rock."

Rocky looked across the table at Jazz. "You look—"

"Good in that black suit you're wearing today," I said quickly.

Rocky shrugged. "So what if you're white and Bell is black. Can't we all just get along?"

"Hey, Rodney King," Jazz said. "I'm all for racial unity, but I'm not white. My father is."

I thought I'd interject a thoughtful, penetrating profile of Jazz and said, "He's probably had to struggle all his life for racial identity. Because of his family's makeup, and where and how he was raised, he naturally identifies himself as a black person, and in truth he is, but he could clearly pass for white."

"No, I can't," he lied.

"He's defensive because he has to constantly prove himself as a black person. Consider, for example, his use of the black vernacular when he's working. It's a compensation defense mechanism."

"I grew up in the hood. I speak a little slang now

and then at work. It's not like I'm in the station house basement making gangsta rap CDs," Jazz said, looking frustrated.

"She did that to me when we dated," Rocky said to him.

Now they were bonding.

"The last thing I need is my woman profiling me," Jazz said.

"So," Rocky said, "you *are* having a fling with Bell?"

"What fling? We're just working together."

"You said 'the last thing I need is *my* woman profiling me,'" Rocky said.

"I meant *a* woman."

"You had one of those Freudian slips," Carly said.

Jazz glared at her. "What is it with you and Freud, Carly? And what is it with you people and the word 'fling'? We're not having a fling."

I made yet another attempt to clear my good name. Jazz could clear his own. "We're simply working on the Vogel-Crawford case," I said.

Carly jumped in with, "Oh, yeah, Jazz, did I mention what their stomach contents were?"

He sighed in a very tired-detective way. "What were they?"

I braced myself for a yucky vision.

"Grape juice and bread—and strychnine, of course."

"That sounds like a freaky Last Supper," Rocky said.

The three of us looked at him. Score one for Rock. "Last Supper" as in "Communion."

"Did you find grape juice and bread in the house?" I asked.

"I found a lot of popcorn and ramen noodles. No grape juice, or anything else, laced with strychnine. I don't remember seeing any bread, but we can check for that." Jazz stroked a bit of stubble on his chin. "I need to find out who this guy Gabriel is, and fast."

Rocky laid his elbows on the table and rested his head in his hands. "That's some bold communion." He looked forlorn.

I watched him to see if he'd try to play catatonic again. Carly distracted me by touching Jazz's shoulder.

"Don't worry. You're a super cop, Jazzy, even if you can't keep wives," she said. "And Bell has faith in you, don't you, Bell?"

"Uh, yeah," I said. "How many *Mrs.* Jazzes have there been?"

"One. And that was too many."

I don't think I convinced him of the faith in him Carly had proclaimed, but he recovered quickly.

"On that note," he said, "can you please get dressed and come to the crime scene with me, *Dr. Brown?* I'd like to work fast so you can get back to my catatonic witness."

"You want to go back to the crime scene?" I asked, somewhat loudly and bordering on hysteria.

Jazz answered with one of those megawatt smiles and a look that said, "I'm challenging you."

I returned his look with one that said, "I know you are, but I'm a diva." I squared my shoulders and stuffed down the fear that rose in my throat. Ma Brown used to say, "It ain't courage if you ain't scared." I said, *Thank you, Jesus, for an opportunity to be courageous.*

"Give me fifteen minutes, Lieutenant."

"I'll give you ten," he said, like he just had to win.

We left ten minutes later.

chapter
fourteen

WE STOOD ON THE PORCH of the home where Jonathan Vogel Junior had died. Worry wove around me until I felt Jazz place his hand at my elbow—a kind, supportive touch. I felt reassurance in it. "They're not in there anymore."

"It's not Vogel and Crawford I'm worried about."

"What are you worried about?"

"My memories."

"Come on. I've got your back." He paused, gave me a little squeeze and a gentle smile. "That just means I'll protect you. It's not an attempt to use the black vernacular to compensate for my fair skin."

"If you say so," I teased.

"You're a trip, Bell."

"There you go with the slang again. And don't call me Bell."

He shook his head to dismiss my protest. "Let's start here at the door."

We didn't head right in. I think he was giving me time to pull my frayed nerves back together. "Who found the bodies?"

"The father, Vogel Senior."

"Why wasn't he here when we arrived?"

"A rookie cop got to the scene first. Vogel Senior proved he was the victim's father, and Daniels let him go because he looked pretty shaken up. Daniels called me on my cell phone and gave me the full story. He figured I'd check him out later anyway."

"Did Vogel Senior report how he ended up finding them?"

"He called his kid on the phone and didn't get a return call. Tried his job and found out he was a no-show."

"And you interviewed the father for this information?"

"Of course."

"And?"

"His wife was out at the time the murders took place. He claims he was home alone. He's a suspect until he's cleared, as is the leader, Gabriel or Michael or whatever his name is, and now so is Susan, your client."

"She's not my client. Why do you suspect the father did this?"

"He was first on the scene and he's family. Too many homicides are committed by someone the vic knows: family, friend, associate. He also had beef with his kid over the cult thing." Jazz blew air from his lungs. "With a homicide, anything can happen." He took my hand. "You like to play make-believe?"

"Depends on who I'm playing with."

"You *are* spicy, Dr. Brown."

"I have my moments. Are you touching my hand?"

He let go.

"You wanna play cop or robber?" he asked.

"I'll let you play the good guy."

"I *am* the good guy, baby."

I took a deep breath. "Okay, maybe the killer . . ."

"That's you," he said.

"Maybe *I* had a key."

He nodded and moved the yellow crime-scene tape, used a key to open the door. "Let's go inside, profiler." He escorted me inside.

The house looked exactly the same except for some telltale signs of the investigation. The crime-scene unit had removed a swatch of the terrible green shag carpet. One or two of the floor pillows and a cushion from the couch were missing—no doubt taken to the crime lab for bodily fluid and fiber collection. Everything else was surprisingly the same. I saw the same shabby sofa on which Damon Crawford had lain dead just days ago and the rest of the floor pillows and the basket table near where Jonathan had died.

"Let's see those skills Carly told me you learned by being an avid consumer of crime shows."

Never mind those eight years I went to college. I made a mental note to rough Carly up a bit when I got her alone. Forget crime television shows, I understood cults and criminology, so I took another deep breath and said a silent prayer that the Holy Spirit would use this as a chance to bring whatever was needed to my remembrance.

The house still stank. Jazz must have seen me hesitate.

"You wanna pray?"

"Would you mind?"

"You already know how I feel about your praying-slash-theologian-slash-crime-scene-analyst work."

"You said it's interesting." I gave him a nudge.

He lifted a manly eyebrow. "Oh, so it's okay for *you* to touch."

"You touch in a different way."

He opened his mouth to say something but decided against it.

"No comment?" I raised my own perfectly arched—because my mother and Maggie speak ill of me if I don't groom them into submission—eyebrows.

"I'm trying to be a good boy today."

"Be an unavailable boy. That will keep you out of trouble."

He stopped for a moment. "Did it ever occur to you that maybe I'm unsure about the whole divorce and re-marriage thing? Theologically speaking."

I stopped, too. Turned to gaze at him. His expression was serious. I didn't want to sound like I was mocking him just because I was chronically defensive when it came to his love choices. "'Theologically speaking'?"

Jazz lifted an arm like he was about to cross it over his chest, putting on his protective-body-language armor, but he must have thought I was watching him too intently. He dropped it to his side again. Shoved his hand into the pocket of his suit jacket. "I mean, what if I get married and cause her to sin?"

"Honey, she's already sinning. Trust me on that one." I sounded mocking anyway.

"You know what I mean."

I looked into his face. He had the needy, approval-seeking expression of a little boy. What a mess Jazz was. What a pair we made. My compassion grew exponentially for him in that moment. At least he cared about what God thought. He even cared about his ex.

I softened my salty tone. "Did it ever occur to you that God doesn't expect you to be a theologian? And frankly, theologians don't even agree on those issues.

I think you're scared. Period. That's a whole different theological issue, one God stands ready to make haste to help you with. Best not to get them confused."

He nodded. I think he could see that I was being straight up with him.

"Now you're looking *way* too gorgeous, miserable, and fixable. I need to focus on the fact that you're U-N-A-V-A-I-L-A-B-L E."

He grinned at me. "You won't let me forget it."

"You might want to consider that it's *me* I'm reminding." I took a deep breath. "Let's pray, if that's what we're going to do."

He took my hands, and I wished he hadn't. The last thing I needed was the laying on of Jazz's hands; but as touching goes, this was pretty benign. After a moment I was able to settle into the prayer, and honestly, he didn't say a lot of lofty words, but what he did say got straight to the point. He finished with "Lord, give us wisdom and help us catch a killer. In the name of the Father and the Son and the Holy Spirit."

"And in Jesus' name," I said.

"You're such a Protestant."

I shrugged my shoulders. "Amen. Now, back to murder."

I'll admit it. That "back to murder" transition didn't work, but I just wanted to get us back to business. I tried to hold up my end of things and place myself in the mind of a killer. "I get in the door without using force. And find myself here in the living room."

"What do we know happened?" Jazz asked.

Easy so far. "Strychnine poisoning."

"Did you bring it or find it here and take it with you when you left?"

"I think I came packing the poison."

"How did you get it here?" He was really getting into this.

"I brought it in something nondescript. A regular shopping bag."

"Good girl. A bag full of plastic bags was resting on the countertop," he said. "They went to the lab to be processed. All we found were prints for Vogel and Craw-ford and a few unidentified ones that are likely from bag-gers or cashiers at the grocery store."

I continue with our game. "I take out the bread and juice and bring it into the living room." At that I lead him to the spot where the bodies were found. "No glasses were left in here, so they drank right out of the bottle."

"Tell me about the bread."

"Probably cheap sliced white bread if the food in the cabinets is any indication. I yank a piece out of the bag."

"Souldier found a twist tie like the kind from a bread bag in the living room. So, what now?"

"I like Souldier with an S-O-U-L."

"Don't like him too much, okay? He said you're pretty."

"He did?"

Jazz ignored that.

"Sweet Communion?" Jazz said, redirecting the conversation.

"Or Last Supper."

We both get on our knees near the basket table.

"Vogel is found here, on the floor. Why?" Jazz asked.

"He's the notetaker. He's more devoted."

"Less scared?"

"Not particularly, but he'd want to impress the man he believes is his spiritual father: Michael Wright."

"*If* we're talking about Wright."

"I have no doubt that we are." I tried to forget about the fact that we were kneeling where a dead man had been. The stink made me feel a little woozy.

"The notebooks have two names, Bell. Michael and, later, Gabriel. Jonathan didn't mention a name change."

"I still think they're one and the same." I tried to hold my breath a little bit.

He frowned at me. "Don't do that; you'll get sick."

I tried to suck it up. "Did the notebooks indicate they got a new spiritual leader?"

"No warning or explanation." Jazz motioned for me to continue. "So, what happens here on the floor?"

I close my eyes, but it's not Michael Wright or Jonathan Vogel I see.

———————

He asks me to kneel before him, and I do. I love him. He has taught me that, as a wife, I must submit. I want to have a marriage ceremony, but he says I am not worthy yet. I keep thinking if we just have a ceremony, even if it's merely a private exchange of vows between the two of us and the other wives, God will understand.

I want to correct the mistakes I've made.

I'm having his baby; therefore, this must be where Yahweh wants me, *I tell myself, hoping it's true.*

I call him Master because he teaches me to do so.

I hope Yahweh understands.

I have to keep my family together. It's what's required of me. I'm not Carly—beautiful and successful, with more admirers in one day than I'll have in my lifetime. This baby is all I have. Maybe all I'll ever have.

He asks me to kiss his feet, and I do. He asks me to lie supine on the floor, and I do. He places his foot on me, and this is submission. But there are more ways to submit. I think this is Yahweh's will.

He unzips his pants and takes his foot off me. He tells me to get back on my knees. And I do. I do everything he asks. I tell myself it's God's will to submit to my husband. I know I'm

lying to myself, but I try to make myself believe. Sin, shame,
and a little knowledge of God can be dangerous things.

———————

I don't know how long the memory captivated me, but
when I open my eyes, Jazz is studying my face.

"What is it?" He takes my hand and cradles it as if it
were a delicate, wondrous thing.

"I need to take a break."

He nods and keeps holding my hand, but I don't
protest.

Jazz doesn't force me to do anything.

chapter
fifteen

J AZZ AND I SPENT the next two hours enjoying the kind of warmth and sunshine that will elude Detroiters by the end of October. We strolled past Comerica Park, with its stone tigers looking ready to pounce.

Jazz treated me to lunch—a mountain of corned beef on rye—after which we made our way to Hart Plaza. We were blessed to stumble upon Detroit's annual jazz festival, which takes place every year on Labor Day weekend. True to his name, Jazz knew every headliner and most of the local bands.

I gave him bonus points for extraordinary sensitivity and a really cool diversion. Of course, a complete respite from the turmoil in my mind would have been too good to be true.

"Are you feeling better?" Jazz asked. He walked us over to the Dodge Fountain—the centerpiece of Hart Plaza. Isamu Noguchi's architectural wonder rises out of the concrete, with arms of stainless steel lifting a circle of metal that sprays a fine, cool mist to the ground. Children were running in and out of the water with such infectious joy that I was about ready to take the plunge myself.

"Yes," I said. I fished in my purse for a penny to toss in the water, but Jazz beat me to it and chucked a coin into the fountain.

Men. Pockets are so much more efficient than purses.

"So tell me what you were thinking about at the house," Jazz said.

"My penny wish was going to be that you wouldn't ask me about that."

"Too late. I already wished for you to tell me about it."

"I should have been trying to figure out why Vogel and Crawford were killed."

"Nice try, but I'm a skilled interrogator. Were you thinking about the freak you lived with?"

"Please don't tell me Carly told you about that, too."

"Why don't *you* tell me about it?"

I sighed and looked wistfully at the fountain. "We were having such a good date."

"Date?"

"I didn't say 'date'; I said 'day.'"

"Ha," Jazz said, his smile competing with the sun. "You had another slip."

"No, I didn't. You slipped, imagining I said that."

"You want me, don't you?"

Who *wouldn't* want him, other than the dumb cow he'd married?

Did I call that woman a dumb cow? Lord, have mercy on my soul.

"If I did, as you said, have another slip, I was merely thinking about how nice dating you would be."

"Really?" He grinned at me.

"What I meant is that you'd be a good date, if you weren't *unavailable*." I frowned. "You *are* a skilled interrogator."

He stepped up to me, invading the two feet designated to be my personal space. He took one of my hands in his. "Nice work," he said. "You almost distracted me. Now, tell me about the nutcase you lived with."

"Tell me about your marriage."

"You're a formidable opponent in a standoff, but you already know about my marriage. For the record, I will say I was adversely affected by Kate's infidelity with my former, and her current, partner. Now it's your turn."

"It would seem that, thanks to Carly, you already know about the nutcase I lived with, but I will say that I was out of my mind to allow him to do even a fraction of what he did to me. I'm not a psychologist now for naught. And the only people I ever talk about him with are Rocky and Mason May, and those discussions are, thankfully, rare."

He stepped closer. "Maybe you need to let it go."

I closed the tiny space between us. "Maybe you need to give me some space."

He rested his forehead on mine. "I'm thinking there's something else I need to give you."

"What's that?" I whispered, trembling, and not because it was cool outside.

"A kiss."

His hand that was not holding mine came to my cheek, caressed it, and lifted my chin.

Oh, no. I realized he was going to kiss me and that I'd been seized by some strange paralysis—except for my head, which was moving toward his—and I couldn't stop myself.

Only I wasn't paralyzed; I was in love.

I wish I could say I was saved by the *Bell*, but sadly, Bell was well on her way to bliss.

Just as Jazz zoomed in for the smooch, a voice sounding like a prophetess's spoke. "Jazz Brown, what do you think you're doing?"

At the sound of the voice, Jazz yanked away from me like I had thrown a pot of hot grits on him.

The woman wasn't really a prophetess. She was more of a diva—a sixtyish, gorgeous, African-American woman. She held her short stature so well that she seemed tall in my mind. She was round in all the right places—big in a good way. Her hair was a tiny, honey blond halo of an Afro.

She wore a lightweight Kente cloth duster—real Kente cloth, not a cotton print. Beneath the duster she wore a cream-colored blouse and matching pants. She sported the best, boldest African-inspired jewelry I'd ever seen. I named and claimed her as my very own mother with such zeal that I'm sure Oral Roberts, wherever he was, heard me and said, "Amen."

I want to be like her when I grow up.

"Mom?" Jazz said.

Apparently, she was the least of his concerns, because beside her stood a silver fox in the full, undiluted fineness that he'd clearly passed on to his son. He wasn't dressed like Mother Africa beside him, but Daddy made a green silk shirt with matching, nubby, raw-silk pants look like the fabrics had been made for him. He wore a caramel-colored Kangol hat, turned backward. A bit of a scowl played about his mouth, like some serious correction was in order, but when he looked at me, he caved and gave me an amazing Jazzesque grin. I could see why Jazz's mother fell in love with him.

"Dad?" Jazz said, looking like he'd been caught with his hand in the cookie jar. "What are y'all doing here?"

Silver Fox did not mince words. His gruff voice bore the hint of a Bronx accent. "It's a jazz festival, clown. Where else would we be?"

"Fancy finding you here, son, standing at the fountain with all kinds of wishful thinking going on." His mother's speech sounded Southern born and Northern bred.

Jazz looked at me helplessly. "My folks have got a thing about jazz. They went to a jazz festival, had a great time, and nine months later, had a bouncing baby."

"Good thing we didn't go to a soul-music festival," Mr. Brown said. "Maybe we'd have named you James Brown." Mr. Brown exploded with laughter. He removed his hat and extended his free hand to me. "Speaking of names, I'm Jack Brown, and this is my wife, Addie Lee."

I shook his hand, but instead of meeting his green-eyed gaze, I gaped at Jazz's mother. *"Addie Lee?"* Upon hearing her name, I instantly recognized her. Jazz's mother is a famous folk artist. Her paintings and jewelry are legendary in the arts community. I'd been to showings of her work and had paid big money to buy it, but I'd only ever seen a small publicity photo of her. "Addie Lee is your mother?" I nearly screamed.

"Sad but true," she said. "And speaking of being his mother . . . boy"—she frowned at Jazz—"what were you doing?"

Papa Brown couldn't hide his amusement. "Maybe he was about to give this pretty lady mouth-to-mouth. Maybe she's got asthma."

"If she's got asthma, she needs an inhaler," Addie Lee said, rebuking Jazz.

"He was about to inhale her," Jack quipped. Addie Lee and Jack both laughed.

"Don't mind us," Addie said to me. "We have to make sure this one"—she gestured toward Jazz—"is in line with the Word of God. It looks like brother Jazz needs to hit Bible study."

"That means you'll have to go to Mass with me on Sunday," Jack Brown said. "And to church with your mother on Sunday night, Tuesday, Wednesday, Friday, and to YPWW on Saturday." He smiled at me. "Now, we Catholics can have Mass every day, but somehow, when the you-know-what hits the fan, we always end up at Addie's church, and I *still* don't know what YPWW stands for."

Addie smacked his shoulder. "Oh, Jack, you know that stands for . . . Young People . . ."

Jack gave her a hearty laugh. "Oh, what does it matter? I have to go to it." Papa Brown turned to me. "What's your name, sweetie?"

Without giving it a second thought I said, "Bell Brown."

Jazz shot me a dirty look. "I have to call her Amanda,"

he said, as sullen as a teenager. "Actually, she makes me call her *Dr. Brown.*"

"Brown?" his father said. "Boy, don't tell me you went and got married without telling us, like you did with the nightmare."

"Dad," Jazz said in a slow staccato, "there are other Browns in the world besides our family." Then like a normal person—almost—he said, "You *know* I'm never going to get married again, because of *the nightmare.* And I'm a little unclear about what Scripture says I can do after being married to her. But if anything changes and I get a green light, I'll be sure to bring Bell home before she and I get hitched."

"Hypothetically speaking," I said. "And you can call me Dr. Brown, Jazz."

His mother approved of me with a hearty "Good. You can handle him." She paused. "Did you say 'doctor'?"

"I'm a psychologist," I said.

"Jazz needs one. He's a little confused, as you can see," his dad said.

"Apparently he is, Mr. and Mrs. Brown, but I'm definitely not trying to see him or handle him."

"Looks like he's trying to handle you." Papa Brown waved his arms about like he was pretending to be touchy-feely.

"Chill out, Dad. We're just trying to work on a case."

"Yeah," he said. "Kissing always helped me solve

crimes. Lock lips with me, Addie, and maybe I'll be able to tell ya where Jimmy Hoffa is buried."

"You're assuming he's dead," Jazz said with mock seriousness. At least I hoped it was mock.

"For Pete's sake, Jazzy. I was a cop before you were even born. I think I can reasonably assume Hoffa is dead."

He decided to give his folks the left foot of fellowship. "Dr. Brown and I are going to get back to work. Have a great time at the festival."

His mother embraced him. "Give Mama a kiss, but otherwise keep your lips to yourself."

Jazz kissed his mother like a good son.

She winked at me when she released him. "At least, no kissing until your confusion on matters of love and remarriage are clearer."

"And be careful," his father admonished me. "I took Addie to a jazz festival back in '66 and the next thing I knew, we were buying cloth diapers."

"I'll keep that in mind," I said.

Jazz clearly got embarrassed easily. "We're not planning on reproducing today, Dad. However, I'll keep you posted on our progress."

"You two stop by the house tonight." His dad chuckled. "We can talk about the case." He started making smooching sounds, which Jazz tried to ignore. Finally, he stopped torturing his son and put his arm at the small of his wife's back in that maddening way that Jazz did to me.

"We'll be busy," Jazz said.

"I'm sure we'll see you later, Bell," Mr. Brown said and escorted Addie toward the music.

We watched them saunter away past the children and what looked to be an indigent man rolling in the waters of the fountain.

"Nice folks," I said.

"Can we sit for a minute?" He ran a hand through his short brown curls.

"Sure."

We walked away from the main stage toward the grassy waterfront where you can see Canada across the Detroit River. Jazz found a comfy spot under a small oak, and we sat, the sun clinging to us like a hug, even in the shade of the tree.

"I apologize, Amanda."

He looked so serious, his brown eyes mournful and cast down. I touched his knee. "Hey, you don't have anything to apologize for. Your parents are great."

"I'm apologizing for almost kissing you."

"Perhaps I should apologize for almost letting you."

"This is all your fault, you know."

I stared at him and leaned back against the tree. "It's my fault?"

"First you wore that red dress, then you kissed me. Twice. Next thing I know, I'm all in love."

"Now don't start using four-letter words," I said.

"You started that, too." His expression sobered. "Let's be honest, Bell, we *are* falling in love, but it's not going to work. And speaking of work, we need to find Gabriel."

"I know."

"You know we're falling in love, or you know we need to find Gabriel?"

I looked at him and decided I would be honest. "I know both of those things."

He tried to hide the grin that was threatening to spread across his face. "Okay, now that we have that straight, let's lay down some ground rules."

"Like 'no touching' and 'don't call me Bell'?" I said. "I'm glad you thought of that."

"Okay, you thought of it first, but I agree."

"You're such a guy." I gazed at him. Dear Lord, he was pathologically fine—so good-looking it was just wrong. I picked up a stray leaf and traced patterns in the grass with it, my mind still lingering on him telling me he was falling in love.

"So," he said, "no touching and no praying together."

That got my attention. "No praying? What's wrong with praying together?"

"Every time we've prayed together, we've touched. I don't know about you, but I was thinking about more than agreeing in prayer."

I had to agree—I mean concede. "I suppose for two

people with a powerful attraction to each other, praying together becomes an intimate act."

"Prayer between two people in love *should* be an intimate act, both between the lovers and the God who loves them."

"You're using that four-letter word again."

"You know, I never prayed with Kate." He shot a look at me. "She was kinda New Agey. Always praying to the universe or the higher power. Now me, I don't pray like that. I'm afraid I'll get an answer from Neptune or the president."

"And you wouldn't want that, would you?"

"With all due respect, I prefer my answers to come from God."

I lay back on the grass, facing the sky and watching the clouds. I felt both winsome and a little melancholy. "We shouldn't talk about how we feel about each other."

"You think if we ignore it, it will go away, Doctor?"

"I didn't say that; I said we shouldn't talk about it."

"A part of me doesn't want it to go away," Jazz said. "I wish God could bless it."

"But you're not prepared to do what He requires to have a relationship."

"I think being honest about how much I want you is a start."

"We're moving toward dangerous waters, Jazz."

"You know what the Bible says: 'Many waters cannot quench love.'"

"The same book also tells us not to stir up love before it's time; and the truth is, we may never have that time—not with your closed and conflicted heart."

"Obviously my heart isn't so closed. If it were, I'd be able to stop thinking about you. Look, I know I'm giving you mixed messages. I'm as surprised as you by how I feel."

I couldn't speak. His words made me feel vulnerable and only stirred my love for him even more.

He turned to me as if he was offended by my silence. "Did you hear me? I can't break the habit of you, Bell. My walls come tumbling down like Jericho whenever I look at you, but I don't want to sin. I don't want to cause you or Kate to live in adultery."

"Jazz, it was Kate who chose adultery, not you. I think God will see to her."

"Oh, I believe He will, but I'm not sure if that means I can get married while she's alive."

I didn't want to continue this conversation. "Let's talk some more about the rules."

"Fine. What rules do you want?"

"Just one."

"Spill it," he said.

"Don't call me Bell. It's like you're saying 'I love you' every time you do it."

He sighed. "Anything else, Bell?"

I bolted up. "See, that's what I mean, Jazz. You're stoking a fire you say you don't want."

He bowed his head and hugged his knees to his chest. "How about we talk about something else?"

Strains of mellow jazz swirled about the skyscrapers surrounding the twisting spires of Hart Plaza while lively scents of ethnic cuisine sweetened the air.

"Let's talk about this wonderful music I'm hearing. Who is this band?" I asked with the false hope that we'd actually talk about that.

"Tell me about Adam." He cocked his head and sheepishly peered at me—the Jazz version of puppy eyes.

He called him Adam, like Carly would. He didn't pronounce his name "Awdawm," as Adam had required of his wives.

So much for music appreciation. "Tell you about *who*?" That Carly. She needed a mouthectomy.

"Let's talk about the man who hurt you and your baby. This time I won't let you out of it." He stretched out his legs again.

I opened my mouth to say something glib, but levity wouldn't come.

My baby.

"I'll tell you about Adam. The baby is a closed subject."

"I'll take what I can get. For now."

chapter
sixteen

INSISTED WE LEAVE the festival. Nothing destroys the experience of jazz—don't miss my double meaning—faster than thinking about something awful.

We were in the Crown Vic, riding in uncomfortable silence, on our way to Jonathan Vogel's father's house. In spite of my protests, Jazz didn't think Vogel Senior was beyond suspicion. I kept my gaze out the passenger's side window and felt grateful to Jazz for not forcing any conversation. Minutes passed. Surely we were nearly there. I didn't want us to get out of the car before I'd had a chance to tell him about Adam. With a sigh I broke our silence and finally said something about those dark years.

"I never had the boyfriends that Carly had, and I didn't have her focus either. She'd almost finished medical school while my head stayed in the clouds, and I did a whole lot of nothing. I didn't know a thing about men and not much more about life. But Adam seemed to know so much. I thought he would teach me." I kept looking out the window.

"What were you trying to learn?" I could hear the tenderness in his voice.

"The love of God. I mean, I didn't know it at the time, but that's what I wanted."

"You didn't learn that in church?"

"I went to a predominately white megachurch. I felt so alienated in that sea of white faces. The thought that they loved me seemed to be more a mental assent than anything else. I felt like an outsider, the lone black woman. But nobody, including me, dealt with that. It's hard to deal with a problem you refuse to acknowledge exists."

"I know what you mean. My father and mother got together before people sang 'We Shall Overcome' at sit-ins. You know that verse about black and white together? Well, not in their world. Even when they moved to Detroit, they weren't accepted in white neighborhoods, so I grew up in a black one. My dad was at work more than he was at home." Jazz took a breath, flicked on the turn signal. He completed the turn before continuing. "I grew up black—but looked white—in a sea of black faces. They saw this pale skin and picked sides for me. And they picked the wrong side. Every day I had to run from or fight somebody who called me 'white boy.' Like there's something wrong with being white. Crazy, huh? My dad, whom I love, is white, but at school the kids treated me like a leper. I hated the way I looked."

I turned to look at Jazz. He seemed not angry but resigned.

"Maybe you still feel that way, Jazz, and you wouldn't be alone. I internalized 'I look wrong' because society said I did. The movie stars and models with all the praise were white, with very few exceptions. But I kept going to church, trying to be accepted, learning the right phrases and movements. After a while, I couldn't see God loving me for me. I was 'the other.' God loved me *generally*, not *personally*. I couldn't find my own face in the heart of God."

"Why didn't you go to a black church?"

I laughed cynically. "I wanted to be a part of a body of believers where it didn't matter what your skin color was. I set out to integrate that church."

Jazz laughed. "You're ambitious."

"You have no idea. To this day I have urges to be a hero." I laughed with Jazz. But thinking of Adam sobered me. "And then I met *him*."

"Did you think he could give you what you were looking for?"

"His God looked like me. To Adam, I was one of God's chosen people."

"A Jew?"

"That's what he believed, and, because I wanted to, for a while I believed it. Adam spoke four languages, including Hebrew. He'd mastered mathematics and geography. I'd never met a man that brilliant. At first he treated me like a queen—a black queen. I thought he could see right into my heart."

"How do you explain that?"

"He was a skilled manipulator."

"He must have been."

"He didn't have to work too hard to impress me—a grown woman who felt like a little girl. Who felt like she lived in the shadow of her gorgeous, brilliant older sister. I'd never, ever felt lovely or special, but he made me feel that way. The next thing I knew, I wasn't a virgin anymore. He would always say, 'You belong to me.' Before Adam, I hadn't felt like I belonged to anyone, including God. I loved that feeling of belonging to someone. And then I got pregnant."

"And you weren't in black Jew paradise either?"

"Not at all. During that time I managed to ignore everything I knew about Christianity and to treat Christ like a religion instead of God incarnate. I opened myself up to all of Adam's pathology."

"When did the beatings start?"

"After we started sleeping together. He owned me then."

"*Owned* you."

"That whole 'you belong to me' thing turned ugly, fast. You don't play God's mysteries without suffering the consequences."

"Are you speaking of sex?"

I stared ahead, out the windshield. "I am. I opened up to him like a flower, and he was my sun. After that, I couldn't see him clearly. I made excuses for his abhorrent behavior. I lied to the people who loved me about the way he treated me. What's worse is that I felt like the baby I was carrying proved that God wanted me to be with Adam. All of my beliefs were skewed."

"I know what you mean," Jazz said, his voice tinged with sadness. "I got together with Kate one lonely night. We cops didn't take her seriously. The guys called her a cop groupie and treated her as such. To my shame, I decided I'd have a turn with her. Then things got complicated, and I ended up marrying her. Like you, I thought God wanted me to."

Jazz stopped at a traffic light. We waited in silence for the light to turn green. He spoke first. "Carly told me it took you seven years to recover."

"If you call what I've done recovering."

He glanced over at me. "Why are you still beating yourself up? Didn't he do enough of that for both of you?" Thankfully, he turned his gaze back to the road.

"He beat me up enough for a whole tribe of people.

I didn't tell my family he abused me until after I left him, but they knew."

"Of course they did," he said. "You got a daddy?"

"Yes."

"He should have kicked his—"

"I made him promise not to."

"Be glad I'm not your daddy."

I thought wryly, *You can be my "daddy," all right. Okay, Lord, forgive me.*

"What's Adam's last name?" he asked.

"His *real* last name is Allen, but he said it was Ben Israel, and he pronounced his first name like it sounds in Hebrew, Awdawm."

Jazz laughed. "Wait. Let me get this straight. He pronounced Adam, Awdawm?"

"All day long."

"Let *me* find him. When I'm done, he'll have to change his name again."

"To what?" I asked, knowing full well that I shouldn't.

His speech turned hood rat again. "Folks gonna call him awww da—"

"Don't you dare say that, Jazz." I giggled thinking of the expletive that sounded so close to "dawm."

He laughed. "How did you know what I was going to say?"

"Because you're wicked, and I've thought the same thing a million times."

"That's what people *would* say when they saw what I'd done to his face."

I cracked up—couldn't help myself. I had no sympathy for the man who'd christened me "Dog."

Our laughter settled, and we grew silent again.

"Where is the jerk now?" Jazz asked.

I shrugged. "I don't know. I don't care. I don't want to know. Maybe still somewhere in D.C. Hopefully cracked out and gone. Maybe one of his wives got smarter than me and prosecuted."

"Don't you want to be sure he doesn't hurt anyone else?"

I looked at him. "Why do you think I'm doing what I do now?"

He nodded once. Went silent.

I looked out the window. How could I tell him that I could fight the battle for others but not for myself?

Jazz finally spoke after a long time had passed. "He'll never hurt you again. I promise you that, Bell."

I didn't ask him not to call me Bell.

———

We arrived in the driveway of Vogel Senior's brown-stone in the heart of Detroit's New Center area. The restored house had been sandblasted to a high gloss. It had all the trimmings, was landscaped to perfection, and reeked of money.

We hadn't gotten out of the car before I gave Jazz a hard time. "Didn't you already talk to Vogel Senior?" I asked with an annoyed edge I didn't bother to hide.

"Yeah, and I still haven't ruled him out. Think of me as Columbo. I keep coming back until I don't have to anymore."

"Hasn't the man suffered enough? I can't imagine finding my own child dead."

"He's not you, and Jonathan isn't your kid, Bell. You know full well that it's not unusual for the person who finds the body to be the perp, not to mention it's standard protocol to check out the family first."

"It's Dr. Brown, and yes, I'm aware of that. However, this man is a Christian who hired specialists to try to help him get his son back."

"Everybody is a suspect until I rule them out, including you."

"Me?"

"You've been to the house. You knew one of the victims and his father. You were even at the crime scene. For all I know you could be a short, fine hit woman trying to throw me off the trail."

"Are you nuts?"

"Nuts? Is that a clinical term, Dr. Brown?"

I gave him a light shove. "Jazz Brown, if you think I'm a murder suspect, why on earth would you want to work with me?"

"No touching, woman! I'm working with you because you're a smart, cute murder suspect, and you smell good, though you don't dress the same as you did that first night."

"I did not kill those men. For your information, the Mob is not in the habit of hiring black women as hit persons. And what's wrong with how I dress?"

"You don't have to respond without a lawyer present. You have the right to remain silent . . . you know the rest."

"Are you arresting me for murder or for bad taste in clothing?"

"I don't think you have bad taste—those pajamas being the exception, but I'm hoping they were an anomaly. Take what you're wearing right now for instance. Basic black pantsuit, conservatively cut, with a little bit of spice that lets a brother know you can let loose when you need to; perfectly acceptable attire for a psychologist. It ain't that red dress, though." Then he laughed. "You should see your face, Bell. You are so easy to frustrate."

My shoulders were touching my ears.

Okay, relax. Do not kill him, thereby proving his point.

A few deep breaths and a little more self-talk later,

and my shoulders returned to their rightful place. "I don't think I like you, Jazz."

"I beg to differ, but we'll discuss that when we're not working."

Mr. Vogel must have grown suspicious of the unmarked cop car lurking in his driveway with two arguing people in it. He walked toward us.

He was taller than I remembered. It had been seven years, but he seemed to have aged considerably. He probably wasn't much older than Jazz's father, but he sure looked like he was. Sorrow had etched deep grooves in his face.

Before Vogel reached the car, Jazz said, "I want you to give me your impression of the guy."

Before I could respond, Vogel had reached the driver's side window. Jazz lowered it and greeted him. "Good afternoon, Mr. Vogel. I was wondering if we could have a word with you." He gestured my way. "This is Dr. Brown."

"Hello, Mrs. Brown."

"Miss Brown," I said.

"Oh, my apologies. When I saw your picture on Lieutenant Brown's desk I assumed . . ." Vogel said.

"My picture?" I turned a burning glare in Jazz's direction.

"We get that all the time, Mr. Vogel. Right, Amanda?" He grinned as if that would make everything all right.

I wondered where he got a picture of me. I had to hold my hands together to restrain my violent impulses. *Who gave him a picture of me, and more important, which picture of me is it?*

When I didn't respond to him, Jazz turned his attention back to Mr. Vogel. "Sir, we'd like to ask you a few—"

"Amanda Brown," Mr. Vogel cut in. "That's it. I knew you looked familiar. You worked for Mason May."

"Yes, sir."

"Please come inside. There's a lot of family in the house, but I'll find us a quiet place to talk."

We got out of the Crown Vic and followed Vogel into the brownstone. His house had the familiar bustle of activity that accompanies loss—grief and family togetherness making a bittersweet blend of action and emotion. My professional opinion so far: Jonathan Vogel Junior was loved. His choices may have been disappointing to his family, but it was clear to me that he came from a strong, supportive clan.

Vogel Senior ushered us to a small alcove toward the back of the house where there was a bistro table and two chairs. He offered the seats to Jazz and me and went to find an extra chair.

Jazz, a gentleman once again, pulled the seat out for me and made sure I was properly settled at the table before he seated himself.

Neither of us spoke until Vogel returned, dragging a

metal folding chair. He looked self-conscious. "I'm sorry to drag it. I'm afraid I'm not as strong as I use to be. Parkinson's, you see."

Jazz stood. "Let me help you with that, sir." He took the chair from Vogel, unfolded it, and seated the man just as he had seated me.

"Thank you," Mr. Vogel said. "Now, what can I do for the two of you?"

Jazz charged right in. "I hope you'll clarify some things you told Officer Daniels in your initial report. You said you hadn't seen your son in several months."

"That's true," he said with a weary sigh. His eyes were red-rimmed and swollen. The man looked devastated by his loss.

Jazz continued his interrogation. "What made you seek him out on Thursday?"

"I wanted to talk to him. Haven't we been over this?"

"I want to make sure I have my facts straight. Can you describe your relationship with Jonathan Junior?"

"Strained. Ever since Michael Wright came into his life."

"What do you know about Wright, Mr. Vogel?"

"Not much. He was very secretive."

"Was?"

"Was. Is. The man is out of my life now. As far as I'm concerned, it's him who should be dead. Not my son."

"Did you ever meet Michael Wright?" Jazz asked.

Vogel's eyes went dark. His chest moved with shortened breaths. "Yes," he said through gritted teeth.

"What did you think of him?"

"What do you think I thought of him?" The tone of Vogel's voice heightened, blown deeper and louder with anger. "What would any father think? I *hated* him. He stole my *son*." Vogel took a deep breath and looked toward the floor as he let it out. He looked back at Jazz, then at me. "I'm sorry. I'm just so . . . so . . ." He wiped an eye with the back of his hand. "I just wanted my boy back. I would have done almost anything to get my boy back. Can you understand that?"

I nodded, but I couldn't tell if Mr. Vogel even saw me. His eyes burned past us with anger, hatred, and maybe . . .

Jazz persisted, unrelenting. "Then for you to go see Jonathan Junior must have been difficult. What you wanted to talk to him about must have been important."

"Not really. I just wanted to see him. He is . . . was . . . my boy."

"And you got into the house using the key when you got no answer."

"Yes."

"Were you in the habit of going into your son's house when he wasn't home?"

Mr. Vogel seemed to grow more uncomfortable with each question. "No, I wasn't."

"Mr. Vogel, it must have been hard for you to see your son so devoted to another man. I knew a man in a similar situation. He ended up writing his son off, as if he were dead."

"I can understand that," Mr. Vogel said. He looked visibly shaken. In fact, he *was* shaking.

Jazz probed on. "That man once told me that there were times he wished his kid was dead. Terrible thing to feel that kind of loss, isn't it?"

Mr. Vogel reddened at this. "Am I a suspect, Lieutenant Brown?" His hand shook so violently that he placed the other on top of it on the table to steady it.

Jazz smiled at him, a disarming dazzler of teeth, but he did not answer the question. "I hope I haven't given you that impression, Mr. Vogel. I'm just thinking of how hard this must be for you. You've suffered a terrible loss. I'd like to find the people responsible. They should be punished. At least that's what I think."

Vogel nodded.

"We didn't find any fresh prints for you at the scene, sir. Can you explain that?"

"I wear driving gloves when I drive. I didn't think to take them off."

Jazz nodded, and his eyes looked sympathetic. "I have a guy on my team like that. He wears those leather gloves every time he gets into a car. Me, I can't be bothered with that."

Jazz turned his attention to me. "Any questions for Mr. Vogel, Dr. Brown?"

I made sure my voice was soft and kind. "Mr. Vogel, I know you said you don't know much about Michael Wright, but do you have any idea if he changed his name to Gabriel?"

"I don't know what he called himself. In the last four years, my son referred to him as Father." At that, Mr. Vogel dissolved into sobs, wailing, "I can't take it. I can't take it."

I reached out to him, touching his shoulder. "I'm so sorry we can't get your son back, Mr. Vogel."

He continued weeping, never looking at us again. Jazz and I thanked him for his time and excused ourselves.

We didn't speak to each other while exiting the house, but when we got outside I let him have it. "Was that necessary?"

"Yes."

"Why is that, Lieutenant Brown?"

"Because this is a homicide investigation."

"That poor man lost his son. *Again.* Only this time there's no hope he'll get him back. Isn't there a time and a place for interrogations? Like maybe *after* the funeral?"

"That wasn't an interrogation. That was an interview."

"I think it was cruel."

He clenched his jaw, but he spoke as if he were un-fazed by my comment. "A murdered kid is cruel. Why don't you let me do my job, which I've been doing very successfully for a long time. I didn't hire you to judge me or lead my investigation."

Ouch.

I sighed. Maybe I *was* judging him, and maybe that comment was unprofessional of me. The truth is, I wouldn't have dared to say such a thing if he were any-one other than a man whom I'd been kissing!

I tried to calm myself. It has to be hard to do what he does day in and day out. The more we worked together, the less it seemed like a good idea. Everything between us felt charged with too much emotion. "I'm sorry, Jazz."

"Oh, I'm 'Jazz' right now? Not 'Lieutenant'?"

"Do you think you can take an olive branch when you're offered one?" I thrust my hand out, hoping he would shake it, and he did.

Bad idea.

I felt those sparks again. He held my hand way lon-ger than a socially acceptable handshake required. We stood there looking into each other's eyes, when I finally said it. "You feel it, too, don't you?"

"Um-hmmm."

"It's pretty bad when we can't even shake hands, right?"

"Yep. It's bad."

"You do realize that we're in violation of our clearly articulated no-touching policy."

"You started it when you stuck out your hand, tempting me, you wanton seductress."

"Wonton? I don't recall seducing any Chinese food, but I *am* hungry. Would you like to go get something to eat?"

He kept holding. "Sounds good to me."

"Will you let go of my hand?"

"What's your hurry?"

"Jazz?"

"Yes?"

"Let my hand go or I'm going to slap you."

"I think you actually mean that."

"I do. Fair warning." I really said it to divert his attention, but he kept holding my hand anyway. Obviously, I didn't threaten him.

"I need you to trust me, even though this is complicated," he said. His eyes told me he was talking about his job *and* his intentions.

"I need you to let go of my hand; I'm sure that will simplify things."

He nodded, and after a moment, he dropped my hand.

I felt relieved when he opened the car door for me. I didn't watch him slide into the car on the driver's side. But after he'd shut the door, turned on the ignition, and drove off, he slid his hand over mine, and my own hand grasped his in turn. Neither of us said a word, until I asked him fifteen minutes later, "Where are we going?"

"Home," he said, and I had no idea what he meant by that very inflammatory response. Coming from him, it sounded like a four-letter word, like M-A-L-E, L-O-V-E, or K-A-T-E.

I didn't dare ask where exactly home was.

I didn't protest, either.

chapter
seventeen

H E TOOK ME HOME, all right. We drove up to a very chichi, brown-brick Tudor house in Palmer Park. Impressive. Jazz apparently lived large. Once again, I questioned the former Mrs. Brown's sanity, but I soon discovered this house didn't belong to Jazz.

It belonged to Jack and Addie Lee Brown. Jack swung the door open, still in his green, raw-silk pants, but he wore a caramel-colored cotton T-shirt instead of the button-down silk one he'd had on earlier. He held a Guinness stout in one hand. Upon seeing us he exploded with laughter, making me laugh, too. He yelled behind him, "I told you he'd bring her. You owe me ten dollars, Addie."

He took me by the elbow, guiding me into the house and ignoring his son, but not before planting a kiss on my cheek. "Hello, baby," he said.

Jazz followed us in. "Baby? You're going to let him call you that? And he gets to kiss you?"

"Stop your whining," Jack said, first frowning at Jazz, then beaming at me.

Addie Lee joined us in the foyer. She'd traded her Kente cloth duster for an indigo caftan. "Oh, I can't win a bet with you, Jack Brown." She gave her husband a playful smack on the arm and gathered me into a mama-bear hug. "It is so good to lose a bet and gain you, honey," she said.

Jazz looked annoyed. "Honey? What? Y'all know each other like all that? You just met her today, Mom."

His mother gave him a withering look. "Stop being rude," she said, silencing him.

They ushered us past a living room that stunned me into silence with its artful beauty and into their kitchen, which I decided I would live in after I honeymooned in Mason May's office. The floor was made of handmade, hand-painted tiles featuring Addie Lee's signature-style blocks of African-inspired patterns. The tiles had a Moroccan flavor, full of bright bursts of color and energy. All the furniture in the room was made of wood with warm tones that complemented the multi-jewel-toned fabric covering the windows and table. Wooden utensils with an ethnic flair decorated the walls, along with several whimsical antique clocks. The dishes set on the table were bold black-and-white-striped china.

"Oh," I said. "It's incredible. I want to live here."

Addie Lee laughed. "Honey, you hang around long enough and you just might get to do that."

"Mom," Jazz said, sounding horrified.

I found a seat at the table. The Browns immediately started feeding and spoiling me.

"You like gumbo, sweetie?" Addie asked, spooning out a huge bowl from a cast-iron pot before I could reel in my overstimulated senses enough to answer her.

"It smells so good," I said, sniffing the air in ecstasy.

She laughed. "I'll take that as a yes."

"Just a taste. I'm watching my figure."

"Looks like Jazz has been watching it, too," Jack Brown said.

Jazz sat at the table facing me. His dad sat right beside me and occasionally gave my shoulder affectionate little squeezes.

"Can I get you a beer, baby?"

"No thanks, Mr. Brown. I'll have a soda if you have one."

"You got it," he said, and jumped up to get it for me. "There's some Guinness in that gumbo's roux," he said, giving me a wink before he went to the fridge. "That's not gonna be a problem, is it?"

"Not at all," I said, already salivating. "I've never eaten anything cooked with beer that I didn't like."

Jack Brown's hearty laugh warmed the room like the smell of his wife's gumbo. "And she's Irish, too!"

I looked at Jazz and mouthed, "Wow."

"I don't think they like you, Bell," he said flatly.

I grinned at him. "It's *Dr. Brown* to you."

He rolled his eyes at me.

Addie Lee set a steaming bowl of gumbo and rice in front of me. I was about to enter Cajun heaven.

She sat at the table on the other side of me, grinning like the Cheshire cat. "So," she said, "you don't have a family history of mental illness, do you?"

I didn't miss a beat, or spoonful of food. "No, ma'am," I said. "Unless you count my Uncle Bobby. He gets drunk at all of our family barbecues, and tries to fight everybody. Even the women and kids."

She waved away my concern. "Everybody has an uncle like that."

Jack Brown chimed in, "Do you happen to have latent homosexual tendencies?"

"No, sir. Could you please pass the bread, Mr. Brown?"

"Sure, baby." He handed me a basket of assorted breads and rolls.

At that Jazz protested. "Wait just a minute, Dad."

"She can have carbs. She's too skinny as it is."

"Can I call you Dad?" I said, thrilled to be too skinny.

He nodded as if to say, "Of course you can. Don't be silly."

Jazz huffed. "I don't mean she can't have bread, Dad. I mean, what's up with this interrogation?"

"'Interrogation'?" Mr. Brown said. "It's just an interview."

"Interview for what?" Jazz said.

"Are you a Christian, honey?" Jazz's mother asked, ignoring him.

I nodded vigorously between bites of bread and spoonfuls of gumbo. "Love the Lord with all my heart. So much so that I won't even let Jazz touch me." Well, it was mostly true.

I looked up to see Addie Lee Brown's eyes misted with tears. "I told you she was the one, Jack."

I could hear Mason May in my head saying of Jazz, "He's the one, all right." My heart was so moved that I actually stopped eating for a moment and gave Jazz a second of my attention.

He shrugged, looking confused.

"By the looks of your son here, I take it that you don't give every girl he brings home this royal treatment," I said to Addie, whom I decided I would call Mom, even if I never laid eyes on Jazz again.

But Jack Brown answered, "He don't bring nobody home, baby. Nobody."

"What size do you wear, Bell?"

I hoped *she* didn't think I was too fat! "Uh, size ten," I said, tentatively.

She smiled. "That's perfect."

Jazz slapped his hand onto his forehead like he had been seized by a migraine.

The three of us looked at him.

"What?" I asked.

"That's the size of her wedding dress—the dress she'll be furiously preparing for you."

I couldn't help myself. I started laughing. Surely they weren't serious, but Jazz didn't laugh at all. He really is quite fair, but the poor soul, he blanched at that one.

After his parents got him calmed and fed, Jazz relaxed. He didn't even seem to mind when his father started calling people on the phone, telling them how nice Jazz's girlfriend is.

"I'm not his girlfriend," I said, but Jack Brown didn't pay attention.

I didn't mind, at least, not *too* much. Coming from Jack Brown it seemed funny. I hadn't been anyone's girlfriend for over a year. Even then I hadn't been altogether comfortable with a guy who was seven years younger than me, *and* was my pastor—even if he did have pretty eyes and made me laugh all the time. I always thought, when I'm fifty, he'll only be forty-three. When I'm sixty, he'll only be . . .

After Addie cleared the table, she brought me some

of her work to look at. I kept going back to one piece—a delicate charm necklace she had not yet finished. Strands of tiny white peyote beads, shimmering like pearls, were snuggled next to larger, clear glass beads, alternated with whimsical silver charms. I fingered a cross, a dove, baby shoes, a potbellied stove, a wedding cake, a little man and woman, a Bible, the cutest minivan, a police car, and a prayer box. The necklace delighted me and filled me with sadness at the same time.

"I made one of these for each of my kids when they got married," Addie said. "I call it Marriage Wish."

I fingered those beads; coveting that necklace, thinking how I had messed up everything. I had given the gift of myself, meant only for my husband, to a man who wasn't my husband and didn't deserve that sacred part of me—or any other part. I regretted every man—and God help me there were other men—who I gave myself to after Adam out of hurt, confusion, or desperation.

I should have waited. There are worse things than being a thirty-five-year-old virgin. There are babies born too early who fit in the palm of your hand. There are broken places and fissures in your soul that never heal. There is no wedding quilt to inherit that your great-grandmother and namesake made for you when you were born—back when everyone had the highest hopes for you. There is the ache of knowing that even if you did find yourself blessed enough to get something as incredible as a Marriage Wish necklace, like the prodigal, once you squandered your fortune you ate with the pigs. And you will never forget it.

"Did Kate like hers?" I said, ashamed that I asked as soon as it came out of my mouth.

Jazz took a really big swig of Guinness. "She didn't get one," he said.

I looked at Mom, confused.

She shrugged. "He said he didn't want me to give it to her. I called him after we'd found out he'd gotten married, because he hadn't even brought her over to meet us."

"That must have been difficult for you," I said, sounding like a psychologist. Sometimes I can't turn off what I do, either.

She nodded. "He'd been married three months. We found out from his sister. And he said it was already over. Broke our hearts."

"Biggest mistake of my life," Jazz said. "One I won't repeat."

"You sure won't," his mother said. "I have no doubt that next time you'll marry the right one."

"Who said there's going to be a next time?" he said, raising his voice to his mama! "I'm not even sure I believe in remarriage after divorce."

She gave him a look that said "Who do you think you're talking to, boy?" which Jazz buckled under like he was five.

"Sorry, Mom," he said.

She rolled her eyes at him and turned her attention back to me, patting my hand and saying mysteriously, "Where sin abounds, grace does so much more abound."

I smiled, trying my best to be comforted, but still not being able to connect that kind of grace with myself.

Again Jazz had made it clear that he'd never marry anybody else, myself included. At least not in the timeline I needed to be married in if I wanted a baby. I didn't have too much longer to wait. We were impossible, Jazz and I, but God knows, I'd never gotten the kind of attention from a man's parents that the Browns gave me that afternoon. And I let myself love it. It would all disappear as soon as we walked out that door, and I knew I'd never go back there. The thought of it was painful. I'd never be Jazz's girlfriend or wife.

Suddenly, I felt exhausted. As if Jazz could read my mind, he was up and standing by my chair. "You ready to get out of here, *Dr. Brown*?"

His mother chuckled. "I love it that you make him call you that, Bell." She got up when I did, and embraced me.

Dad waved me over, and I went to him, pressing a kiss on his cheek. "See you, Dad," I whispered.

He winked, never breaking the flow of his phone-bragging about me. I'd treasure that wink.

Jazz put his hand at the small of my back in that exasperating way of his, violating our no-touching policy again. Just as he was moving me toward the door, my cell phone rang. I hurried and rummaged my purse for it before my voice mail could pick up.

"This is Amanda," I said.

"You mean you're actually carrying your phone?" my caller asked. "What are you up to, babe?"

"I'm working with Jazz, Rocky."

Jazz scowled. "Don't tell me your man is hunting you down."

I ignored him. That seemed to be happening to him a lot today.

Rocky's voice sounded urgent. "You might want to cut that short and get over to the house."

My face must have showed my concern.

"What's going on?" Jazz said.

This investigation was wearing me out, but what Rocky said before we ended the call immediately perked me up.

Jazz continued to fish for information. "What? Your boyfriend doesn't trust me with you?"

"I know you find this hard to believe, Jazz, but that call wasn't about *you*. Susan Hines is asking for me."

His brown eyes lit with enthusiasm. "We'd better go."

"Take me back home so I can get my car. *I'm* going to see her. Not *we*."

He looked flabbergasted. I took that to mean he didn't get a lot of nos, but he complied. The man got me home faster than a bad date.

And he didn't even have to use the siren.

chapter
eighteen

A N HOUR HAD PASSED before I made it to the safe house. Rocky was waiting outside on the porch. With him stood Toni Patterson, the music ministry department head. Completely in love with Rocky, she was leaning close, looking all starry-eyed at him. I imagined the willowy blonde sizing him up for the tuxedo he'd wear at their wedding. He could do worse, I thought.

"Babe," he said when I got out of the car. That word, a mere annoyance to me, seemed to crush Toni. I felt bad for her—for about two seconds. *You're beautiful, thin, and tall. Don't expect much sympathy from me.*

"Hey, Rock," I said. "Where is she?"

"Um. One thing, babe."

This didn't sound good. In fact, his big brown eyes

were saying, "This is bad, but I didn't want to tell you on the phone."

"What is it, Rocky?" I couldn't imagine. I thought he'd tell me something awful, like she'd jumped out of the window or something.

"She asked for you—but not verbally."

"Not verbally?"

"Not quite." Rocky winced a bit, like I was about to slap him.

"Exactly how did she communicate that she wanted me?"

"She did it like this." Before I could stop him, he'd gone catatonic again and was gesturing in his dazed state like he was writing.

"Rocky, if you do that one more time . . ."

Rocky jerked back to consciousness. "Whoa."

"I'm beginning to worry about you."

"I just do it as a quieting spiritual discipline; *she's* the one you need to be concerned about."

Leave it to Rocky to find God in a catatonic state.

I ran my hand through my short, kinky hair. "I burned up I-94 to get here, thinking she was talking."

"She wrote your name. Sounds like progress to me."

Then he attacked me. "You're just mad because I took you away from your boyfriend."

I'd had enough. This whole *boyfriend* thing was beginning to wear on me. Rocky had finally pushed me to histrionics. "Hey," I yelled, pointing at him, "Jazz is not my boyfriend. *You* are not my boyfriend. I am boyfriend-less. Sans boyfriend. *Nada, cheri amour,* or whatever 'no boyfriend' is in French, Spanish, or both. Do you understand that?"

Whether or not he understood, I did; it depressed me.

"No," Rocky said. "What I understand is that you're in love and very sensitive, not to mention defensive. You should try being catatonic sometime. It's very relaxing."

That statement drained me of the wee bit of energy I had left. I'd almost gone catatonic from sheer exhaustion when I decided to walk into the house to find Susan myself. At first Rocky trailed behind me, but then he detoured into his office. I continued toward the counseling office.

I found Susan in the corner, perched on one of the mahogany chairs from the dining room.

I sat in a wooden folding chair at the conference table. I hoped that I'd put enough distance between us for her to feel safe.

I waited.

And waited.

And waited.

Once enough time had passed and I thought she might need a break, I spoke up. "You can go to the bathroom or get up and stretch your legs if you want. You're safe here, Susan. I'm willing to sit with you, to give you the opportunity to share your story, but I'm not here to force you to speak. I don't think you're catatonic. I think you've suffered a terrible tragedy and are afraid."

She didn't move or look at me.

I slouched in my seat and stretched my arms. I'd hoped that briefly opening my arms would act as a physical symbol of my openness to her. "Do you know why people have defense mechanisms, Susan?"

I didn't expect an answer, and she didn't give one.

"It's so they can protect themselves. If you strip someone of their defenses, you strip them of their hard shell. The soft, vulnerable part of them gets exposed. You don't have to talk to me if that's how you choose to take care of yourself. But please, be comfortable. I understand that you're in pain. It's okay to go to the bathroom. I won't negate your feelings because of a little ol' bodily function."

She didn't speak, but lowered her head. Her shift in posture signaled that she trusted me enough to change her stance. I sat with her another half hour, then I said, "Let's take a bathroom break. I'll see you in ten minutes."

I didn't bother to look at her. I walked out of the room.

She came into the bathroom five minutes later.

I returned from the bathroom first and waited. She came back. *A good sign.* "Is there anything you want to talk about today?"

She didn't speak or move.

We sat together for another half hour. She still refused to talk, no matter what kinds of prompts I tried. I didn't want to press her, especially since I seemed to be breaking through. I thanked her for her time and said good-bye. I didn't see Rocky or Toni as I left. I went out to the parking lot, glad to finally end my day and drag my weary bones home to the safety of my little apartment.

Only, it didn't feel right when I walked in. I had that creepy sense that someone was in my place. I picked up the first thing I could get my hands on—a giant, decorative bean pod that I had seen in the home-design section of *Essence* magazine. I had been under the misguided impression it would make my place feel earthy.

I crept toward my bedroom. From within my room the television blared a football game.

The TV was off when I left home.

My heart slammed in my chest.

A burglar, homicidal maniac, or weird apparition is in my room watching . . . sports?

With my spidey senses on full alert, I peeked my head through the open door.

The burglar, homicidal maniac, or weird apparition looked good. Too good to be on my bed. "Jazz," I screamed, "what are you doing here?"

He looked awfully comfortable with his shoes off and his suit jacket sprawled across the quilt. The Wolverines were giving a smackdown to some poor Big Ten losers. "It's the only place you have a television. What is that in your hand?"

I took a deep, calming breath. "It's a decorative bean pod."

"And you were planning on doing what with it?"

Now I felt annoyed. "I was going to hit you."

"You were going to hit me with a bean pod?"

I tried to distract him, because I already knew having a giant decorative bean pod was ridiculous. "It was the first thing I grabbed. How did you get in?"

He ran his hand across his chin. "In all my years doing police work, I've never known anyone to use a bean pod as a weapon."

"What are you doing in my apartment?"

"Why do you even have a three-foot-long bean pod?"

"It goes with the furniture. How did you get in?"

"I picked your lock. With ease, might I add, and in the middle of the afternoon. I've called a locksmith. You should have a couple of good dead bolts before the night is over."

"Why are you ordering me locks?"

"The ones you have are a psycho's dream, and your next-door neighbor is a registered sex offender."

"Henry? Is that why you told me to stay away from him?" I said, appalled. I sat on the bed beside him. He moved over to accommodate me, taking the bean pod from my hands and shaking his head at it.

"Yeah. Hank's a freak. I'm not too worried about him with you, though. He likes kids."

"Henry's a *pedophile*?" I had to lie down and fan myself with my hand.

"That's what his record says. The bigger problem would be the two rapists that live within five blocks of here. Didn't you check out the neighborhood before you moved in?"

"No. This is Ann Arbor. It's supposed to be one of the safest cities in the United States." I started moaning in disbelief. "Henry is a pedophile."

"I printed out mug shots of the rapists. They're on your dresser."

"There are rapists on my dresser?" I said slowly.

"There are *mug shots* on your dresser. That's different, and might I add, better."

I sat there bewildered. *Henry*.

"You know what's really scary?" Jazz said.

"What?"

"We're in bed together."

I jumped up from the bed as if his voice had scalded me. "That leads me back to my question from before your shocking revelations. Why are you in my bedroom?"

"I'm watching the game. It's not my fault you don't have another TV."

"Why are you in my apartment?"

"I told you. I knew you had a few freaks in the neighborhood and thought I'd check out your security system. It ain't adequate, baby."

"Don't you call me 'baby,' especially while you're lounging on my bed. Get your behind up and into the living room. Pronto."

"I like it when you take charge." He stood, gathered his jacket and shoes, and followed me out of the bedroom. "I'm just protecting and serving," he mumbled. "Be good or I'll make you pay for the locks."

I sighed and plopped down onto my cushiony sofa. Honestly, men are draining. I'm giving them up in favor of a life of deep contemplation and an exhaustive practice of the spiritual disciplines.

Jazz sat beside me. "So how did it go?"

"How did what go?"

"With Susan?"

"It went *confidentially*."

"She's not talking, huh?"

"Will you please go home, Jazz?"

"I don't want to go home. I like it here. You have yellow walls. My mom would love it."

"That's ochre. It's supposed to be peaceful."

"It *is* peaceful. I slept like a log." He yawned. "So when do you think she'll talk?"

"Maybe after a few more sessions. You slept in my bed?"

"Did you know your sheets smell just like the vanilla and sweet amber you wear? I have one of your scarves in my pocket."

"You stole my scarf?"

"Now that you know, let's just say you gave it to me."

"I did not *give* you anything."

"What were you saying about Susan?" he asked, deftly trying to distract me. It worked.

"I was saying I'm not a detective. I'm a psychologist. As much as I'd like to assist you in solving crimes, what I really do is help people who are experiencing mental health crises. That delicate young woman is my priority."

"And you don't think finding the person who killed her friends is a meaningful endeavor?"

"Jazz, I don't want to argue."

"I don't want to argue, either. I want to do my job."

I sank deeper into the sofa, kicked off my sensible heels, and rubbed my feet. "You know, things are getting more and more like you said—complicated. I don't know if I'm the person who can help you."

He took my feet in his hands and started massaging them far better than I could. "Like it or not," he said, kneading my tootsies into a blessed state of relaxation, "you are at the center of this investigation."

"You're touching me," I said, halfheartedly.

"For medicinal purposes."

"What a rule breaker you are."

"Will you shut up and stop acting like a girl?"

I didn't know what he meant or whether or not I should be offended. Plus, he really did have magic hands.

"Bell, I don't know how to make a catatonic potential witness talk. She may be the only way we find that nutjob, Gabriel, and finding him would tell us a lot."

"Finding him would close the case. He did it."

"We don't know that, but we'd be closer to the truth."

I used remarkable willpower to pull my feet away from his skilled hands. "Will you please go home now, Jazz?"

"I'll leave after we have dinner. I ordered Chinese."

"I don't want Chinese with you."

"C'mon, Bell. I didn't get to see you seduce any wontons."

I got off the couch and dragged myself to the dinette table. Jazz followed and seated me, ever the gentleman. My feet still tingled from his touch. I sat, willing my hormones into submission. I thought listing his transgressions would help my cause. "First you break in, you sleep like Goldilocks in my bed, then you order Chinese food and dead bolts, and you steal my scarf."

He sat opposite me at the table, giving me a full,

frontal view of his gorgeous face. I noticed he had a touch of gray hair at his temples.

"Actually, I ordered the dead bolts first, and I only took a brief power nap. You don't have to thank me for the locks, but a foot massage would be nice." He held up a socked size eleven to what I'm sure he hoped were my eager hands.

He was mistaken. "Put that thing away. I follow the rules, Lieutenant. *No touching.*"

"You didn't seem to mind acting like you were my girlfriend at my folks' house. Now when we're alone you get coy?"

"I'm not coy. I'm *unavailable.*"

He flashed me a wicked grin. "I'm going to make you pay for that." He put his elbows on the table and beamed me an endearing look.

Why did my furniture seem so very small?

Jazz said, "I realize you find me so attractive that you can hardly stand it, but can you be about business for a minute, Dr. Brown?"

Honestly, the man is exasperating. "I'm not the one stalking. Breaking and entering."

"I was merely taking the first steps in securing your home. Now, back to the case. We've got two prime suspects: Michael, possibly slash Gabriel, and Vogel Senior."

For a moment, he looked serious. I got up from the

chair, and he jumped to his feet to pull my chair out. "Will you stop?" I said.

"I can't. I was raised right."

I walked back to the sofa, trying to look demure, and sat, knowing he was watching me.

Jazz sat right beside me. The man couldn't take a hint.

"Mr. Vogel," I pointed out, "is battling a raging disease. He probably doesn't have the energy to plot his son's murder."

"Having a disease doesn't mean he can't kill somebody," Jazz said. "It wasn't a big, violent, bloody scene. The killer used poison."

"Why would he kill his own son?"

"Maybe to put him out of his misery. Haven't you read any Toni Morrison novels?"

"This is not about literature," I said, though the fact that he'd read Toni Morrison impressed me.

"In the real world, people kill their kids, too. I've seen it. So have you. Maybe Vogel thought the poison was humane."

"I don't think so."

"He had a half-million-dollar life insurance policy on the kid."

"He doesn't look like he's hurting for money." I could feel a headache throbbing at my temples. I laid my head back against the couch cushions.

Jazz wanted to keep arguing. "Who's not hurting for money?"

"Wealthy people. Like Jonathan Vogel Senior."

"We're looking into his finances, and they're not so stellar. Think about it. The kid gets involved with a cult. He dies at home after having some weird communion. Sounds like a perfect setup. Plus, Vogel wears gloves when it's ninety degrees outside."

"He said he wears driving gloves. I thought you said one of your guys did the same thing."

"I only said that to put him at ease."

"Is there nothing you won't do to get what you want?"

"Sometimes, a man can't have what he wants. No matter how much he wants her."

That got my attention. "You slipped," I said.

"What slip?"

"You said, 'No matter how much he wants *her*.' You want me, you really want me."

"Ignore it, Sally Field, okay? Better yet, let me ignore it."

I nodded, still smirking in triumph.

After an uncomfortable pause, I decided to continue our "debriefing." "So why would Vogel Senior kill Damon Crawford?"

"Collateral damage."

I didn't think so, and I wanted to get him off the idea

that Vogel Senior was his perp. "Can we talk about the other suspect—the real killer?"

"This may not be the slam-dunk case you think it is. Just because Michael or Gabriel, or whatever he wants to call himself, is a freak, it doesn't mean he's a murderer. And don't forget, we still don't know if they're two different people or not."

"If Michael slash Gabriel, as you say, is a narcissist, I believe there's little he wouldn't do for his own interests—including kill."

"Tell me the impression you had of Michael Wright when you met him."

I tried to picture the man. *Holy Spirit help me to remember.* Two things came to mind. "First of all, I noticed he was short."

"How short?"

"Maybe five feet."

"He's like a G.I. Joe."

"Exactly, only with glasses, but I think he'd like Barbie's clothes better."

"Meaning?"

"I mean he dressed like a Prince wannabe, from the *Purple Rain* years. I don't know about his sexual orientation. He seemed to favor women, and they favored him."

"How so?"

"They were fiercely protective of him. It's like he used the women to both gratify and mother him."

I got another raised eyebrow from Jazz. "And you noticed this in one visit?"

"I went three times, but it didn't take three visits to notice that. He wasn't very discreet."

"Anything else?"

"He's probably a violent pathological liar."

Jazz seemed to contemplate that for a few moments. He settled a little more into the sofa and loosened his tie.

"What are you doing?" I asked, alarmed.

"I'm just relaxing. Don't worry."

He looked at me with a smirk on his face that turned into a wide grin. "You're really pretty, especially when you're worried about bodice ripping."

"I am not worried about anything. You know, you have some narcissistic tendencies yourself, Lieutenant."

"Tell *me* more about it, so *I* can recognize it when *I* see it in *myself.*"

"Very clever," I said. "Do you remember the Greek myth about Narcissus?"

"No. Tell me."

"He was very handsome."

"Like you think I am." He moved closer to me on my tiny couch.

"Scoot." I waved him away.

"I'm not touching." He smiled like a little cherub.

I moved over, away from him. "Anyway, there was this woman who was desperately in love with him—Echo."

"Echo?"

"Echo."

"Is there an echo in here?" He laughed at his sad attempt at humor.

"There is no one in here who is desperately in love with you, if that's what you're implying, except maybe you."

"I'm not convinced, but finish the story."

"Anyway, he wasn't interested in Echo. He treated her with indifference. She was so brokenhearted she ended up wasting away."

"That would never happen to you."

"You are correct. You may go to the final round, Jazzy."

"So, what happens next, pretty little Bella?" He put his arm across the back of the sofa.

"Why are you calling me that?"

"You asked me not to call you Bell. You didn't say I couldn't call you Bella. It means beautiful."

"You looked it up?"

"I did. On the Net. Back to the story."

I sighed. Honestly. "Nemesis was the goddess of retributive justice. She didn't appreciate how it all went down."

"'How it all went down'? Are you using the black vernacular while you're working to compensate for your fair skin?" Jazz asked.

"I am not that fair-skinned."

"You're the color of peanut butter. I bet you have to prove yourself."

"No one doubts that I'm black, Jazz."

"You don't think you're tall enough or dark enough, do you? You want to be a statuesque ebony queen, but you're a sixteen-ounce jar of Jif."

"I'm golden bronze, and make that a ten-ounce jar. Besides, choosy moms choose Jif."

"My mom chose you," he said.

"Can I finish the story?"

"If you must." He stretched, shifted his weight, and made himself a little more comfortable.

"Nemesis punished Narcissus for the death of Echo by making him fall in love with himself."

"Ouch," he said.

"Then he pined away for himself and turned into a flower."

Jazz frowned. "The ending is a little anticlimactic."

"Yes, but my point is this: Narcissus was into himself."

"Can you put that into more clinical terms, Dr. Brown?"

"Oh, I'm *Dr. Brown* now?"

"Hey, I'm trying to get my flesh under control here. Work with me."

"Move your arm then." I willed my voice to sound steely.

He slid his arm back to his side and shifted away from me.

I continued. "Here is the narcissist in a nutshell: inflated sense of self, lack of empathy, and grandiose ideals, including thoughts that they are above the laws of God and man."

"Sounds more like a nutjob than a nutshell."

"Michael Wright was a nutjob, all right. If I remember correctly, he also had this whole apocalyptic thing going on. He believed he was chosen to lead his people to the new world."

"You think Michael Wright is his real name?"

"Could be. I'm certain he was self-absorbed enough to use his real name, but I also got a sense that he was paranoid. Let's look at the name, Michael Wright."

Jazz stood and walked to my door. "Wright is pretty easy; drop the W and the man thinks he's a god."

"Exactly," I said, stretching my legs out. "In the Bible, Michael is the archangel of God for Israel in the last days. I think Wright believed he would lead his little tribe to God."

"So why would he be Gabriel now?"

"Gabriel is God's messenger. He interpreted visions for Daniel and Jeremiah. He was also the angel of the Annunciation. My guess is he changed his name to express what he felt was his growth. No longer just a deliverer, he may believe he speaks directly for God. Of course, according to Vogel's notebooks, Gabriel's people call him Father. He probably thinks he *is* God, or at least God's equal."

Jazz unchained the door and opened it. A delivery man stood there, looking baffled.

"Oh, uh. I didn't even knock," the deliveryman said.

"How much do I owe you?"

"Twenty-five even."

He paid the man thirty-five dollars and watched him leave before he closed the door. "Always tip and intimidate."

"Why do I have to intimidate delivery people?"

"Because you don't know which ones are sociopaths. I don't recommend the bean pod for letting people know you mean business."

"Leave my bean pod out of this."

He took the food to the dinette. My nose and tummy compelled me to meet him there.

He went into the kitchen, and I could hear him opening and closing cabinets. I peeked into the kitchen and watched him for a moment. He sure was a lot of man for my little apartment, and I wondered how long I'd be able to contain him.

I rushed back to the table and sat before he came back.

He returned carrying plates. "You checking me out again, Bella?"

"How do you do that? You know when the food is here before the poor guy can knock; you know I'm looking at you when you're not supposed to know. What are you, the psychic detective?"

"You'll find that I'm very perceptive, but it helps that you're so completely obvious."

"Shut up and eat," I said. "Then go home."

"I will, after the locksmith comes. You may not be safe."

Was he kidding? It wasn't the rapists I was worried about.

And the locksmith never showed up.

chapter
nineteen

WOKE UP THINKING, *Thank God it's Sunday*. Rocky wouldn't have to worry about my attendance today. I planned to beat a path to God's house. I almost wished I went to a good, old-fashioned Pentecostal church instead of the Rock House. I'd rush the sanctuary in one of my dainty Sunday suits, looking all prim and proper, and yet be allowed to wallow at the altar like the biggest sinner in town.

Oh, God, deliver me from Jazz.

Rocky doesn't have emotional services. Church is simple; come as you are, worship, praise, hear the Word, and handle your business with God. No yelling, no running the aisles, no prostrate moaning and begging forgiveness. God is approachable at the Rock House, like a pal whom you can just chill out with. But the music—now, that's special. It's not called the Rock

House for nothing, and frankly, I play a fierce tambourine. It's not quite the same as crying out to God in the modern-church equivalent of sitting in sackcloth and ashes. But it's home, and it would have to do.

Before I went to service, I stopped at the staff house to check on Susan Hines. She sat in a wicker chair alone on the porch. When she saw me, she gave a subtle nod of her head in what I assumed was a greeting.

"Good morning, Susan."

She didn't speak.

"It's a beautiful day."

Duh. Like she couldn't tell.

"I hope you'll join us at the worship service."

"I don't think I should," she said in almost a whisper.

I tried to act like I wasn't surprised she was capable of speaking. "Why not?"

"I don't remember Jesus." She dropped her gaze.

"He remembers you, Susan."

"I love him," she said with the innocence of a child.

"Jesus loves you, too."

She was quiet for a few moments. "I mean I love Father."

So much for my evangelism.

"Why did you leave?" I asked, trying to keep any inflection out of my voice that might suggest judgment.

"I didn't want to leave. Father made me."

Now this was interesting. It put a whole different spin on matters. "Why did you come to the Rock House?"

"What does it matter? Where do I go without Father's love?"

That didn't sound good. It sounded worse than catatonic mutism, which she didn't have. The girl had a serious Gabriel jones, and clearly was still grieving his loss. I had my work cut out for me. I figured I'd start with the basics. "Susan, who told you about the Rock House?"

"Jonny. He said you would take care of me."

"Who is Jonny, Susan? Do you mean Jonathan Vogel?"

She nodded.

Okay. I wasn't expecting that. How did Jonathan Vogel Junior know about our services for people fleeing cults? It's a very informal setup. To my knowledge, most people believed we had stopped taking people in. I doubted if even Vogel Senior knew what we did. Why would Vogel Junior endorse us if he was devoted to Gabriel?

Susan continued without me prompting her. "Jonny said he thought about coming here himself."

Did Vogel Senior know that? "Why didn't he come?"

"His father."

"Gabriel knew he wanted to leave?"

"Jonny's earth father knew."

If Vogel Senior knew his son had been considering leaving, why would he stop him? His son's leaving would be the answer to his prayers. Maybe Jazz was right. If Vogel Senior needed to collect on the insurance policy, the logical solution would be to make Gabriel the fall guy. It *was* a good setup, but I still had my misgivings. I waited for Susan to say more, since I was not sure of where she was going with this.

She nearly growled, "You're better off dead. I should kill you myself." Her voice didn't sound like her own. I didn't know if her dissociation mimicked Gabriel or Vogel Senior. She grabbed me, her nails scratching my arm. Her voice was her own again. "You have to warn him. You have to tell him he's coming to kill him."

"Who's coming to kill who, Susan?"

"You have to tell Father that he's going to kill him."

"Who's going to kill Father?"

"Jonny's father."

Then she shut me out again.

chapter
twenty

I LED SUSAN INSIDE the house and into the sunny kitchen. I made chamomile tea for the two of us and sat with her. As we sipped the warm, calming tea, I pondered what to do with her.

From our brief conversation, I could see Susan's condition improving—she'd even touched me. From what Rocky said about her habits, she posed no obvious threat to herself or anyone else. And I'd finally made some progress. I wanted her to feel a little more comfortable with me, and then I would see if she got better or worse. According to Rocky, she'd been calm and quiet at the house. She showered, dressed herself, ate, and used the bathroom without incident. She just wouldn't talk to anyone.

On the other hand, the things she said troubled me. She seemed desperate, and that, in my mind, made her unpredictable. I knew I had to get her talking a lot more if I was even to begin to help her. I felt like I was flying blind, and still, so much depended on what she could tell us. People's lives were possibly at stake. I had to tread very carefully.

At the Rock House we give the few who come to us from cults plenty of time to reflect and regroup. We offer prayer, support, Bible study, and counseling—both group and individual. It's nothing like the deprogramming techniques that gained popularity in the seventies. We don't kidnap people, deprive them of sleep, or batter them with the Bible until they finally surrender. If safety, love, prayer, the Word of God, and absolute support don't help them, they don't want to be helped. At the Rock House, you have to want it. We don't force anyone to come or stay. God doesn't trample on free will, so neither do we.

I continued to reflect on the things Susan had told me, convinced that the voice she imitated belonged to Vogel Senior. *You're better off dead. I should kill you myself.* The words bounced like a rubber ball inside my brain. How could a father think such a thing?

How could a mother?

I said something about my family. He told me I had no family. "I am your father, your mother, your husband. I am your God."

He slapped me soundly on the mouth. "Do you understand that?"

I nodded, feeling my lip swell, tasting blood I didn't dare spit out.

He'd gotten the idea to slap our mouths out of a book—a book written by a black Muslim woman. She touted her book as a guide to understanding the black woman. If your woman says something wrong, the sister advised, slap her soundly on the mouth.

I remember how my eyes burned with tears when he read that to us.

I wished I wasn't pregnant. I closed my eyes and clasped my shaking hands together, remembering Jesus. The loving, gentle Savior. Not Adam's distorted view of Yahweh with harsh vengeance—a mirror image of himself. I remembered the God-man who said, "Come unto me, all ye that labor and are heavy laden, and I shall give you rest."

Jesus, I prayed silently, don't let me have this baby. If I have it, I'm going to stay here. It's better off dead. If I had the nerve, I'd kill it myself. I'm sorry about all this.

———————

Susan stared at me over her teacup. I realized I'd said "I'm sorry about all this" out loud.

———————

I left Susan at the staff house and tried to find some shelter for myself inside the church.

The first two verses of the Ninety-first Psalm from *The Message* hummed in my weary soul:

> You who sit down in the High God's presence,
>   spend the night in Shaddai's shadow,
>   I will say this: "God, you're my refuge.
>   I trust in you, and I'm safe!"

I'd missed most of the hour-long service. Rocky sat in the center of the stage strumming his guitar and calling the worshippers to prayer.

I moved to the rear of the sanctuary. Rocky had set up something of a station there, complete with a seven-foot-tall wooden cross and a few folding chairs and floor pillows to lean on. The lighting back there is softer than in the rest of the sanctuary. The space is made for quiet reflection and doing some serious business with God. I found our single station of the cross empty and sat in one of the folding chairs, glad to be alone. It gave me the freedom to pray in a quiet voice.

"Abba, my Daddy, God. I know I've asked You this before, but please forgive me for that terrible thought I had about my baby girl. Take care of her. I hope she's happy in heaven with You. Kiss her for me, and tell her I'll be there whenever You bring me home."

I grew quiet, closing my eyes.

Sometimes I just don't know what to pray, so I sit in God's presence, speaking to God in sighs. He understands that language. I love the Lord for that.

The worship music calmed me, and after a while I felt ready to talk to God about more practical matters. The rest of the congregation seemed to disappear, and I became engrossed in the presence of God.

"Jesus, I've got this situational challenge. Susan told me some information that Jazz may need to know, but I don't know if it's reliable. In one way she's getting better, talking and all, but in another she's getting worse, and I'm asking You to help her and to help me know what to do for her. I'm also a little confused about what's going on inside of me. Please reveal my motivations to me. This is all starting to feel personal. The flashbacks are upsetting me, Lord. Help me remember that this case isn't about me and Adam."

I took a breath—just one more thing to talk to God about. I hesitated, even though I knew the Lord's mercy endures forever. Best to dive right in: "And Lord, I've got this little lust problem, and I'm hoping You'll help me. Actually, it's a love-slash-lust combination, and that's not good. Did You have to make Jazz so beautiful? How am I supposed to resist him? I hate to sit here in church talking about my baser instincts, but if I can't tell You, who can I tell?"

"You can tell me," a male voice said.

Uh-oh.

Did you ever say one of those futile prayers that you know will not, no matter how strong your desire, be granted? At that moment I did. My silent prayer shot to heaven. *Oh, God, please let that be an auditory hallucination.*

It wasn't.

I cautiously opened one eye and peeked at Jazz.

"It's me again," he said, his grin melting me. "Long time no see."

I couldn't look at his face. I zeroed in on the name tag affixed to his chocolate brown suit. He'd scrawled "JB" on the tag underneath "Hello my name is."

"Didn't we spend enough time together last night?" I moaned.

"Not enough for me," Jazz said. "Looks like I missed most of the service. I expected you Pentecostals to meet for at least three hours."

"How much of my prayers did you hear?"

"I heard that boring stuff, starting with Susan, who told you things that you should *definitely* tell me. Then things got really interesting." He nudged me. "When this case is over, I'll tell you about my prayers. They're surprisingly similar."

I leaned over and told him in a stage whisper, "I don't want to hear about your prayers. I don't want to think about your prayers. I don't even like my own prayers. Can't you see that I'm struggling here?"

"*We're* struggling. Why do you think I'm here instead of at Mass?" He clasped my hand in his.

"That's against the rules."

"Going to church together?"

"Touching. We're in the house of God. Control yourself." I snatched my hand away from him and stood to leave. Unfortunately, at the same time, Rocky had asked the visitors to stand.

I heard Rocky laugh into the microphone. "I know you've missed a few Sundays, but you don't have to start all over."

Every eye in the building zoomed in on me, standing in front of the cross, with a mortified expression on my face. I grabbed Jazz as fast as I could. Fortunately, he took the hint and stood, facing what felt like our judges.

"Uh," he said. Either he wasn't comfortable with public speaking, or he wasn't comfortable at church. "You're not going to pray for me, are you?" Jazz said.

Rocky laughed. "Would that be a problem?"

"Yes," Jazz said, looking terrified.

"We won't do it to your face," Rocky said. The congregation laughed, and I hoped that would put Jazz at ease.

Rocky is kind. He didn't ask Jazz any more questions,

and I sat down to let Jazz know it was okay for him to sit, too. Rocky read a few announcements, then asked the congregation to stand so he could say the benediction.

Jazz used the opportunity to grab my hand. I shot a hard look at him.

Rocky's voice urged us: "Be careful for nothing, but in everything, by prayer and supplication with thanksgiving, let your requests be made known unto God. And the peace of God, which passeth all comprehension, will guard your hearts and your minds in Christ Jesus."

Amen, I prayed silently, *and I forgot to mention, thanks.*

"Amen," Jazz said.

For a long time he continued to hold my hand.

chapter
twenty-one

W E COULDN'T HAVE LEFT the sanctuary faster
if we'd been shot out of a gun. Jazz still looked
spooked, and I allowed him to hold my hand
while I led him to one of the Sunday school classrooms—
which had emptied for junior church—where we could
talk alone. The walls were decorated with a whimsical
mural of Noah's Ark—fat, smiling animals rendered in
vivid primary colors. He sat on a yellow, plastic kid's
chair, and I watched him try to adjust those long legs to
get comfortable—an impossible task—until he gave up
and stretched them out before him, crossing his ankles.
He also crossed his arms.

"What's the matter, Jazz?"

"I wasn't expecting to have to stand up and say
something. These kinds of churches make me nervous."

"He went easy on you. You didn't even have to say your name. But what's up with that no-prayer request?"

"I don't trust Pentecostals."

"But your mother is a Pentecostal."

"I know. That's where it started."

I figured this ought to be interesting—an opportunity to get inside Jazz's head a little more. I sat with ease in a kiddie chair facing him. Being short has its advantages on occasion. "What happened to you that makes you so uncomfortable in these situations?" I gave him the ol' empathy eyes and a nod to let him know it was safe to disclose.

"I was a kid," he said, glancing around the room as if someone would hear his confession. "I think I was fourteen or fifteen at the time. My mother took me to a Benny Hinn crusade."

His signals—closed stance, nervous shifting that went beyond the discomfort of the small chair, and biting his lip—told me that whatever he was going to say was difficult. I felt genuinely concerned for him and leaned forward a bit to let him know it.

"Everything was cool, and then things went bad." He shook his head, his expression pained.

"What happened, Jazz?"

He dropped his head to his chest and muttered, "I got shot."

"What?" *No wonder the man became a cop.*

I tried to sort through the news archives stored in my brain, searching valiantly for any sign of a teenager gunned down at a Benny Hinn crusade. Try as I might, I couldn't think of a single shooting incident. I'm sure it would have gotten press. It had to have happened in the eighties, around the time of the fall of the big teleministries.

"Who shot you?"

"Benny Hinn."

"Benny Hinn shot you?" I said, horrified.

"With his Holy Ghost machine gun."

It took a few moments for this to register.

Jazz must have noticed me trying to compute this information. "It was traumatic," he said. "I spoke in tongues for two hours straight."

I started laughing. I didn't mean to, but honestly. Poor Jazz was scarred for life by a charismatic experience?

"See," he said, "I shouldn't have told you. That's why I'm Catholic. Nothing weird happens at Mass."

"Yeah, but Pentecostals don't see the face of saints in their grilled cheese sandwiches, which they later sell on eBay."

"We don't do that at our parish."

"I'm just saying," I said. "It can get a little weird everywhere. Pentecostals don't corner the market on strangeness."

"Can we just change the subject?"

"Yes. I'm sorry Mr. Hinn shot you . . ." I really tried to pull myself together, but he looked like a sad little boy sitting in that tiny chair, smarting over my response. ". . . with his Holy Ghost . . ." I couldn't help it. I cracked up again. I got so carried away that he ended up laughing with me.

"You ain't right, Bell."

I was too busted up to ask him not to call me Bell.

He waited for me to calm down.

I wiped a few tears away and gathered myself enough to talk to him. "You're overdressed."

"At my mother's church, you have to dress."

"I'm dressed," I said, standing up to model my jeans and white T-shirt.

"Personally, I like it," Jazz said, the wicked gleam in his eyes making me realize that modeling for him was a mistake. "But if you went to Mom's church dressed like that, they'd expect you to accept Jesus Christ as your personal Savior."

"That's already been taken care of."

"You should have told me about the relaxed dress code."

I took a moment to enjoy his dress code. He looked like a big chocolate kiss in that brown suit. "I would have warned you if you'd told me you'd be joining us today."

He flashed me a smile. "You gonna model some more for me, or are you going to have a seat and tell me what Susan said?"

I went with the safer option and sat. "It's surprising that she talked to me at all."

"So, what did she say?" he asked, leaning in to me, and smelling really good, like trees and bug spray, but in a good way. Mr. Soap and Deodorant must have changed brands to impress me.

It worked, but I had to shift gears and get down to business. "Even if she's not my client, I still respect her right to privacy. I'm going to tell you what's pertinent to your investigation—only because she believes someone's life may be in danger."

"I'm waiting."

"She implied Vogel Senior may be responsible for the murders and that he's going to kill Gabriel."

He rubbed his expertly shaven chin. "I see."

I see? Is that all?

I stared at him. "You don't want to start in with I-told-you-sos?"

"Maybe I would if I had something. The word of a nutjob who talks when it suits her isn't enough to take to the DA."

"She's not a nutjob. She's a vulnerable woman in pain."

"Yeah, yeah, yeah. Did she say she saw anything?"

"No. She didn't talk much, but she did do something strange."

"Lovely. What did she do?"

"She dissociated."

"I'm afraid to ask you to elaborate."

"Her voice changed, and for a moment, she sounded like a man." I stilled myself to assume a blank affect and did my best Susan-acting-like-a-sociopath impression in a growly voice: "You're better off dead. I should kill you myself."

Jazz stared at me for a moment. "You've been hanging around Rocky too long."

He was right. I snapped out of it.

"Are you sure she's not possessed?" he said in a mocking tone.

"I'm thinking not, but if she is, I have a Holy Ghost bean pod."

That got a chuckle out of him. "That's the last time I tell you my worst fears."

"That's doubtful."

"You think you can get more secrets out of me? I have superpowers that you don't understand, Dr. Brown."

"That's what Samson said."

"I thought he said, 'Just a little off the top.'"

I smiled. What a charmer he was.

I may be short, but I'm still getting older. My knees

began to ache in that little plastic chair. I stood and moved to the window to peer through the blinds, out into the church parking lot. A couple held hands, laughing with Rocky. I wondered what it would be like to leave church with Jazz every Sunday, our hands clasped together, looking happy and in love.

His voice drew me out of my reverie. "So what's your take on this dissociation?"

I turned away from the couple to look at Jazz. "I think she needed to emotionally distance herself from the speaker."

"By doing incriminating Vogel Senior imitations?"

"She most likely imitated Vogel Senior," I said. "Even though she seemed to implicate him, I still have my doubts about him being the murderer and about her as a credible witness." My gaze swept to the sky, gloriously baby-blue in the sweet September day. *I really should avoid the word "baby" around this man.*

He must have realized the futility of sitting in that chair. He got up and came over to the window where I stood.

"Why is it so hard for you to believe that Vogel could be good for this?"

"My instincts say it's not him. The man is a dedicated Christian."

"So was John List, and he killed his entire family."

"John List was a sociopath who *seemed* to be a dedicated Christian. There's a difference. I do understand what you're saying, Jazz. My great-grandmother used to say, 'Everybody talking about heaven ain't a-going, but that doesn't mean *nobody* is a-going.'"

"How do you know if Vogel is a sheep or a wolf?"

"I don't have proof, but so far I'm not seeing that kind of pathology in him. He is seriously hurting. I hope he gets help through his grieving."

"I'm still not convinced. You know as well as I do that sickos can look perfectly normal."

"I also know they always reveal what they are, eventually. He's a nice man. Mason would never have sent me to investigate Vogel's son if he wasn't."

"So that means the man's incapable of murder? Maybe he *was* a nice man. A lot can happen in seven years."

"The pieces don't fit, Jazz."

He stepped closer to me and adjusted the vertical blinds to let in more sun. He didn't speak for a few minutes. When he did, he seemed to choose his words carefully. "Is this getting personal for you?"

I thought of him slipping next to me without my noticing while I prayed. "Are you speaking about something I said in my prayers that wasn't meant for you to hear?"

"Perhaps it *was* meant for me to hear."

"Are you concerned about my professionalism, Lieutenant?" My tone turned cool. "Perhaps you should find another consultant."

"I'm not questioning your professionalism. I just wanna make sure you're okay."

I fingered the blinds again. Dust clung to my hands. "You asked for my services. I'm telling you my professional opinion based on my instincts and my knowledge of human behavior and criminology."

"Your knowledge doesn't leave room for the possibility that a man of means, maybe with financial problems, could eliminate a troubled, estranged son for half a mil?"

"We've been through this. Shall we continue to be redundant, or would you prefer to shoot from the hip, as I know you're capable of doing?"

He moved closer to me still. "Okay, Dr. Brown. I'm wondering if you are identifying with Vogel Senior."

"Is that a problem?"

"I don't have a problem with you being empathetic. I don't want it to go beyond that."

I turned to face him. "Shoot a little straighter, Lieutenant, I think you missed me that time."

"Okay. You're working with me. You're thinking about these young guys; they should be getting married, starting families. They're about the age you were when you met Adam."

I didn't say anything.

"All these things must be triggering your own memories. Bad memories."

"I've been working with people involved with cults for years, Jazz."

"How many dead people were involved?"

I didn't answer.

"That wasn't a rhetorical question."

His presence suddenly felt overwhelming. I didn't want to keep talking, but I answered him anyway. "Until now, I haven't dealt with any cases involving murder."

He kept firing questions at me like I was a criminal. "Are you sure, Dr. Brown?"

"I believe I would know if I had."

"Maybe there was one."

"What are you getting at?" Tension mounted in every muscle in my body.

"A baby. A little girl."

I took a step away from him, moving to the left of the window, my back to the wall.

"Your baby girl."

I didn't utter a word.

"It's tough to think about. You're young and pregnant. In love. But he's the wrong guy. He's not kind Awdawm anymore. He humiliates you, beats you, is coked out of his mind. You think about dying a lot, even though you want your baby."

He hovered over me. "So now you're thinking about Jonathan, and he's got a bad situation, too. He's gotta know it on some level. His dad knows it. His dad loves him, just like you loved your baby."

My heart thudded in my chest. I didn't respond, but he went on.

"You think to yourself, 'I love my kid. She'll be born soon. But is this the life I want for her?' Maybe not, huh, Dr. Brown?"

I swallowed hard. "The last I heard, loving your child wasn't a crime."

Jazz folded his arms across his chest. The lines in his face looked oddly hard to me, in a way they hadn't before. "When Adam was beating the crap out of you, did you wish—for your child's sake—that the baby would go away?"

His words struck me with surprising force. "I'm done with this conversation."

He hemmed me against the wall. He didn't touch me, but I felt suffocated by him. "Didn't know you'd get what you wished for? Or did you provoke Adam on purpose so he could do the dirty work for you?"

My hand flew to his face, and I slapped him hard. Twice.

He grabbed my wrist.

Tears sprang to my eyes. Neither one of us spoke. Hot tears fell down my cheeks. Time suspended, and we stood there, my hand stopped by his grip. He wouldn't let go.

I tried to yank my arm away from him.

"Calm down," he commanded.

I couldn't speak anymore. I didn't trust myself to reveal my feelings.

"Tell me how you feel."

I bit my lip.

"You need to let it out, Bell."

I wouldn't.

He pulled me closer. "Carly said you'd never let go of it."

With every bit of strength I had in me, I restrained myself from hurting that man. "How do you let go of your child?" I asked.

"Talk to me." His demand grated my senses.

"You're not my therapist. Let . . . me . . . *go*."

He released me, and I moved from the wall and as far away from him as I could get.

"Wait, please," he said before I could dart out the door. I stopped for him.

"I've been a cop for half of my life. I don't know how to turn it off sometimes. I'm sorry."

When I said nothing, he came closer to me. I didn't want him near me.

"Please forgive me, Dr. Brown." He came closer still. "I wasn't trying to hurt you."

I believed him. I hated that I believed him, and I craved whatever method he'd use to make up with me. But he'd hurt me. I wasn't a criminal. I'd had just about enough of his strong-arm tactics. He'd have to play "bad cop" with someone else.

Jazz stood just behind me, moving me away from the classroom door. His arms circled my waist, and he urged me around to face him.

"Get your hands off me," I hissed.

He removed his hands.

"It's clear to me," I said, turning to face him, "that we are unable to work together. It's my fault. I started a little fire when I kissed you. I should extinguish it."

"Look, I upset you. I didn't mean to."

"The Scriptures say that if your right hand offends you, cut if off."

"Bell, listen."

"I'm tired of listening to Jazz. I'd rather hear gospel."

For a moment he stood silent, watching me. "How did you get your psychology degrees without dealing with your Adam issues?"

"Thank you for your time, Lieutenant."

"Okay. I'm saying all the wrong stuff, but I mean well. Can't we work this out?"

"We don't have anything to work out."

"I don't want to end our friendship because I'm not as good as you are at communicating."

"A friendship between us is not possible."

"Bell, *please.*"

"I'm not going to ask you this again. I'm going to tell you. You have no right to call me Bell. People who love me call me that. I am Dr. Brown to you."

He nodded, frustration evident on his face. "I happen to enjoy your company, *Dr. Brown.* I really would like to be your friend."

"If you'll excuse me. Please respect my wishes and don't contact me again."

"Don't cut me off."

"I don't have anything for you."

"You're angry because of what I said."

I stepped away from him. "Good-bye."

He didn't stop me from leaving.

Be careful what you ask for. You just might get it.

I had asked to have my motivations revealed. I didn't expect the answer to come so speedily and with so much anguish.

I needed my fuzzy blue pajamas.

I waited in the ladies' restroom until the stragglers still hanging around the church had cleared out. I slipped out of the church without Rocky seeing me and retreated to the safety of my little yellow Beetle.

A part of me wanted to see the Crown Vic in the parking lot and Jazz standing there, with a gigantic floral arrangement, apologizing profusely. Another part of me was glad he was gone. I could move on. No problem, save one.

I am my beloved's.

But my beloved is not mine.

————————

I made it home. No sooner had I kicked out of my Nikes than someone knocked at my door. My heart beat fast. I don't get many visitors. I stood there wondering what to do. What if it's Jazz? Could I handle making up?

Nope.

What if it isn't Jazz? Could I handle that he wasn't coming back and that we were really over?

Nope.

I decided to ignore the door.

The knocker, however, did not go easily. I had to open the door before my nutjob neighbor thought I had a stalker and got ideas.

I pulled the door open to find a smiling Carly with several Victoria's Secret bags in one hand and a Godiva Chocolatier bag in the other—evidence of the mercy of God.

"Sissy," I said, embracing her, "why didn't you use your key?"

"My hands are full." She managed to wrestle out of my bear hug, get inside my apartment, and close the door. "What happened, boo?"

"What do you mean?"

"You've been crying. Are you having perimeno-pausal symptoms again?"

"I don't think so."

"Did Ma tell you Don King's hair looks better than yours?"

"Ma said that?"

"Never mind. I got some Vickie's," she said. "Some nice pajamas and some smell good."

She placed the pink bags on my couch, and I went through them as fast as she put them down. I pulled out midnight blue satin pajamas, styled like a man's, a sky blue lacy camisole with matching tap pants accented with white roses, a gift set of peach shower gel and body lotion, and a red number that was hot enough to singe my hand.

She politely took the last one away. "The red one's not for you."

Praise the Lord for that.

"Now sit down and tell me what's bugging you," she said, moving bags and girlie things out of the way.

"What's bugging me? Try murder, mayhem, and a *fine* man."

She chuckled. "I hear you, sis. Tell me all about it."

"Why did you tell Jazz about Adam?" I should have asked what I really wanted to know, which was, why did you tell Jazz about the baby?

She scooted nearer to me and placed a hand on my shoulder. "He cares about you. He really does. I thought he should know why you stopped living."

"Do I look like a corpse to you?"

She stroked my arm. "Not the kind that comes to me with a tag on its toe; but, sweetie, you haven't put your past behind you in a healthy way. It changed you. You're not yourself yet—and it's been seven years."

"Why does everyone want me to let her go?"

"I was talking about Adam. Who are you speaking of?"

My sister the doctor. She knew the wound reveals the cure, but I wouldn't speak of it anymore. She didn't push me.

"I had a fight with Jazz. I told him I didn't want to see him again. Again."

"He's persistent, and why wouldn't he be? You're amazing."

I pushed bags, but not merchandise, onto the hardwood floor. I rubbed the satin pajamas against my face. "Do you believe in love at first sight, Car?"

"I certainly did on your birthday."

"Was I that obvious?"

"He was."

"I'm a psychologist. I don't believe in love at first sight."

"And you've been crying for . . . what?"

"I'm in sin."

She eased over to me and widened her eyes. "You slept with him?"

"No, but he stayed here last night far longer than I should have allowed him to."

Carly shook her head and chuckled. "I think God can work with you on that one."

"Every time I see him, we get more intimate."

She pounced on me again for details. "Are you feeling each other up?"

"No. It's just that . . ."

"You *want* to feel each other up?"

"Well, yes."

She looked disappointed. "You know what that's called?"

"Lust?"

She placed her hand on top of mine. "Try *normal*. I know it's hard to do therapy on yourself, but if it were anyone else, you'd say this is a common reaction for two people who care about each other and find each other attractive. Seems to me like the most you two are doing is some hand-holding and talking."

"He thinks he loves me."

"And you think you love him."

"It's impossible."

"Is it, Bell?" she said, reaching for the box of choco-lates. "You're a Bible girl; do you think David and Bath-sheba had love at first sight?"

"I think it was lust at first sight."

She opened the box and started looking over the selections. "But they did come to love each other," Carly said.

I picked up my new pajamas and lay them across my chest, sinking into the cushions of my sofa. "So they eventually loved each other. Look what they went through. And speaking of David and Bathsheba, what if Jazz and I are merely sexually attracted to each other?"

"Bell, you're always talking about love. You're the love guru. Now you're telling me that when you meet a man who gets your attention, it can't be about love?"

"I just don't want to be stupid."

"Sometimes love *is* stupid. And reckless and irratio-nal. I think you're afraid of him." She nibbled on a piece of dark chocolate. "Yum."

"Yes, I'm afraid of him. I don't want to be stupid, reckless, and irrational. I like how I used to be, before Jazz came into my life."

"Can you calm down for a minute? Let's just say the two of you started with love. You're a loving human being, and so is he. For example, when I told him everyone who loves you calls you Bell, right away that's what he called you."

"He was flirting."

"Maybe. Maybe not."

"What's your point, Carly?"

"My point is, maybe that's a God thing. How do you know he doesn't want what everybody wants—to love and be loved. Everybody needs friends and family. It's not just sex people want."

"I know, but . . ."

"But what? Are you disappointed that he could possibly just want to be your *friend*?"

I decided not to answer, nor to ponder that question deeply.

"I'm not the one who went to seminary, Bell, but I did read that love chapter in First Corinthians. What does it say in that Bible translation you like so much? I know you've got it memorized."

"*The Message*?"

"That's the one."

"It's a paraphrase by Eugene Peterson, not a literal translation."

"Just quote it, girl."

"It says, 'Love never gives up. Love cares more for others than for self. Love doesn't want what it doesn't have.'" I nudged her. "See? I've messed up already."

"Keep quoting," she said.

"'Love doesn't strut.'"

"You messed that up on your birthday in that little red dress," Carly teased.

We both laughed, and I continued.

"'Doesn't have a swelled head.'"

"Another strike against Bell. God is definitely winning here," Carly said.

"If you don't quit throwing stones at me, I'm going to stop this impromptu Bible study."

"No, you won't. You're on a roll. Give me some more."

"'Doesn't force itself on others.' I almost violated that one last night, too."

"Girl, spare me the details. If it had been me, I'd have on a scarlet letter this morning, and it wouldn't be *C* for 'Carly.'"

I laughed, thankful I didn't have to wear a scarlet letter *A* that wasn't for "Amanda."

"'Isn't always "me first." Doesn't fly off the handle.'" I sighed. "I suck at love according to this, Carly."

"I know, but keep going. You're almost at the part that closes the deal."

"'Doesn't keep score of the sins of others.'" I cleared my throat. "Add another strike against me, but I digress. 'Doesn't revel when others grovel.'"

I considered that one. I may not have slept with him,

but based on this passage of Scripture, I *still* have a lot to repent about.

But I went on, *The Message* spanking me. "'Takes pleasure in the flowering of truth. Puts up with anything. Trusts God always.'"

"Okay," Carly said. "Stop right there. Repeat that last line."

"'Trusts God always.'"

"That's what I'm talking about, boo. Why don't you take whatever you feel, give it to God, and trust Him to keep you and Jazzy safe?"

"You sure you didn't go to seminary, Carly?"

"I'm sure. But I did go to Godiva. So let's get fat off those chocolate-covered strawberries."

"Sounds like a God thing to me."

"They didn't name the place 'God Divas' for nothing."

Carly was right. People do need love, friends, and family. Clad in my new-and-improved blue pajamas, after she left I basked in the afterglow of the sisterly fun we'd shared. God's word softened my heart and tempered my worried thoughts.

I went into my bedroom and lay across my bed, smelling of peaches.

Love doesn't fly off the handle.

It was late, nearly eleven, but I picked up my cordless phone from my night table, punched *67, then dialed Jazz's cell phone number. That way, if I bailed, he wouldn't know it was me who called. This maneuver is a primary in my arsenal. I had not completely surrendered my bag of tricks to God. It was part of my personal stash of manipulations I'd reserved for self-preservation—and I mean self-preservation in the bad way.

After the first ring, I hung up.

I dialed again.

Hung up again.

I repeated the sequence once more, in case I had any doubts about my capacity for being ridiculous.

Hearing a knock at my door interrupted this futile endeavor.

My heart caught in my throat.

Is that Jazz? Who else would it be at this hour?

My heart rate quickened, and I prayed that God would give me the strength to stay in godly love and remember the Bible study Carly and I had had earlier.

I opened the door, thinking to myself, *If it is Jazz, he's going to get mad because I didn't say "Who is it?"*

Rocky stood there, a manila folder in his hands and worry etching lines in his youthful face.

"Rock, come in. What's wrong?"

"Susan Hines is gone."

chapter
twenty-two

I SNATCHED ROCKY into my apartment as though he were my last chance for love.

"Nice pajamas, babe."

"What do you mean she's gone?"

"She split. Hit the road. Took off. Gone with the wind."

"No more goneisms, Rocky." I motioned to my dinette table. "Have a seat. Let's see if we can figure out what's going on."

He settled into a chair and plopped the manila file he carried down on the table. "This is the information I got when she first came. It's just emergency contact stuff and a few notes I took."

"I saw her this morning, and she talked, but just for a few minutes." I stopped, considering what I'd experienced. "How was her behavior the rest of the day?"

"As far as I know, she didn't say anything to anyone else today, but she did seem unusually agitated. I figured she just stepped out to get some air or something, but when she hadn't returned a few hours later, I got concerned."

Rocky slid the file to me, and I opened it and pulled out her contact sheet. "Have you called any of these numbers?"

"They're all wrong numbers."

"What about her last known address?"

"She lists this one in Detroit as her most recent previous address and this one in Romulus as her present address."

I looked at her contact information. The Detroit address was number 2345 on the same east-side street I'd been to. "This is Jonathan Vogel's house."

Shoot. Ready or not, I had to check with Jazz. And whether I liked it or not, I was stuck working on the investigation with him.

Rocky pointed to the Romulus address. "How much do you wanna bet this address is where she really comes from?" Rocky said. "Parents, maybe?"

"Or Gabriel."

"She wouldn't give us his address, would she?"

"She would if she wanted us to find him."

His puppy eyes looked concerned. "Why would she want us to find him?"

"To save him. Exactly what did Susan say when she arrived at the Rock House? Did she say why she left the group?"

"She said someone she trusted told her about us and that things hadn't been going well. She said she wanted to get herself together. The same kind of stuff anybody else would say."

"Did she say someone she *trusts* or *trusted* told her about you?"

"I dunno. What difference does that make?"

"It can make a tremendous difference. Anyway, she told me Gabriel forced her to leave."

He rubbed his hand over his chin. "Now that's interesting. She didn't tell me that."

"Rocky, I believe she's convinced that Vogel Senior wants to kill him. She's not stable, and she's still enamored with Gabriel. I found that out in our little chat today."

"Whoa. You think she might try to hurt somebody?"

"I think she'll do anything to protect him." I paused momentarily to compose my thoughts. "If two men are dead, and she thinks she knows who is responsible, she might do something. Whatever the truth, there's bound to be trouble brewing in Gabriel's little paradise." I drummed my fingers on the tabletop. My mind spun. "Parts of Romulus are rural enough to hide out in. I wouldn't be at all surprised if that is where his lair is. I'm going to try and find her."

"Bell, you'd better not go there on your own. Get dressed and I'll go with you."

"I'll call Jazz to meet me."

He responded with his "I'm not sure you'll actually do that" puppy eyes.

I gave him my own version of "you have my word" puppy eyes. "I'll be fine, Rock. Jazz won't let anything happen to me. You go back to the house in case Susan returns."

He hesitated.

"It's fine. I'm going to call Jazz to meet me at that address."

Still not convinced, he narrowed his puppy eyes at me.

I gave him my brightest smile. "I promise I'll be good."

He still didn't look convinced, but he relented. I always wear Rocky down. "Okay," he said. "You'd better call me. I want to be sure you're okay. Susan, too."

"I will, Rock. I'll take my cell phone."

"Babe, you and that cell phone are a bad combination. You're always forgetting it, not turning it on, or forgetting to charge it."

"I have it with me, on, and charged most of the time," I protested.

"Yeah, if, in your world, thirty percent is 'most of the time.'"

"I'll take it with me and make sure it's on, honest."

He grazed his fingers through his hair, his blond spikes now styled in a tiny faux Mohawk. "Fine. I'm hoping it's just her folks at that address."

"She thinks Gabriel *is* her folks."

Rocky massaged his neck. "If it's Gabriel, let Jazz handle the heroics. Okay?"

"I'll be careful, babe." I jumped up and kissed my pal on the cheek.

A grin spread across his face and his cheeks colored. He usually loves it when I call him babe. "Don't call me babe, Jazz's girlfriend, and thanks for inviting him to church."

"Don't call me Jazz's girlfriend, and I didn't invite him. He showed up on his own."

"Then you might want to take cover. God is doing something."

Take cover, indeed.

I saw Rocky out, then I rushed into my bedroom to get changed. I went from blue pajamas to a conservative blue suit in record time. Thank God for the teeny-weeny Afro. I could make a quick work of hair grooming.

As I left, I locked my front door and said a little

prayer for protection and guidance. I could hear my cordless phone inside the apartment ringing. I hoped it wasn't the answer to my prayer, because, with Susan's file and the MapQuest directions I'd printed tucked under my arm, I kept going.

chapter
twenty-three

AS SOON AS I HIT I-94 heading east toward Romulus, I dug around my favorite purse for my cell phone. I located it and flipped it open. The low-battery warning flashed on the screen, and I realized in my haste I'd forgotten the charger for my car.

Shoot.

I hoped I had enough charge to call Jazz. Even though it was after eleven, I figured Jazz would answer.

I still didn't feel quite ready to talk to him, but Rocky was right, I didn't need to go after Susan alone. *Psychologist, heal thyself.* I helped people sort through their problems for a living, but I couldn't decide how to handle Jazz. Susan needed help, though. I had to put my nerves aside and make the call. I punched in his number.

He answered on the first ring.

"Aha. I got you this time," his mellow voice said. "Are you ready to make up?"

"This is about business."

"Is that why you called me and hung up three times?"

"How did you know it was me?"

"I'm a cop. I know how to find out who's calling me."

"That's cheating."

"I'm sorry about earlier, Bell. I just want you to find some peace about your baby."

My stomach flipped and dipped again. The truth: I had fallen in love with Lieutenant Jazz Brown, and I wanted to try to work things out, at least enough for us to be friends. "I'm sorry, too, but listen, about this business . . ."

"You just refuse to talk about her, don't you?"

I sure did.

"Jazz, Susan Hines left the Rock House this afternoon. I have reason to believe she may be trying to find Gabriel."

He swore. "She's talking?"

"According to Rocky, I'm the only one she's spoken to since she watched the news broadcast on Thursday and saw that Jonathan and Damon were dead."

"I've looked up every Michael Wright around here. None of them are the cult guy. I don't know where this guy is. Or who he is."

A feeling—edgy and worn—settled on me. "It must be an alias. Susan left some bogus emergency phone numbers with Rocky."

"Maybe they're not bogus. Maybe she just hasn't called them in a long time. What are they? I'll run a check on them."

I gave him the numbers from the file.

"Jazz, I'm in my car. She left two addresses. I'm sure one of them is the house where Jonathan Vogel Junior lived. The other is a place in Romulus."

"Whose place is it?"

"That's what I'm on my way to find out. It may be her parents, a friend . . ."

"Or a nutjob. *Lucy,* you're not heading over there alone, are you?"

I laughed at his Ricky Ricardo imitation. "I want you to meet me. I think it's imperative that we find her as soon as possible."

The phone connection started to break up.

"Can you hear me, Jazz?" Something garbled.

Shoot.

"Can you hear me?"

I stared, disbelieving, at the dead phone and then tossed it onto the seat next to me.

———————

If my MapQuest directions were correct, I'd be there in a few minutes. I chewed on my lower lip and pondered the possibilities—a family member or friend of Susan's could live there.

Wright is still an option.

But, I argued, it was likely that Wright's paranoia and narcissism had increased over the years. He would have diligently trained his disciples in the fine art of secrecy. Surely, Susan wouldn't reveal his whereabouts.

Unless she wanted him to be found.

My stomach flipped. Now I hoped and prayed the address wasn't Michael/Gabriel's.

I found the address on a mailbox at the end of a long gravel driveway. I stopped the car and turned off the headlights. My instincts about his desire for secrecy had been correct. I could barely see the long ranch house hidden and shrouded by trees. It sat on an expanse of fenced land that stretched well beyond what I could see in the dark. It had to be well over an acre.

I drove with the headlights off, the tires crunching the gravel like an alarm. I hoped the occupants couldn't hear me quite yet.

As I approached the house, I could see it looked worn yet not quite dilapidated. It certainly didn't bear the well-kept look of a "Home, Sweet Home." Metal bars guarded all the windows and the one door I could see. *Love don't live here anymore,* I thought.

I parked my Bug halfway down the long driveway.

It occurred to me that I could pretend to be a damsel in distress. I was conservatively dressed and certainly not threatening-looking. A little car trouble. Could I please use your phone?

It could work. Right? It would give me a peek into the house. If I were fortunate, Susan would be there and would be willing to talk. If not . . .

God help me.

I proceeded to the front door with caution, all the while having a little chat with myself.

What do you think you're doing? Turn around, go home, and leave this to the police, spoke the voice of reason.

But the other side of me needed a chance to voice her opinion, too. *Go ahead, girl. You know you're dying to know who's in there. What if it's him? What if he's got the women and kids in there, about to kill them? You can be a hero.*

I chastised myself. This could very well be Susan's parents' home. Or an annoyed middle-aged man wearing ratty pajama bottoms, with a T-shirt stretched unbecomingly over his paunch, could answer the door and send me off, damsel in distress or not.

By this time, I was at the door. I gave it a hard knock and hoped this experience wasn't going to give me one.

The door opened cautiously, and a pair of eyes, hidden in shadows, peered out.

A woman. A living, breathing one—but not a

healthy one. Looking into her face, I knew. *I've found Gabriel's lair. Thank You, Lord. Help me find the babies.*

The woman stuck her head out the door to get a better look at me. She looked no older than Susan, but she had a soul weariness about her. She reminded me of me, this honey-colored African-American girl. I saw my own face in hers—seven years ago—and felt my heart shatter, the pieces scattering in a wild free fall, like glass shot through with a bullet.

She did have one thing I hadn't had when I lived with Adam: a spark—albeit tiny—of defiance in her eyes.

"Hello," I said.

She paused, as if she could read the sympathy in my eyes, and quickly looked down. "What do you want?" she whispered.

Good question.

"I'd like to use your phone."

"Why?"

"I'm having . . ."

What? A flashback to my misspent youth? A suicidal need to rescue you from cursed communion? *Answer her, Bell.* "Is Gabriel here?"

"You shouldn't be here." She looked behind her. In that moment she could have been crowned Miss Terrified Paranoia.

And what is that smell?

A man, about the size of an action figure, appeared behind her. He stretched to the full height of his five feet. He pulled the woman aside, apparently to stand in the doorway and look at me. My heart flipped into overdrive.

Michael Wright, now called Gabriel.

A half smile crept across his face. "I knew you'd return to me, Amanda."

My blood turned to ice water.

———————

"It's Green, right? Amanda Green."

I forced a smile. "What a memory you have." That would serve to flatter him and keep him from knowing my last name. I wanted him to know as little about me as possible. As it was, I could hardly believe he remembered me. Then again, as soon as he came to the door, I remembered him.

Michael had changed more than his name. Seven years ago he really did look like a red-haired, bespectacled G.I. Joe—from the shirt-bulging muscles down to the stubble on the chin. He wore those big, plastic-framed glasses every predator with less than 20/20 vision wore. Michael had had serious issues with his height and tried to compensate by dressing like his idol, Prince. He was no Prince, however. He would even have been turned down as a prom date by a desperate girl in a horrid yellow dress that made her look like Big Bird.

Gabriel was still short, but he'd aged, and not gracefully. Gray flecked his oily red hair. His eyes seemed to be larger than I remembered. He looked hot, and not in a good way. Perspiration beaded on his face, and moisture trailed down his chest and made circles at the armpits of the dingy white T-shirt hanging on his bony body. Something had ravished him—most likely drugs.

The sick little elf stood there and undressed me with a bold look. I doubted that in his mind I was wearing my classic blue suit. His intense gaze burned into me. I took a step back to distance myself from his unrelenting stare.

"You remember me?" I asked, forcing my mouth into a grimace I hoped I could pass off as a smile.

He gave me a curt nod. "I know it's been a long time, but I remember everyone who belongs to me." He leaned against the doorframe. Again, his eyes swept up and down my body. I'd changed, too, and he'd noticed.

"You've gained weight."

He had to be a nutjob to say that to a woman.

I nodded amicably. "Yes, well. Like you said, it's been a long time."

"You came to three of my studies, maybe six or seven years ago. I thought I'd see you again sooner. What took you so long?" Honestly, the man looked like he wanted to devour me.

I knew I shouldn't give him any information that he could use against me. "You know how it is, Michael. Life gets in the way."

He didn't seem pleased with my answer. "Nothing should stand in the way of spiritual perfection and oneness with God, and I'm not Michael anymore. That is the name of an inferior being. I am Gabriel."

At that moment my fight-or-flight instinct emerged, giving me a clear, unmistakable urge from God to *run*.

Unfortunately, an inflated sense of heroism prevented my flight. Now that I'd been discovered, I decided to stay and fight to find the women and children. How many women could I save?

He leered at me. "Your hair is different now."

"I cut it for my birthday."

"You will grow it back. A woman's hair is her glory."

How do you really feel, Gabe?

"How did you find me?" he asked, his green eyes darting from side to side with paranoia.

Now there's a good question. I had to be shrewd. What would best appease this man? Do I rat out Susan? What if she's here? I decided on an answer that wouldn't implicate anyone—anyone alive, that is—and hoped his ego was big enough to buy it.

"Seek and you shall find."

He nodded appreciatively and gave me that really bad half smile. "You've been seeking me?"

"You have no idea how badly I've wanted to find you."

"And how *did* you find me?"

God, help me say this the right way. Easy girl.

"Through Jonathan and Damon. I remembered their house and went from there."

This actually quieted the moron. I let the little shrimp usher me inside.

Whoa. My lungs tightened, as if his house were one big allergen. I swallowed to suppress my urge to cough.

This house contrasted dramatically with Jonathan's. Where the one had been sparsely furnished, the décor of Gabriel's lair was a study in excess. The place reeked of bad taste in black, red, and velvet. And speaking of reeked, an odd chemical smell permeated the air. To his credit the place was tidy—a tidy cross between a brothel and a very cheap Chinese restaurant. The focal point—a mural of Gabriel standing on the backs of four women—took up one wall of the living room. The feral eyes of Gabriel gazed at me from the mural, looking devilish and powerful.

I shuddered.

I had to admit, the subject was atrocious, but the work was exceptional—thick, bold strokes of vivid color met with photo realism. I figured the artist must live in this house. I doubted Gabriel had the skill or discipline to create such a work, nor would he commission it from someone outside his lair.

Underneath the mural, cursive words read, "No one can take you away from me. My Father has given you to me. I and my Father are one."

Not good.

The life-size portrait of him standing on the women's backs boldly communicated what I already knew—the women were chattel and were subject to whatever whim moved him, sexually, spiritually, and emotionally. I silently prayed that he was still into the number seven. At least that would minimize the amount of people he could damage.

And God, please save the children from his urges.

The girl who had opened the door now closed it with a thud and turned a key in the dead bolt to lock us inside the house. The clanking keys conjured images of the county jail. She trailed behind us and handed the keys to Gabriel. I looked at her, and her head shook, an almost imperceptible "no."

Gabriel placed his hand at the small of my back the way Jazz did. He was not Jazz, however, and I couldn't help recoiling at his touch. I didn't mean to react and glanced at him to see if he'd noticed. He had, and he didn't like it.

"I'm sensitive," I said.

"You'll get used to my touch," he said nonchalantly, as if he'd said, "We serve Cheerios for breakfast."

Frankly, I'd have preferred to hear about Cheerios.

He was nowhere near this bold seven years ago.

Lord, what have I done?

Gabriel stopped and placed his hand on my shoulder. He looked me squarely in the eyes. That's when I saw the dilated pupils. He was high. "You are starved for touch." A putrid, medicine-like smell wafted from his mouth.

I didn't respond to what he'd said, glad he couldn't see that my heart was about to jump out of my rib cage.

"You haven't been loved in a long time."

I started mentally calculating the list of people who love me. My mom, my sister, Rocky, Mason and his wife, my church family, Maggie, everyone who calls me Bell.

Jazz.

I suppose Gabriel thought I hadn't caught his implication. "You haven't been made love to in a long time."

Great. He *had* to remind me of that. He seemed to search my face for confirmation.

What was I supposed to say, "Yeah, it's been seven years since I left Adam, and it should have been longer than that"?

When I didn't reply, he stroked my face with the back of his hand.

Oh, God. What could I say? I had no clue. He, however, had plenty to say.

"Every woman needs a man's touch."

I needed to know what he was on. I bet he'd taken

an upper—which kind could determine my fate. Thanks
to Adam, I was all too familiar with a cocaine high, but
Gabriel's intensity made me think something more insidious than crack had him zooted up.

Gabriel continued his slimy rhetoric. He talked loud
and fast. "Every woman needs a man to complete her.
Even you." He grazed a clumsy hand down the lapel of
my suit jacket.

I came up with a new meditation. *Father, God, help
me not to scream. Please help me not to scream.*

He leered at me. "But I'll take it slow. Slow is good."
Not at all is better.

He gave me a tour, bouncing around with Tigger-
like energy, showing me different rooms in the house. I
didn't see any children or any evidence of them. I saw no
television, radio, or print media in the sadly tacky place.
Then, for a finale, he showed me *his* room. This one was
fully equipped with books, state-of-the-art stereo equipment, and a big-screen television. *Right again, Bell.* He
did keep a tight rein on what got into the heads of his
followers. Other than what he allowed them to see, they
were cut off from the world.

Gabriel's room had orange walls with a yellow and
brown couch from the early seventies. He'd apparently
ditched Prince in favor of Elvis Presley. The King's 45s
donning an entire wall will be burned evermore in my
memory. One wall bore another giant mural of Gabriel.

In this one he was dressed like his new idol: white sequined jumpsuit, high collar, and awful Elvis sunglasses.
A snake hung around his neck in this rendering.

"This is my domain," Gabriel said, gazing proudly
at the mural. "I used to really have that outfit," he said.
His lips twisted into a pout, which, trust me, was prefer-
able to his smile by a long shot. "Some reprobate stole
it from me."

Thank God for said reprobate.

Another waif—this one a dirty blonde and looking like someone Gabriel had dragged out of a crystal
meth lab—stabbed at a button on a remote when she
saw us. Elvis's voice burst forth in surround sound, de-
claring himself a "hunka hunka burning love." Then the
girl jumped up, ran over, and placed her arms around
Gabriel's neck, planting a flurry of kisses there. She got a
smile out of the troll. She dropped to her knees after the
neck-kiss fest and started in on his feet.

Girlfriend had indulged in a little feel-good herself.
High out of her mind, she definitely belonged to him.

Gabriel stood there as if this were a natural display
of affection. He rubbed her head as if she were a dog.

Dog.

My fleshed crawled. I found it hard not to hate him.

"What's her name?" I said, to make sure he let her
have one.

"That's Faith." He didn't bother introducing us.

Faith. Ain't that deep?

I scanned the room again. I decided from then on I'd refer to the Elvis room as the ER—'cause I'd only set foot in there again in an emergency. Of course, if I did have an emergency, it would be the perfect choice. It had a phone.

"Do you want dinner?" he asked me, as the woman continued to worship him.

"I'm good," I said.

"I'm sure you are, but are you hungry?"

Fabulous. I had to listen to his game, too. I felt sorry for those poor, fragile women. Anyone with a whit of self-esteem would have laughed at his tacky innuendos.

"No, thank you," I said. The smell in the house still bothered me. A dry coughing fit seized me.

"Would you like something to drink?"

"No," I croaked, trying not to cough. Even though the smell in the house made me intensely thirsty, I didn't want anything from him but the babies and the women.

"Amanda, I'm just being a good host."

Just then it occurred to me to accept the drink he offered: first of all to keep from choking to death, and second, for the opportunity to hang out a little longer to get the information I needed.

Unopened cans or bottles only, I heard my mother's voice warn. *I hope you wore clean underwear; you never know when you'll end up dead or in the hospital.*

Okay, not a good time to think about my mother or contemplate the possibility of being maimed or murdered.

My coughing ceased long enough for me to ask, "What do you have to offer?" I made the mistake of asking this like he was a normal human being.

"I have a lot to offer, Amanda," he said, going over to the ugly couch and lounging on it. He kicked back in a pose that had to be a pathetic attempt at looking sexy. I tried really hard not to roll my eyes. Finally, he made a sweeping gesture with his arm like the room was a showplace. "All this can be yours. But for the moment, I was offering you a beverage."

All this can be yours.

The little devil spawn. Did he know I'd understand his reference to the temptation of Jesus?

Why taunt me?

"What do you have to drink?" I asked. I tried to maintain my cool and play along.

"We've got diet cola, grape juice, and bottled water."

I'd definitely pass on the grape juice. Thank God he didn't offer any poison-laced Kool-Aid. "Bottled water would be great."

I hoped God would understand what I meant when I prayed, *God, don't let that sound like it sounded.*

It sounded like it sounded, but Gabriel didn't let on if it bothered him.

He barked an order at the girl who had opened the

door for me. "Elisa. Take Amanda to the kitchen, and make sure she's comfortable."

He didn't follow us.

Thank God for favors, big and small.

On the way to the kitchen we walked through a corridor. The first thing I saw was another massive mural of Gabriel painted by the same artist. I noticed that in this one the artist rendered the subject more intensely, every color bolder, every stroke angrier. This mural had an almost manic energy. *He ticked somebody off,* I thought. The passionate, chaotic result reminded me of Van Gogh's work. I wondered if the painter endured the same self-struggles as Van Gogh had, a kind of love-hate relationship with self—or with Gabriel.

I glanced at Elisa. If she were fabric, she'd be threadbare burlap. Obviously thin and wearing baggy clothes, the green-eyed black girl didn't have the same drugged-out look of Gabriel and Faith. Maybe he didn't allow her to partake of whatever he was on. I wondered if any of them got decent meals.

"Nice work," I said about the mural, and then slipped in, "It must have been expensive to pay someone to paint that."

"We give good gifts to Father," Elisa said in her flat voice.

I assumed that meant "he makes us work like dogs

to give him whatever he wants while he does absolutely nothing but get high and gratify himself."

"Do you have a job somewhere?"

"No, not me. I'm called to be at home. Some of Father's children work on the outside. He doesn't think I'm strong enough. He likes me to paint at home."

"It was you who painted the murals of him?"

"Yes." She didn't look proud, only sad.

I placed my hand on her shoulder. "You're an amazing painter, Elisa."

"My gift is for Father. I only use it for Father."

I didn't want to hear any more. It would break my heart. I'd seen men like Gabriel before, who choke the creativity of others because they are afraid of it.

I touched the wall. "This kind of work has to be time-consuming. Do you get out much?"

"Oh." She looked startled. "Please don't touch that. We can't touch anything that belongs to Father. We only touch his things to clean them."

"He doesn't want you to touch things in your own home?"

She looked at me as if I'd said something shocking. "We don't have things. Father insists that we give him all. We must totally transcend the things of this world so that we can receive his enlightenment."

"How convenient," I said, before I could stop myself.

"Father is wise above all."

She'd missed my sarcasm.

We moved from the corridor into the kitchen—the least scary place in the house so far. But believe me, it was its own version of scary. The room looked as if someone had transplanted it from a bad Western movie circa 1970. Faded wallpaper of wagon trains adorned the walls. I didn't think those wagon trains were the best choice for a kitchen—even in the seventies—but hey, I didn't decorate the place. Still, the wallpaper gave the room warmth and matched the small, Western-style dining table surrounded by wooden chairs with backs that looked like wagon wheels.

Elisa fumbled in the cupboards, searching for a bottle of water. They had plenty of bottled grape juice.

"Elisa." I glanced around me, to make sure Gabriel wasn't coming. "You said some of you work outside the home. How many of you are in your . . ." I struggled for what word to use. "How many are in your group?"

Wrong word choice.

She laughed. "We're not a 'group.' We're children of Father. His chosen."

"How many children of Father are there?" I cringed as I said it.

"Six. Four sisters and two brothers. Father does not count himself or the babies, but he favors seven. He's been waiting for a new chosen one to reveal herself."

"Really," I said, trying to remain calm.

"Yes. We don't count Father because he is eternal, and the babies . . ." Her voice trailed and she looked out the window over the sink.

"What about the babies, Elisa?"

She turned to face me again. "It does not appear what they shall be. That's what Father teaches us."

"What does that mean?"

Her green eyes darkened. "You should ask Father."

"I will ask him, but I'd like to know what you think it means."

She took a step closer to me. "You shouldn't be here. You shouldn't have come."

"God is with me, Elisa."

"Father is God," she said. I saw in her eyes a weariness that I feared would kill her, but she wasn't hostile toward me. She even seemed concerned.

If I could gain her trust, I could find out the information I needed. Maybe get Susan and those children out of there, and Elisa, too. "Have you seen Susan?"

"Are you his chosen one?"

"His chosen one?"

"He said another would come."

I had to go easy on her. "I'm not his chosen one. I just want to help."

"You can't help me. If you aren't his, you shouldn't be here."

I moved closer to her. She nervously rummaged around a shelf. "Why shouldn't I be here, Elisa?"

She whispered, "He won't let you go."

"He can't keep me here."

She sighed wearily and turned to face me. "You're already locked in. You can't get out of this house without him."

"He'll let me out."

"You don't understand," she said. "If he thinks you're his, he's going to keep you."

I refused to believe it. "Have you seen Susan? I can help you both."

"You can't leave him if you belong to him."

I kept digging for more information. "Susan left, didn't she?"

She shook her head vigorously. "She didn't really belong to him."

"Did she leave on her own, Elisa?"

"He sent her away."

"Why?"

"She wanted to be like the most high."

"What do you mean?"

"You have to ask Father to reveal the Scriptures to you. He will. He loves to share the knowledge of God." Finally, she handed me the water. It had a twist-on plastic cap. Unopened. "Don't eat or drink anything else he tries to give you," she said. "And hope he sleeps tonight."

Her warning gave me courage. I touched her arm. "Elisa, what kind of drug does he use?"

She seemed to struggle to answer.

"I won't tell him you told me."

She didn't tell me. She walked over to the sink and opened the cabinet door underneath it. I saw boxes of cold and allergy medicines stacked on a box of mason jars. Hoses, coffee filters, ammonia, starter fluid, and, Lord, have mercy, strychnine—and that just for starters. *Methamphetamine lab supplies right under the kitchen sink?* That explained the potent chemical mix burning my lungs. I didn't miss the fact that the house had both grape juice and strychnine readily available. My mind raced. "Where does he make it?"

"Right here."

Poor Elisa.

I thanked God for her generosity, but I still needed more. I had to tread carefully. Surely she knew that showing me that could get her killed. Her courage told me she wanted out. "Does he force you to use it?"

"Not since I got pregnant."

I felt what was left of my heart drop to the floor. I couldn't have been more affected if she were my own child, but I had to put my feelings aside. I didn't know how long I'd be able to talk to her. "Does he sell it?"

"Jonathan and Damon used to sell it for him, but now he's using it all himself."

I went to her, placed my hand on her arm, and looked into her eyes. "Elisa, you have to know these chemicals are highly toxic. Even breathing them is dangerous."

She nodded.

"Not only are you at risk, so is your baby. Meth labs have been known to explode. Let me help you get out of here."

In response she gently closed the cabinet door, headed over to the table, and sat. She stared at her hands clasped in her lap. "I can't leave him. We're going to have a baby together."

Again, I went to her. This time I knelt by her chair. I put my hands on her cheeks. "Listen to me, honey. Once, I knew a very bad man, and I thought I had to stay with him because I was pregnant. My baby died, and he almost killed me, too. If you let me help you, I promise you won't have to have your baby alone. Please trust me. You don't want to bring up a child like this."

She wouldn't look at me. As much as I sympathized with her and wanted to comfort her, I still needed a little more information . . .

"What about Susan? Did she use crystal meth, too?"

"Yes, but he made her stop. He said it made her crazy."

Too many men at the jail came to me with drug-induced psychotic symptoms after using methamphetamines—symptoms that closely resembled schizophrenia. I wanted to press Elisa for more, but the fear in her delicate features told me she knew she'd already said way too much.

Her wide green eyes regarded me. I could see both fear and compassion in them. "Don't eat or drink anything he gives you, all right?"

I took what she said to heart.

Deliver us from evil.

chapter
twenty-four

I TWISTED THE BOTTLE of water open and sat down in one of the seats that gave new meaning to the word "wheelchair." I took tiny sips, trying to sift through the strands of thought dangling in my mind. I didn't have long to make sense of anything because at that moment a nightmare came in.

Actually, "nightmare" was too generous a description. That Amazon looked like she could be the spawn of Charles Bronson and Xena: Warrior Princess. She had the demeanor of Nurse Ratched in *One Flew Over the Cuckoo's Nest*. I could picture her distributing lobotomies as though they were Bayer aspirin. I wished she'd use such ministrations on Gabriel.

Nightmare stomped over to me with frightening efficiency. "Hand me your purse."

Ask me nicely, I thought. "My purse?" I found parroting to be an effective time purchaser.

"Hand me your purse."

I had to admire her focus, but I wasn't through playing Polly-wanna-keep-my-purse. "You want me to hand you my purse?"

She clenched her jaw and held out her hand.

Next strategy? Go elementary school. "Huh?" I said.

"I want your purse."

Go cosmopolitan. "It's a Coach. I got it at the Coach boutique in Briarwood Mall ages ago. Had to save for three months. It's their classic bucket bag. The black leather goes with everything, and this baby will still be around when I'm in the nursing home."

Nightmare Girl had come to the end of her patience. "Give it to me."

Back to parrot. "You want me to give you my purse?"

"Now," she said through clenched teeth.

And elementary school again. "Why?"

She snatched my purse off my arm, nearly dislocating my shoulder. I sized her up. She was at least six feet tall and two hundred and fifty pounds. She could probably beat me like cake batter, but I was fast. I'd have to outrun the cow.

She left the room, carrying my three-hundred-dollar bag.

Elisa intervened. "They're going to check it for weapons."

"I'm not packing any. I'm a lover, not a fighter."

"You'll get it back. They just want to make sure you don't have anything harmful."

"By 'they' you mean . . ."

"That's Beryl, Father's most devoted child."

I didn't remember Beryl, and she was unforgettable. "She's been one of his longest followers?"

"She's first in rank, not chronology. His first child is Jonny."

"Jonny who?" I played dumb. "What is his last name?"

"He doesn't have a last name anymore. We give up our earthly families for the family of God."

"Was it Vogel?"

"I don't know."

"Surely you must have some idea?"

She stared at me. "This is not a good place for questions like that."

I studied her face. She was trying her best to warn me of the precarious position we were in, God bless her. I backed off.

She stayed focused on my purse. "He won't let you have anything bad to read," she said softly.

"I don't have any books in my purse except for a small New Testament."

"You can't have that until Father says so. He has to make sure you understand the Scriptures first."

Other than my keys and identification, the items in my purse were just girlie things: A hairbrush, makeup, a gel pen, a highlighter, two miniature Snickers bars, and my wallet. I had credit cards in my wallet, and about forty dollars in cash.

The cash I could replace, but they could do some damage with my credit cards. My keys gave them access to my car and my home. And if those people ate my chocolate . . .

I tried not to awfulize. I'd get my purse back as soon as they made sure I wasn't a threat.

They would *see that I wasn't a threat, right?*

I wasn't quite sure whom I was asking.

"Elisa, the girl in Gabriel's room—Faith—how old is she?"

"Twenty."

"Who is the other woman in your family?"

"Catherine, and now, I guess, you. He's been waiting. He needed another one after Susan."

"How does he pick the members of his family?"

"He makes Jonny and Damon find them. He tells them what he wants, and they get them for him."

"How?"

"Like they found me. They took me away from infidels."

"Took you away?"

"They delivered me from the hands of evil and gave me unto the Father."

I knew Gabriel was bold, but *my God*, he had his henchmen snatching women off the street? I reached across the table and clasped her hand. "Oh, sweetie. What happened to you?"

"I am Father's, and Father is mine."

"Tell me what your last name is."

"I don't have that heathen name. It is gone from me."

I knew if I could get her to reclaim her name, I might be able to get her out of here. "I will help you, Elisa. Tell me, please, who are you? *Who are you?*"

She hesitated. I saw such sorrow in that child's eyes, I could hardly bear it.

"I used to be Elisa St. James."

"You are still Elisa St. James." I squeezed her hand. "I will remember that."

I moved my hand when I heard footsteps creaking in our direction. It was burly Beryl. She didn't have my purse. "Father wants to speak with you. Follow me."

What choice did I have? I followed her to Gabriel.

chapter
twenty-five

THERE ARE TIMES when it is necessary to empty yourself of preconceptions to the best of your ability. These are times of deep concentration on nothing. I needed to free my mind of the images of Elisa, Vogel, Crawford—and Adam.

This would be a difficult role—perhaps the hardest I would play in my life. This was for Elisa, Susan, the children. It was for Bell— broken Bell—seven years ago. I would play this role, and maybe I would free them.

Beryl took me to a room, smaller than the others. The room was understated—opposite of the brash living room. I presumed it expressed a different part of Gabriel.

He sat in the corner on a pristine, white natural-fiber futon placed on the bare, tiled floor. The walls were also white and Martha Stewart clean. Next to the futon stood a small, flat basket table like the one in Jonathan's living room. I sat on the floor, facing him. My heart thundered inside of me.

I hoped he was in a talkative mood. I'd appeal to every trick available to me to stroke his ego, and Adam had taught me many.

He motioned for me to sit and dismissed Beryl. She left, a tight smile on her face.

A lock clicked. *We're locked inside this room.* A sense of panic rose in me like bile, and I pushed it back, burying it deep.

A tangible comfort hung around my neck, hidden underneath my high-collared blouse—Jazz's prayer beads. I wanted to reach for them.

"You are as beautiful as you were seven years ago. Tell me, Amanda, why did you go away? You only came to study three times. Didn't you like my teachings?"

Play this role, Bell. For the women and kids.

"I wasn't ready for you."

He actually licked his lips. "And are you ready now?"

"I—I don't know." I didn't mean to stammer. Fear moistened my skin with sweat.

"Are you afraid of me?"

I didn't answer. I didn't have to.

Just then, I heard the lock click again, and in came burly girly. In her right hand she held a tray with a plate of fresh fruit and bread, and two wineglasses that appeared to be full of grape juice. She walked through the room, as adept as a waitress in a fine restaurant. I had to admit, he'd trained them well. She carefully placed the food and drinks on the basket table.

My throat felt raw and burning. I needed to cough, but I couldn't risk taking a drink of what was in those glasses. I longed for my bottled water, left standing on the table in the wagon-train kitchen.

God, don't let him ask me much.

Gabriel leaned back, positioning himself against the wall. He watched me for a long time with his intense, methamphetamine-driven stare. "Tell me about yourself. What have you done in the years since I saw you last?"

I coughed, and quickly tried to recover, clearing my throat. "I went to school—off and on. Worked a few jobs. Over the years I thought about your teachings." I hoped he wouldn't discern this double-talk. I'd have to be careful.

"What did you think?" he asked.

I could smell him. He reeked of patchouli and his own revolting scent—a metallic, chemical odor.

"Your teachings were unforgettable. From there I went to study at a seminary to try to understand the little that I'd heard you teach in those three sessions."

"You can't find what I teach in any school."

Thank God.

I nodded. "I grasped that," I said, followed by a cough that practically hocked up a lung.

"Drink?" he said, like the devil himself.

"No, thank you."

My answer displeased him. He eased himself nearer to me, and I knew he'd finished indulging me. He got right to the point. "I will teach you the things of God, little Amanda."

I didn't reply.

He laughed a soft but sinister laugh. "Don't be frightened of me."

"I feel like things are moving a little faster than I thought they would."

"We have plenty of time. I just want to talk to you. Tell me how you found Jonny. He's a good kid, isn't he?"

Interesting. He didn't strike me as insincere, even if his sincerity was perverted. I didn't understand. What was this freak asking? "Pardon me?"

"Tell me how you got together with Jonny after so long."

Stay cool, Bell.

"I happened to be in the neighborhood last Wednesday. I saw the house, and I remembered being there before."

"You stopped in?"

"Yes."

"Did Jonny remember you?"

Where is he going with this? Take it easy, girl.

"He didn't say."

My lungs, thankfully, seemed to settle down, though I did feel a little wheezy.

Again, Gabriel offered me a drink. "Have a sip of your wine."

What a clown. Sky-high on dope, but he serves grape juice and calls it wine. "I don't want anything," I said.

His jaw tightened, and again, that foul grin spread across his face. *I'm losing ground. C'mon, Bell, slow him down. You've talked to worse at the jail.*

Gabriel rubbed his hands together, fidgeted a bit. "Jonny must have remembered you. I certainly did. Jonny and Damon. They're good sons. Jonny should have brought you to me."

Good sons in the present tense. *Does he know they're dead? Or does he think I don't know?*

I tried to smile. It must have worked. He returned a dingy grin and moved close enough to touch me, but didn't.

"It just kind of went from there," I added before he could ask me more about the dead man. I decided to take an incredible risk—one that could hurt more than just myself. "I met Susan, too," I said. I realized she could be somewhere in the house, but I wanted the attention away from Jonathan Vogel.

He raised an eyebrow. "And what did she tell you about me?"

"That she loves you." Honestly, between my lungs and rapid heartbeat . . .

"She said that?" He looked surprised.

"Yes." I tried to keep my teeth from chattering.

You can do this, Bell.

"Anything else?"

"That seemed to be her focus. We didn't talk much."

He nodded and seemed to consider what I'd said. He scooted closer still and placed his hand on my knee.

I looked into his crazy, Charles Manson–like eyes.

"I'm not going to pretend that I didn't know you would return," he said. "I am a man of revelation knowledge."

I didn't say anything.

"You have been hurt, and it is hard for you to trust. You go through the motions, building a shell around yourself in order to insulate yourself from the world."

I let him go on.

"You want to be loved so badly, Amanda, yet you sabotage yourself."

The depressing thing was he was right. "You think so?"

"I'll bet you choose men who are unavailable. I'll bet you believe you're in love right now with a man who won't have you."

What? Do I have a big sign on my forehead that says "I love unavailable Jazz"? It unnerved me that this man could read me so well. I thought about what Jazz had told me. My eyes. Too expressive. They tell all. *God help me.*

He droned on, but I refused to let him draw me in. I knew the kind of parlor tricks manipulators like him use to gain power. Yes, he'd changed. He was touched by evil when I saw him before—now he seemed to have made a deal with the devil, and the devil rewarded him. He still didn't have numbers, though. His group was small, and this could benefit me or hurt me. Small meant I could possibly get away easier, because there were fewer people who would be obstacles in my flight. On the other hand, small meant he was less visible. He could hide more easily, and it could take authorities forever to find me. In either case, he posed a threat to me, especially while he was high. Methamphetamines can cause a person to turn violent or even psychotic at any time. Only God knew when the time bomb—now rubbing my thigh—would detonate.

At that moment, I again became keenly aware of the beads Jazz had given me—beads he'd touched in his own prayers. I could picture him speaking tenderly to God.

Our Father which art in heaven.

My trembling hand went to my neck. Gabriel couldn't see that I was touching the beads underneath the fabric of my blouse. *God, I'm scared. Protect me.*

Gabriel drew circles on my thigh with his index finger. "You will never want for anything. You are mine. All that is mine, I will give to you."

Liar. Your father is the devil and the father of lies. God, help me.

Thy kingdom come, Thy will be done, in earth as it is in heaven.

"You are a beautiful woman, Amanda. You came here because you belong to me."

My hand crept up a bit to touch another bead. I shuddered at his words. *You belong to me.* That—and calling me Dog—had been Adam's constant refrain.

Give us this day our daily bread.

"Why are you touching your neck?"

I pulled my hand away from the beads. I didn't want him to take them. I remained mute. Where was I in the prayer?

But deliver us from evil.

No, that wasn't where I had left off.

But deliver us from evil.

"You belong to me, beloved," he said.

I don't belong to you. I belong to Christ. But deliver us from evil.

"I am your God. Beside me there is none."

I belong to Christ. But deliver us from evil.

"Renounce the man you love. Renounce all. Come to me."

Deliver us.

"That man. Your family. Your few friends. They will never love you like I will."

Carly was right. I'd stopped living. My miniature world consisted of a few friends and my family. That's all. *Oh, God, if you get me out of here, I'll open my heart. I'll expand my world.*

I could feel the garnet beads warm against my neck—beads his mother had made with love. Again, I touched them, my fingers now where Jazz's had been in supplication.

Deliver us.

He took my hand away from my neck and held it. "Renounce all, and come to me." I couldn't speak. My lungs felt on fire, and my mouth felt full of cotton.

Dear Jesus, deliver us.

Gabriel laughed, an evil, tinny sound, then hissed in a voice taut with anger, "Don't be foolish. Do as I say."

Deliver us. Jazz. Me. Everyone—the few they are— who love me. Deliver us from evil.

He growled, "You are mine."

My pleas to God became more desperate. *Deliver us from evil.*

"I am your God. You belong to me."

I shook my head and prayed aloud, "For thine is the kingdom, and the power, and the glory, forever. Amen."

"I am your—"

"No!" I screamed.

His façade of kindness vanished. His face contorted into a devilish grin. He slapped me across my mouth so hard that my entire face went numb. I tasted my own blood.

I've always loved the free-form prayers I've prayed most of my life. I couldn't understand why others enjoyed fixed prayers when God was so very present. You could just express yourself—creatively, spontaneously—in any given moment.

I tasted the sharp metallic tang of blood inside my mouth and I began to understand how those classic prayers offer a quiet assurance. They did not change, and God was just as present in them. One prayer anchored me now in the mercy of God, since my own words failed me. I was empty, save for the prayer that Jesus taught his disciples.

I curled into myself. Like Rocky in his catatonic state, I gave myself wholly to God. The Lord's Prayer became all I knew.

Finally, the last thing I remember saying—"I belong to Jesus Christ."

chapter
twenty-six

Fuzzy. Dark.

My eyes fluttered. My vision blurred, then cleared a bit. The room was dark. I tried to lift my head from the futon. It ached. My whole body ached.

No, worse than that; my whole body felt trampled, inflamed, and throbbing.

Had he beaten me?

Sticky, warm liquid pooled under my head. I put my fingers to it and looked. Blood. Copious amounts of blood. Further investigation led to the wound—a deep gash on my head. I tried to sit up, but a wave of dizziness thrust me back onto the ruined futon.

Ruined with my blood.

The thought felt odd, displaced, as though distant from me.

I lay there knowing I needed medical attention but

unable to do anything about it. In a motion slowed by agonizing pain in every muscle, I pressed my jacket against the wound, trying to stop the bleeding.

My pants lay crumpled in a heap on the floor just out of reach. I checked my underwear. Although twisted and bunched, it was in the right place. But that tender, private area throbbed with pain.

He hadn't removed my blouse. Some of the buttons had been ripped off, yet the precious prayer beads remained hidden.

"Thank you, Jesus."

After touching the beads reverently, I crawled over to my pants and struggled to put them back on. Trembling, I wondered, *What did he do to me?* Yet, I didn't really want to know the answer. The potential truth scared me to the core of my being.

That fear put me on high alert—I knew I had to get out of there. I looked for a way of escape. Bars on the windows, locks on the heavy door, and I didn't have a key.

Dear Jesus, help me escape.

I chastised myself. I guess I didn't do a good enough job of emptying myself of preconceptions to play the role I'd hoped to play. Maybe there was nothing I could have done. Elisa was right. I shouldn't have come. I curled into a ball on the futon, wondering if I would die here like this—dizzy, bleeding, and half conscious.

The food had been knocked off the basket and was scattered on the floor.

Don't eat, I remembered Elisa saying.

I rubbed my eyes and touched the beads at my neck. The garnet stones felt warm against my skin. My thoughts were hazy, but I could still pray.

Our Father.

My head seemed to echo the words, *Father, Father, Father . . . Abba.* But I couldn't remember the other words.

Forever, and deliver us . . . After this manner therefore, pray ye, forever. Thy kingdom come. I want to see my baby, Lord. Thy kingdom . . . Forever, baby girl.

Tears flowed down my cheeks. I wasn't sure why I was crying, or what my fractured prayer petitioned God for.

The lock on the door clicked. The door squealed as it opened. I squinted at the light. A woman holding a small flashlight. Pretty little brown girl with green eyes.

Elija? Elisha? No, her name is Elisa.

Deliver us.

She lowered the light and scooped me into her small arms. "I'm going to clean you up. He'll come to you today. First you must fear him. Then you must love him."

"No."

"Shhh. You can't fight him."

"Please let me call someone. Please, Elisa. I can help us."

"You can't do that. If he finds out, he'll kill us both. You belong to him. He will show you his love completely when he comes to you today." She hesitated. "You'll get used to it. You might even like it sometimes."

"Please. Please let me call someone."

"It's no use. Surrender to him."

She was terrified of him. I couldn't reason with her. "Elisa, he beat me because I love my family and friends."

"You can love none but him. Don't you understand? It's over for you. It's over for me."

"Then let me say good-bye to just one person. Please. I love him. Just let me say good-bye. You can listen to everything I say."

"I can't do that. I have to clean you up for when he comes to you later today."

"I'm hurt. I may be dying. Please let me say good-bye to the man I love. Please, Elisa."

Several minutes passed while she considered my request. She held on to me, stroking my hair. "They're asleep. Be quiet. I'll let you call him, but I have to make sure you don't try to call anyone else. If Father finds out . . ."

"Thank you." I hoped the Lord had touched her heart, encouraging her to help me in spite of her instincts to do otherwise.

"Save your strength."

She shifted her body and helped me get to my feet. She supported me, helping me creep down the hall with all the stealth we could manage to the ER—the Elvis room.

"You have to be very quiet. He's drunk and high and with Beryl. If she hears you, she'll tell and he'll kill us both."

"Okay," I whispered.

"You can't call the police. If the police come, we won't get out of here alive. We've practiced it many times."

"Okay," I said. I understood. The police would bring on the apocalypse.

Oh, God, what do I do?

Call the police.

I could hear Jazz's voice in my head the day he'd shown up at my door when my phone was off the hook, *"I am the police."*

Call Jazz.

I blinked my eyes, trying to bring his number back to memory. I had only a small window of opportunity. I couldn't let Elisa know I was calling a cop. She was unpredictable and could turn foe as quickly as she had turned friend.

God, help me remember.

One. Three. One. Three. I paused. What was that

number? I strained to recall. After all, I'd called his cell phone three times last night.

One-three-one-three. I couldn't remember any more than that. But the Detroit police homicide phone number—I'd called there many times for my job.

Please, God. Help me remember.

I blinked my eyes. Numbers came to my consciousness, and I pressed the digits quickly before they faded. I was growing weaker.

A man answered on the first ring, and dear God, it was Jazz. He barked, "Brown," into the receiver.

"Jazz?"

"Bell, where are you?" His voice sounded soft, entreating. Hearing him triggered a well of tears. "I've been worried sick all night," he said. "I couldn't sleep, so I came to work to try to see if I could figure out who this Gabriel guy is."

I had to word this very carefully. *God have mercy.* "I have a bad connection, Jazz. Can you hear me?"

"You sound strange. Are you okay?"

"I have a *bad* connection. Can you hear me?"

"Yes, I can hear you, but you sound . . ." He paused as understanding dawned. "Are you safe?"

"That's better. I'm calling to say good-bye."

He was quiet for a moment. "Can they hear what I'm saying?"

"No, but you should talk soft. I have a really bad head hurt. I mean, headache."

I could hear him muffle the phone and say, "Get a trace on this line."

Back on the line, he cooed into my ear, "I'll find you. I'll know your exact location in moments."

"Do you remember when we talked about the kind of man I'm looking for? I told you all about him."

"You found Gabriel?"

Think, Bell. Don't let her know what you're doing. "It was *Rocky* getting here, but I found him. He's everything I thought he would be, and more."

"Lord, have mercy."

"Very soon, I'm going to belong to him completely."

"You think he's going to try to rape you?"

"Yes, and then my life will be his."

"He's going to kill you?"

"I know it with all my heart."

"No, baby. I'm coming for you."

"It's over for us. I wanted to say good-bye."

"It's not over. We haven't even gotten started."

"Good-bye, Jazzy. You tell everybody I said good-bye. You know who to tell."

"Nothing to tell, because I'm coming for you, so help me God. I'm on my way. I'm bringing the troops with me."

Elisa was getting impatient.

304   claudia mair burney

"Go easy, Jazz. Okay?"

"I hear you. They won't know what hit 'em."

"You really are one of the good ones. Thank you for a *minute* of your time, Jazzy. You know what I'm saying?"

I just wanted to be in love for a minute.

"Do one thing for me," he said. "Stay alive."

I hung up the phone. I felt faint; my knees buckled.

"Let's get you to the bathroom. I have to clean this mess before he sees it. Hurry," Elisa said.

I didn't answer. I didn't have the strength to. She would have to drag me.

chapter twenty-seven

ELISA PROPPED ME against a table.

"Hang on," she whispered.

I literally hung on to the table. "I'm praying for you, Elisa. To my God, not to Gabriel."

She nodded. "My grandmother is a Christian."

"Mine was, too. I'll bet they're both interceding—praying for us right now."

On earth as it is in heaven.

Elisa checked the hallway, then practically dragged me to the bathroom. She drew a bath while I rested against the wall. I didn't know how I would make it into the tub, let alone out of the house, alive.

She unbuttoned my blouse. I didn't have the energy to protect my beads. When she saw them, she grazed her finger across them, reverently. Her eyes looked as though she'd been transported to a faraway place. "Jesus

Christ, Son of God, have mercy on me, a sinner," Elisa said.

The Jesus prayer. I didn't know how she knew it, but I suspected it had something to do with that grandmother of hers.

She undressed me, leaving the beads around my neck. With her help, I clambered into the bathtub. The water was warm and soothing. I leaned back against the tiles, still cool to the touch, and closed my eyes as the water washed over me. A washcloth in Elisa's tender hand cleansed me of blood, yet everywhere she touched felt like an open wound.

I tried to speak to her, but I felt so weak. I wished I could say something that would minister to her as she so aptly served me. I decided to leave that to Jesus. My job was to stay alive.

"What time is it?"

"It's five A.M."

I coughed again, feeling sicker than ever. "We have to get out of here, Elisa."

She pulled up the stopper in the tub. The bloody water swirled down the drain. I kneeled in the tub as Elisa toweled me off and then dressed me in a white cotton sheath. She wadded up the towel and tossed it in a basket.

"The police are coming for me."

"What?"

"The police. They're coming. We have to leave."

I watched as understanding dawned on her face. "Oh, my God," she said, and I don't think she was talking about Gabriel. She turned to look at me, puzzled. "Who did you call?"

"My friend. I called my friend."

"Did he . . . but you didn't . . . I heard everything you said."

"You have the keys, Elisa. Get us out of here."

"I can't leave him."

"Yes, you can. I promise you it will be okay."

She looked torn. Tears sprang to her eyes. "I don't know what to do."

"Help me. Get us out of here. I promise I will help you."

"If the police come, they're going to wake up. He'll offer us the sacrament, and we'll all go with him to paradise. We've practiced it so many times. I have to go with him."

"I see a spark in you, Elisa. You don't want to go to paradise right now. Please help me. We'll figure it out. I promise you."

She stroked my wet hair. "Can you run?"

"I can hardly stand."

"You'll have to. That's the only way we'll get out of here."

"Where are the kids? We have to get them out."

"The kids don't stay here. They live with Catherine in another house. Jonny and Damon live in a different house, too."

She doesn't know.

"Jonathan Vogel and Damon Crawford are dead, Elisa. They were murdered."

She froze. "That's not true."

"It's why I'm here, sweetie."

She took my hand.

"Wait," I said. "Give me his toothbrush, but don't get your fingerprints on it."

"What?"

"Grab the toothbrush with the hem of your skirt. Quickly."

"Why?"

"It's evidence. I promise. It'll help us."

"It's covered," she said, pulling his toothbrush, sheathed in a plastic cover, from the medicine cabinet behind the mirror. *Way to go, Gabriel.*

"We'd better go now," she said. She put her arm around me, giving me stability and strength. With all that I had in me, I went with her. She unlocked the front door, letting us out of the house. We moved away as fast as my aching body would let us. I looked back and saw lights come on in the house. Elisa began to run, and I stumbled forward in a half run. I must have had angels holding me up. She guided us through the trees. In the darkness I couldn't tell where we were, or how far we were from the house. I fell several times, and Elisa kept picking me up, silently urging me on.

But then, my foot caught in a tree root. I went down too hard. I knew I couldn't get back up. Elisa bent over me, tugging at my arm.

I shook my head. "No. Run, Elisa. Don't wait for me."

"I can't leave you."

"I'm not going to make it."

"Yes, you will. You have to."

"I can't run anymore," I said. My lungs felt as if they'd burst. I could scarcely breathe, and my aching legs crumbled beneath me, refusing to go on. I touched my neck. "Take the prayer beads."

"I can't," she said. I saw that she was crying.

"Go with God, Elisa. Say a prayer to Jesus to have mercy on us. When you get away, call Lieutenant Jazz Brown with the Detroit Police. Homicide. Take him to the children."

"I'm going to stay with you."

"Don't. You're young. Run, Elisa. Let the Lord save you."

She kissed me on my battered forehead, and I felt her tears fall onto my face. Elisa smoothed my hair again, and pressed her lips to my cheek, then she ran deeper into the woods.

She left me on the ground, praying and clutching a
toothbrush, something that I hoped might help identify
the man who would surely kill me.

A blinding pain exploded in my head, which felt like
it was going to split in two, and I blacked out.

chapter
twenty-eight

*I*T IS PEACEFUL. *I have never felt such serenity. My head doesn't hurt anymore, and sunlight streams through the trees. The air smells like springtime—a sharp, lively smell of fresh pine and earth still damp from the last shower—and something else. I see Jazz, and I hug him. I love him, fearlessly and free of shame. He is my friend. I open my arms to embrace him. He holds me, and he kisses my cheeks again and again.*

Then it is dark again. I hurt. My head, my torso, my thighs. Why do I hurt so? And I smell smoke.

Jazz speaks to me, but I don't understand what he says. I want to thank him for coming for me. I believe I will be all right now.

"You came for me," I mutter, and it hurts to talk.

"I told you I would."

Where am I?

I winced at the light when I opened my eyes. I was lying in a bed. Jazz sat on the edge, his prayer beads, the ones he'd given me, in his hand. He was uttering prayers in a low voice, his head bowed and his eyes closed. Flowers filled the room.

I tried to speak but it was difficult. My mouth felt dry and unused. I tried again and in a raspy voice, managed to say, "Someone let you loose in a flower shop again?"

His eyes snapped open, and he graced me with one of those dazzling smiles. "Hello to you, too." He touched my face and picked up the call button to alert a nurse.

"May I help you?" a female voice asked over the intercom.

"She's awake," Jazz said.

"Where am I?"

"University of Michigan Hospital."

"When did I get here?"

"Monday morning."

"What day is it now?"

"It's Wednesday. You were banged up pretty bad."

"How bad?"

"Bad. You had lots of contusions, some head injuries, and acute bronchial inflammation, and I'm sorry to say you have a bit of a hair deficit now. You don't even want to know what your mother said about that."

"You met my mother?" More horror. "What did she say to you?"

"I met Maggie, too. Let's just say I now know more about you than you know about yourself. And those women *love* me."

I reached up and ran my hand across my poor, aching head.

Jazz cleared his throat. "Uh, there's the stitches issue, too, but my mom made you a fierce head wrap. A couple of them."

He was right. Stitches bound a part of my scalp together. Boy, was I sore.

"The doctor said your hair will grow back, much to your mother's relief."

We didn't say anything for a while, but Jazz kept staring at me, his face serious and concerned. I recognized that face. I was about to get the Jazz version of "the talk."

"He could have killed you."

"I know."

"We pulled two bodies out of that house. I thought I'd lost you, and I can't lose you."

I swallowed hard.

"Promise me that you will never do anything like that again."

"I promise, Jazz," I said, ashamed of my egotistical impetuosity.

"You're fired."

"Does that mean you won't pay me the five grand?"

He gave me a half smile. "We'll have to find another way to have babies."

"Yeah. Let me know when you're available."

"A head injury, and still you remember that?"

I laughed. It hurt.

He got serious on me again. "What else do you remember?"

"I remember getting to Gabriel's house. I know he slapped me. I don't remember much after that until I woke up alone in the room."

Jazz reached down to the floor and grabbed a manila envelope. He opened it, and took out a mug shot. "Is this Gabriel?"

"Yes, and he *is* the former Michael Wright."

"His real name is Michael Pingree."

"How did you find that out?"

"He's an ex-con. We got his prints off the toothbrush you were carrying. Souldier says we can get a good DNA profile, too. Gil Grissom would be proud."

I smiled at his *CSI* reference, but grew serious quickly. "Jazz, I don't think Gabriel knew about the murders."

"Why do you say that?"

"We talked about the guys. He seemed oblivious." I tried to pull my fuzzy thoughts together. "You said you pulled two bodies out. Is he dead?"

"The bodies were female. They were burned badly."

"He set the house on fire?"

"Someone did. We'll get to that part. Elisa contacted me. We got the kids and another woman, Catherine. You're a hero."

"I'm an idiot."

"Elisa didn't think so. She's at the Rock House, and they're loving her up. The children are in protective custody until we can get some of this mess straightened out. Catherine is with her parents."

"Praise God. I know Rocky will take good care of Elisa. She saved my life."

"You saved hers." He touched my chin, a sweet, gentle gesture. "Do you remember anything else about being hurt?"

My memories of the events that took place at that house were like pieces of a broken mirror. I saw myself and whatever happened in shards of vivid recollection, but some pieces were missing completely. "I don't remember everything. He must have hurt me pretty bad, because I ache all over."

Jazz held my hand in his. "We found you in the woods by the house. You were in and out of consciousness."

"Did you kiss me? I vaguely remember you kissing my face, and I said, 'You came for me.'" I blushed a little at the thought of it.

"You did say that, but I didn't kiss you."

"You didn't?"

"It was a dog."

"What?"

"A dog licked your face."

I was horrified. "You know, that's not a comforting thought."

He pulled my scarf out of his pocket. "Thank God for that dog. This is how I found you." He stretched out the length of yellow fabric. "It's scented with vanilla and sweet amber—essence of Bell."

I smiled at him. "The scarf you stole."

"The scarf you *gave* me. We brought in a bloodhound and a cadaver dog."

"Did you find Gabriel?"

"No. We didn't find Susan Hines, either. Rocky said she never returned to the house."

"Jazz, do you still think Vogel Senior killed Jonathan and Damon?"

"What, now you think he did it? I've been arguing with you for days about that, and now you've changed your mind?"

"I'm sorry for arguing with you, Jazz. This is all so confusing."

"This ain't *CSI*, baby. It takes a while to get to the truth sometimes, but we're on it."

"Did he?"

"I don't know yet."

"Do you know where my car is?"

"We have it."

"Is it damaged?"

"No, but we couldn't find the keys. We think they're in the rubble in the house."

"My Love Bug! Yay!"

"You're more concerned about the 'Love Bug' than about your own injuries? Cars can be replaced, but you can't."

My broken body screamed the truth of that statement.

A doctor came into the room. She was a small Indian woman with a warm demeanor and compassionate obsidian eyes. "Dr. Brown. It's good to have you with us. My name is Dr. Pakoor."

"It's good to be here, but everything hurts."

She pointed to a small machine by my bed. "This is your new best friend. It has morphine in it." She handed me a cord with a button similar to the call button to get the nurses' attention. "Just push when you need to. We'll wean you off of it soon, so enjoy it while you can."

I pushed. Fast.

The doctor looked at Jazz, then back at me. "I'm going to order some tests for you now that you're awake. I'll let you and your husband have some time alone."

Jazz winked at me.

My husband. In my dreams.

"I'll be back in a little while to examine you. If you have any questions, I'll be here to answer them for you. We also have a social worker on hand for you to speak with if you wish. Please let me know if you need anything."

"I'm okay for now, just thirsty."

"I'll have your nurse bring you something to drink. How about some grape juice?"

"Anything but that, please."

"Whatever you'd like. I'll be back soon." She left the room swiftly.

"Okay, husband," I said.

I was rewarded with one of his smiles. "Can I help it if people make assumptions because we have the same last name?"

We both chuckled.

"You know what's ironic?" he said.

"I'm afraid to ask."

"Kate didn't take my last name. She was too liberated for that."

The thought of his *real* wife sobered me, even if she was his ex.

"I need to ask you something, Jazz, and I expect an honest answer."

"Ask away."

"Did he rape me?"

His smile faded. "When we found you, it was clear that you were hurt, and the focus was on treating your head injuries and discovering any internal injuries as a result of the beating you'd had."

"Okay."

"We found trauma around your thighs, and . . . other delicate parts." He took a deep breath. "We thought he may have sexually assaulted you. The doctor ordered a rape kit, but someone must have cleaned you up. They said it was inconclusive."

"Elisa gave me a bath." My stomach felt queasy as the truth swept over me.

"Carly raised all kinds of you-know-what. Then she examined you herself."

I didn't say anything. All words were gone from me.

"She couldn't tell for sure, either, but she leaned toward you having *not* been raped. Look, Bell, decisions had to be made, and Carly was the only one with durable power of attorney to make medical decisions for you."

The horror of his words cut into me, stopping my breath. When I could breathe I had to ask the hardest question I've ever asked anyone in my life. "Did she give me an abortive medication?"

"She believed you'd forgo any drugs that would terminate a possible pregnancy."

Tears flowed. His words blessed and wounded me at the same time. I couldn't reconcile the two realities.

On the one hand, I did not take a medication that would have aborted a possible pregnancy, which is what I'd have chosen. On the other, I could possibly be pregnant.

"Hey, hey," he said, shushing me, wiping my tears and kissing the tips of my fingers. "Carly didn't think you were raped. You know she's right about everything."

I couldn't even laugh at his all too true assessment of my sister's ego. "I'm fertile, Jazz. If he . . . I could be pregnant by that slug. Oh, my precious God." I wailed my prayer.

Jazz folded me into himself. "Shhh. It's okay, love. It's okay. He's not the one you're going to have a baby with. God knows he's not."

I sobbed and sobbed in his arms as the warmth of the morphine spread through my body, seeping through the pain, and my weeping subsided. Everything grew hazy. "What if Carly is wrong, and he raped me? I've been begging God to let me have a baby. What if this is how I'll get one, Jazz? How could I raise it? What would I tell people?"

"It wouldn't be his baby."

"What do you mean?" I could feel myself about to float away, the morphine surging in gentle waves through my body.

"If you're pregnant we'll tell everyone it's *our* baby. Over time, we'd come to believe it." His voice sounded far away now. "Do you hear me, Bell? It will be our baby.

Yours and mine. But I think God has a better way for us. I'm almost sure of it. You'll just have to trust me on that."

Yours and mine.

The words echoed in my head, mingled with Scripture.

I am my beloved's, and my beloved is mine.

I squeezed Jazz's hand and drifted off to sleep, dreaming of Ma Brown and her slave mother, Aimee.

> *You are blessed, daughter, and you will heal from this, too, as your grandmother's grandmothers healed of many violations so many seasons ago— on slave ships and in cotton fields, in plantation big houses. You are strong, my namesake, Amanda Bell Brown. You will triumph in the Lord, as I did, and my mother, and her mother. I have prayed for you that your faith fail not. Believe it.*
>
> *Let the weak say, "I am strong."*
>
> *In my dream I said to Ma Brown, "I am strong."*

chapter
twenty-nine

I WAS RELEASED from the "U" two days later, and sent home with a police escort—the handsome protector of my reputation and virtue—Jazz Brown: lieutenant, detective extraordinaire, friend, and husband—at least in the minds of the doctors and nurses at the hospital.

He'd gotten me a new set of apartment and office keys, though I refused to allow him to get and pay for new locks for me. I doubted that would be necessary. I didn't want new locks anyway. I wanted to go home and find my life as it used to be—before young men and women were murdered by strychnine-infused communion or burned in fiery apocalyptic destruction.

Although most of my memory returned, I still couldn't remember all of Gabriel's brutal assault. That, to me, was a mercy.

I just wanted a normal life again.

I think Jazz did, too. He took one look at me and, like he did that first night we met, lifted me off my feet and carried me up the three flights of steps to my apartment. He grunted and sweated as he got closer to that third flight, and I showed him no mercy—teased him, in fact. "You're going to have to work out if you plan on making a habit of this."

"Hey, I can hang with you," he puffed. "However, you might want to consider moving to a place with an elevator."

"You're not going to suggest that I lose weight?"

"I may be crazy, but I'm not stupid."

"So this is how you work off all those Krispy Kreme doughnuts?"

"I'm a Dunkin' Donuts kind of guy."

We laughed as we reached my door. He was a little out of breath, but placed me gently on my feet.

I nudged him. "You remember what happened the last time you carried me up the stairs?"

"Yeah. You asked me if I believed in magic."

"Do you?"

He grinned and gazed down at me. "No. I believe in God. And you'd better not kiss me because I made all kind of bargains with the Lord when I thought you were dead. We are not going to mess up."

"Who said I was going to kiss you, Mr. Arrogant?"

"I don't trust you."

"You don't trust *me*? What kind of damage could I do?"

He looked at me incredulously. "Don't even get me started on that. Now, would you like to go in or stay here and chitchat?"

"I'd like to go in."

He paused. "Maybe you can give me just one little kiss."

"Be strong in the Lord and in the power of His might," I teased.

"So, now *you* want to be good? Now *you* want to preach?" He placed the key in the door and opened it for me. He let out a stream of expletives that would ensure his need to go back and do a little more bargaining with God.

I peered around him. Written across my living room wall, in large red letters, were the crudely written words "You belong to me."

chapter
thirty

JAZZ SLAMMED THE DOOR closed before I could go in, and wasted no time getting his Sig Sauer from his shoulder holster. He also took out his cell phone and handed it to me.

"Call 911, and get back downstairs. I'm going in to see if it's clear."

I grabbed that man and locked lips with him so fast that it made my head whirl.

Or maybe it was the head injury.

"Oh, now you want a kiss?" Jazz shook his head. "You know what? I can't handle you at all. You are completely out of control."

"I'm scared. I wanted to kiss you in case we die."

"Get downstairs, woman." He crossed himself, saying, "God help me."

I left, dialing 911 because we really did need God's help, and the police.

I heard him open my apartment door and yell, "Police. Come out with your hands up." Then a shot fired, a thud, and quiet.

I know. He told me to stay back, but honestly, people were shooting in there.

I turned around, moving as fast as my sore legs would carry me. I stepped inside the apartment as quietly as I could manage. My heart thudded so hard I could feel it in my throat. Again, I saw my new wall mural. *He wrote that with my thirty-dollar-a-tube lipstick.* I knew shock and fear can make a person think strange things. That was my strange thought.

Jazz lay on the floor—alive, thank God. My attention was quickly diverted to more important matters. He clutched his thigh and grimaced in pain.

"You've been shot," I said, louder than I intended.

"Yeah, and I don't think it was Benny Hinn this time."

He still held his .38. I snatched the Sig from him before he could stop me.

"Are you nuts, Bell?" he hissed.

Apparently I was. I headed toward my bedroom, still weak, my head throbbing, and Jazz scrambling after me.

I wasn't Catholic, but I crossed myself, too.

God help me, indeed.

chapter
thirty-one

A ND LEAD US *not into temptation, but deliver us from evil.*

I had a new appreciation for the Lord's Prayer. *And* for the Twenty-third Psalm.

Yea, though I walk through the valley of the shadow of death, I shall fear no evil.

My heart beat like a machine gun firing. I was scared to death, but if Gabriel was in my bedroom, I was going to stop his reign of terror if it killed me.

But Lord, please don't let it kill me.

As I walked into my bedroom I heard a click, then a strange girl/man's voice, "I knew you'd return to me."

I glanced at my closet. It was open, and I could see a pair of feet hanging out.

What a surprise.

Gabriel sat in my closet, tied up and gagged among

my work suits and shoes. Susan Hines, however, stood in the corner, packing more than my decorative bean pod. She had on a hideous white, sequined Elvis jumpsuit, her red hair chopped off in a style my mother would say made her look like a truck driver. She sported awful sunglasses—the kind the King of Rock and Roll loved. I found it disturbing how easily she pointed her gun at my head. I could just see my mother at my funeral, wagging her finger at me, tsk-tsk-tsking, and saying, "I told you not to work with crazy people."

Susan's voice brought me back to the present. "I don't want to hurt you, Amanda," she said in her fake man voice.

"Then you might want to point that gun away from me."

"I didn't hurt your friend, and I won't hurt you."

"You shot him."

"I could have killed you both. I heard you when you opened the door."

"I know you heard me." I'd spoken too loud on purpose. I'd wanted whoever was in my place to know that I'd arrived. It was me they wanted, not Jazz. "But you didn't shoot me." I took a chance and hoped I'd called this next part right. "What do you want from me, *Gabriel*?"

She nodded, as if she knew we had an understanding. "Put the gun down, Amanda."

Suddenly my visions of heroism returned to the realm of fantasy where they rightfully belonged. I lowered the gun to my side; after all, I didn't want to let go of all the power I might have. Maybe I could distract her from blowing my head off *and* keep Jazz's gun by asking her probing questions like "Why is Gabriel tied up in my closet?"

"He is not Gabriel."

Okay, take it easy.

"Why is *that man* tied up in my closet?"

"Because he is evil. He is an imposter."

Good answer, albeit understated.

I needed to see if Susan's psychosis obliterated her sense of self, or if she was still hanging on. I was careful not to call her name yet. "You said you loved him."

"I do love him," her girl/man voice cracked, "but he hurts. The real God is love."

Good. Susan is still fighting in there somewhere.

I nodded toward the man sitting on top of my pumps, including the blue suede Donna Karans. That whole "don't step on my blue suede shoes" thing wasn't lost on me, but who has time to chuckle at irony when they're about to be killed by a psychotic Elvis impersonator *impersonator*? I took another chance at reaching the real Susan. "That fake Gabriel *does* hurt. Did he hurt you?" I kept the Sig Sauer at my side. I didn't dare point it at her. Not yet.

"He hurt all of us: Jonny, Damon, Elisa, Catherine, and Faith."

I wanted to see how much she knew. "Who is Catherine?"

"Catherine belongs to me. She is with the children. We're going to go to her when we are done here. The imposter told me Faith is dead—he killed her in the apocalypse."

"What about Beryl?"

"Beryl is dead, too, but I don't care. She was evil like he is." She jerked her head toward Gabriel.

Susan truly was, as Jazz would say, a nutjob, but I had to agree with her. Beryl *was* evil.

"The imposter told me that when he saw that you and Elisa were gone, he knew you'd called the police. So he gave the women the sacrament, and locked them in the house. But he was too big of a coward to stay and die with them. They are in hell because he took their lives." She gave Gabriel a withering stare. "He is not God. I saw that when he started to hurt the babies."

I needed to keep talking to the Susan who wasn't presently the King of Rock and Roll, though I still didn't think she was ready for me to call her by name.

Be careful. She's already shot Jazz.

God help me.

I also prayed that God would keep Jazz out of harm's way. I couldn't hear what Jazz was doing, but somehow I knew he was watching us, waiting for the right moment. At least I hoped he was. "You're right. He is not God. How did he hurt the babies?"

"He said he was loving them, but it hurt them. He said they wouldn't feel it, because it does not yet appear what they shall be. I'm going to free them. You, too, because you wanted to help me. We're all going to paradise."

"Did you write on my wall?" *With my good lipstick?*

"Yes, Amanda. You are mine. Today, you will be with me in paradise."

I *so* did not want to go anywhere with Susan. "In paradise?"

"Yes. Like Jonathan and Damon. They had communion with me, and now they are in paradise waiting for me to return. I am their God. I am the true messenger. *I* am Gabriel."

While I was glad to see she'd had a verbal breakthrough, and was now speaking with no apparent hesitation, it was clear to me that she was also experiencing a serious bout of complicated bereavement. It happens when a person grieves the loss of someone so profoundly that they become the person they lost in their mind. She grieved the loss of the Gabriel she once loved, and then she became him; only, in her mind, she was a better version of him. She was also angry with him, not to mention suffering from posttraumatic stress syndrome, not to mention psychotic. I felt so sorry for her. I really did, but I didn't think it was in my best interest to partake of the communion she was knocking people off with.

She came over to me, still pointing the gun in the general direction of my head. It occurred to me that perhaps I'd made a big mistake confronting someone who had just shot a man and killed two people.

"This imposter," she said, pointing with her free hand toward Gabriel, "came to get you. He had your purse and your keys, but I was watching out for you. I've been watching you since I left the Rock House."

I shuddered, feeling weak from exerting myself so much after being in the hospital for days. Not to mention feeling weak from the freaky notion that someone had been stalking me.

She came closer, still pointing the gun at my head. She stank of the same chemical odor Gabriel's house reeked of. I scanned her face and eyes to confirm it. In a flash of anger I thought, *Man, if she's been smoking crank in my apartment, I sure don't appreciate it.* True to the drug energizing her, she rattled on in her imitation Gabriel voice. "You are kind and good, so I knew you would look for Susan. I hid in the woods behind the house. I saw when you went in. I stayed all night waiting for you."

She began jumping up and down all over my bedroom. "I am God. I am God. I am God." I could feel goose bumps ripple over my flesh. *Stay cool, Bell. Nice and easy. Don't let her see how scared you are.*

She needs a mother.

Whether that thought was instinct or a little bit of wisdom from above, I couldn't be sure.

What would you say to her if she were your daughter? The words "your daughter" brought a stab of pain, sharp and penetrating. *My daughter.*

I mentally shook myself. *Don't think about the baby now, Bell. Play Mommy to this lost girl.*

How would I know how to be a mother? I never got the chance. My gut knotted when I thought of it. I forced my brain to focus. I spoke softly, hoping a little piece of Susan would hear me. "Susan, sweetheart, what else happened? Tell me, honey."

She stopped bouncing and slowly turned to me.

My legs trembled. I hoped I hadn't said too much. "What else, Susan?"

My tender voice seemed to soothe her—the poor, love-deprived soul. What had happened to her? Had he lured her to his house with empty promises like Adam's? Or had he or his flunkies snatched her off the street, like Elisa? Whatever the case, I had the feeling that Susan was determined to retrieve the love she had lost by any means necessary.

She lowered the gun. Her shoulders sagged, as if the weight of the gun *and* the Elvis clothes were too much for her. She took off the King's ugly sunglasses and placed them on top of my chest of drawers.

"I was sleeping in the woods when I smelled the smoke. He ran out of the house and I followed him to his car." She didn't even try to disguise her voice. I had Susan back. But I didn't know how long she would stay.

She laughed, an empty, shallow sound. "I caught up with him and told him I still wanted to be with him."

"And what did he say?"

"He said he would think about it. He told me I would go through a period of testing. If I passed, and am truly his, I can be with him. He told me that you belong to him, too. He was coming for you. He had your purse and your keys."

"Why didn't he take my Love—my car?"

"He didn't want the police to find him in a stolen car. He said they wouldn't understand that he is God."

"That man told you all of this."

"Yes."

She'd responded well to my questions, and even let the gun hang to her side, but she hadn't let it go. *It's not over, Bell. Not until you get that gun from her. Don't rush.*

"What happened then, sweetheart?" I managed a smile for her.

"I brought him here in my car, and it pleased him that I was obedient and told him where you live. I pleased him in every way he wanted. He said he might take me back."

She pleased him in every way he wanted? I reminded myself to buy new sheets . . . a new bed . . . maybe a new apartment.

"He told me he wanted to start over. Only, instead of seven, maybe it could be the three of us reigning together. He said we'd be the Trinity. But then he got mad at me, and . . ." Her voice dropped off, and she squeaked like a small animal. Tears welled in her eyes. "He punched me." With her left hand she touched her sequin-covered stomach. "I'm going to have his baby." Tears trailed down her face. "He is evil, and he must die."

"Oh, sweetheart," I said, and I meant it. She, Elisa, myself, we belonged to the same awful club—the three of us trapped in heart-stripping grief.

I pulled my thoughts away from that truth and focused on another: I had to get her to give me the gun. The crank made her unpredictable.

"Susan, how did you overpower him?"

"He was coming down off his high. He had to sleep, and I convinced him to trust me. I took care of him here, and we waited for you to come home."

I looked into her face. She was somebody's little girl, looking tiny in the Elvis Presley jumpsuit that sagged off her body.

"He wanted to get high. You had some pain pills in your medicine cabinet so I gave him what you had."

Five pills left over from having a wisdom tooth removed.

"He went to sleep, and I tied him up and took his gun."

Smart, crazy, and fortunate: a bad combination.

"He told me what he did to you. I waited so you could kill him," she said, like a little kid happy to offer up her own great treasure to another more deserving.

My mind urged me not to buy into this, but her words clutched my heart, now pounding wildly in time with my ragged breathing . . . *You . . . could . . . kill . . . him.*

Kill him.

Kill him.

Kill him.

I could feel my pulse in my throat. The two small words now seemed incarnate. They'd grown arms to grab me . . . push me . . . pull me . . . *where?*

Where you've been afraid to go for seven years.

Those words "kill him" pushed my feet deep into my plush carpet, electrifying me with cold, hard hate. Like the shattering screech of an animal about to take its prey, those words tore through me, hungry for release.

Kill him.

I rocked back on my heels, trying to deny my urgent need to pounce on him . . . on Adam. The dizzying thoughts assaulted me. I felt drawn toward something stronger than myself. Susan looked wild-eyed and nervous. The gun trembled in her hands.

"Susan," I said, trying to restrain the monster inside me that was struggling to be free. I drew upon the Mommy voice, keeping it steady, hoping it would help calm both of us. "I'm so sorry you've suffered so much. Come here, sweetheart." I kept Jazz's gun at my side, its muzzle pointing to the floor. I took the biggest risk of all. "Come to Mama," I said. She walked slowly into my opened arm.

I stroked what was left of her red, ragged hair and shushed the sobs racking her small shoulders. "Give me the gun," I whispered to her. Susan didn't protest, nor did she surrender her weapon. I thought I'd try to gain a little more leverage.

"I want you to give me the gun, and then we'll do what we have to do to the imposter." I knew what I'd said was vague. It had to be.

"I can't give it to you, Mama; I'm scared."

"I know you are. You can trust me, Susan, honey. I have never hurt you. I want to help."

"But I need to rid the world of this vermin," she said. She kept her head nestled in the crook of my neck and offered a halfhearted gesture toward Gabriel.

Almost there.

"You know what, honey? I think you sent your friends to paradise to protect them."

She pulled away from me, and her eyes widened as she nodded. "I did. I did."

"I think you should tell the imposter how you feel."

She looked confused. "Tell *him*?"

"Yes. Absolutely. You don't want to go to paradise carrying that kind of baggage."

I sounded like Dr. Phil on LSD. "He's tied up in the closet. He can't hurt you. Tell him how you feel."

"Are you sure?" she asked, her voice her own again, tiny and vulnerable.

"He can't hurt you. Look at him. He's completely vulnerable. Harmless. He can't even talk to you. Tell him, Susan. It's okay. You can trust me. You don't want to go to paradise with someone you don't trust, do you?"

She shook her head no, and I drew her closer into my embrace. I clasped my hand around the gun. She loosened her grip and surrendered it to me.

I tucked the gun into the waist of my pants, trembling because the hardest part was over.

I walked her to my closet. "Tell the man how he hurt you."

She cleared her throat and looked down at him. "You hurt me. You hurt my insides, and you beat me up."

Me, too, my heart cried in recognition.

I chastised myself. *Don't think of yourself right now. This isn't about you.* "Keep telling him."

"I trusted you. I just wanted to be one of God's children, and you said you would help me be one."

Me, too.

I couldn't seem to shake that niggling thought. I heard Jazz creep into the room. "Keep going, Susan."

She kicked him. "I hate you." Her attention never wavered from him once she started telling him how she felt. *"I hate you,"* she screamed.

Me, too.

"Go on," I urged. I felt Jazz's presence behind me, but I didn't look at him.

Susan continued her tirade. "I wanted you to take care of me and love me, but what you did wasn't love." She kicked him again, and a circle of urine stained the front of his pants.

The sight gave me too much pleasure.

God, have mercy.

Another memory assaulted me.

I lay battered, and my dead baby girl lay as a precious bundle between my legs. She was tiny. I was so badly beaten, I couldn't move. I couldn't pick her up. I see her in the palm of Miriam's hand. My baby. My little girl.

One singular thought sped through my conscious mind.

Kill him.

I would kill him for this.

I realized I'd stopped paying attention to the drama unfolding in front of me. Susan's voice continued on. "I'm going to kill you for all the people you hurt. I'm going to kill you for hurting me, for hurting the first baby you put inside of me."

They could have been my own words. I battled to retain my professional distance. But my own pain had a stronger voice.

Kill him.

Miriam gasped when she picked up my baby. I turned my face away from her. She was so tiny it felt obscene to look at her. She looked like something only God should see.

Susan kicked and shouted, "I hate you. You evil, horrible vermin. I hate you!"

They could have been my own never-uttered words. I hadn't dared to say them aloud, not once in the seven years since I'd left Adam. But they'd stayed with me; "I hate you" seeds, having grown into tall weeds in my soul, choking the good in my life, hiding me in dark corners— away from people, from regular church attendance, and from the abundant life Jesus promised.

Kill him.

Gabriel and Adam merged into one, hateful entity in my mind—both evil to the core. The world *would* be better without them.

Kill him.

I felt Jazz's hand at the small of my back.

Dear God, Gabriel was in front of me, but Jazz was behind me. *Choose. Death or life.* Every dark desire I had so skillfully suppressed came to the surface. I pointed Jazz's gun at my tormentor's head. Susan kicked him and kicked him, but he fixed his hard, cold gaze on me. I had only one question.

"Did you rape me?" I asked, my agitated voice piercing, accusing.

He sat perfectly still.

Jazz whispered to me, "Give me the gun, baby."

I ignored him, walked over to Gabriel, and yanked the gag out of his mouth. Susan stood wide-eyed, absorbing this change of roles.

"I asked you a question, you little worm, did you rape me?" *Say yes, so I can kill you.*

"I am the Lord, your God. I am the gate to paradise. I am your God, and you belong to me." His bulging eyes cold as ice.

I pointed the muzzle of the gun right in the middle of his forehead. He didn't flinch. "Wrong answer."

Jazz gently touched my back. "Don't do this, Bell."

I didn't move.

"Drop the gun, Bell."

Susan fell to her knees, rocking back and forth and sobbing.

"I said drop it, Bell. He's not worth it."

"I can't, Jazzy." My hand felt glued to it. My eyes couldn't stray. Gabriel had me locked in. Hate turned the key.

Miriam laid my baby on my bruised, naked chest. My heart shattered. And then I went silent as a grave.

Jazz's bloodstained hands circled my waist. "Give me the gun, baby." But I'd frozen in place, my hands poised to give Gabriel a quick boost into the hereafter.

Jazz took Gabriel's gun from my waistband.

"Bell," Jazz's voice sounded firm, strong. "Give me your weapon. Him, Adam; they've taken too much from you already. Don't let them have the rest of your life."

Forgive us our debts, as we forgive our debtors.

Oh, God. Gabriel. Adam. Both of them pure evil. I can't forgive them.

And lead us not into temptation, but deliver us from evil.

My own refusal to forgive the men or myself—all of it was evil. How could I have known when I prayed that simple prayer at the crime scene that I needed to be delivered from the evil within me as well?

My finger itched to pull the trigger. To kill the evil in front of me, to kill the evil in my life.

"You killed my baby."

"I didn't rape you," he said, his voice clear, authoritative. "First you must fear me. Then you must love me."

"You killed her."

My great-grandmother's image flashed into my

mind. Once, she'd told me a story her mother had told her. Aimee was in the kitchen shelling green beans. The master of the house came in to where she was working and made his evil intentions clear. They were alone, and she had no one but God to protect her. He yanked her up from her chair, and his intentions became reality. A knife lay inches from her fingers. That's all the story that my great-grandmother told me.

Kill him.

I have set before you life and death, blessing and cursing: Therefore, choose life that thou and thy seed may live.

My seed was dead. "You killed her."

"I didn't kill your child. I would have loved her. I would have raised her to know God."

I heard sirens in the distance. It was now or never. Two voices warred within me.

That thou and thy seed may live.

I don't understand what you mean, God.

Jazz spoke softly but urgently into my ear. "Give me the gun, Bell. The police are coming."

His voice was different than theirs. His voice was life.

I said aloud, "Why didn't she ever tell me the rest of the story?"

You know the rest of that story. You are here. What is the end of this *story? What will you choose?*

It was the shepherd talking to me. *My sheep hear my*

voice, and I know them, and they follow me. I knew this verse since my pigtails and laying-on-Ma-Brown's-bosom days.

"Jesus," I told my shepherd, my heart heavy with the sin burden I'd carried for so long. "I let him kill my baby."

I felt like a levee broke inside of me, and the flood of tears I'd denied all these years burst through, destroying me on the spot. I sank to the floor, sick with pain, screaming the only words left in me. "I LET HIM KILL MY BABY. I LET HIM KILL MY BABY. I LET HIM KILL MY LITTLE GIRL."

"He's not Adam, Bell."

"My little girl," I whispered.

Jazz pleaded with me. "I want to hurt Gabriel for what he did to you. God knows I do, but we've got him. He's going to prison. We have to leave his life, as pitiful as it is, to God."

"No," I wailed. I wanted to do something. I wanted to stop what God hadn't.

"Give me the gun now. I don't want to have to hurt you, Bell." Jazz urged—the big, bad cop. He had a job to do, but at the moment I didn't care. I had a job to do, too.

I stayed there on my knees for what felt like an eternity, Gabriel's life in my hands and my life in Jazz's. Thoughts of my unborn baby girl merged with images of

Jonathan and Damon, Elisa, and Susan with her twisted mind; all the death and destruction he caused. I steeled myself to pull the trigger.

The soft but determined voice of my great-grandmother rose up in my soul.

Vengeance belongs to the Lord, baby.

How many times had Ma Brown taught me this lesson when she spoke of unspeakable horrors our people endured, and the special grace God gave us to move on with dignity? How many times had God taught me this lesson? I closed my eyes. *Lord, I'm not strong.* Joel 3:10 rushed to the forefront of my mind.

Let the weak say, "I am strong."

I shook my head, and said weakly, "No."

Choose.

Death or life.

Thy kingdom come, Thy will be done, in earth as it is in heaven.

I thought of all the living my daughter never got to do.

As it is in heaven.

She lives *in me,* my shepherd said.

My daughter lived in Jesus. Would I dare to do the same?

Let the weak say, "I am strong."

"I am strong," I whispered. I didn't feel strong. I felt

faint and dizzy, all the adrenaline draining out of me like a balloon deflating.

I breathed in and out, each inhale and exhale calming me. "I am strong," I said, easing myself away from Gabriel and death, toward my Savior and life.

"Bell?" Jazz spoke gently, his voice caressing me.

"Okay, Jazz," I whispered. "Okay."

I handed him the gun and felt a weight come off more than just my hand. I looked at him, tears flowing down my face. "I'm so sorry. I let Adam kill my baby."

"God forgives you, Bell. I promise you; He does."

"Jesus, please forgive me."

I sobbed into Jazz's chest while he held me. The police burst into the room, but I didn't care. I was busy talking to Jesus.

I cried for a long, long time.

IEUTENANT JAZZ BROWN, who was now my
favorite detective—even more than Columbo—
made me promise that I would promptly deal with
my own issues, and I'd better not miss church. If I didn't
do as promised, I'd have heck to pay. Only he didn't say
"heck."

No one else died because of Gabriel and his mad-
ness. Other than Jazz, no one else was injured. Susan and
Gabriel were on their way to the Washtenaw County
Jail, to begin paying their debts to society and to get the
psychological treatment they both desperately needed.

Jazz was still plenty mad at me and yelled all the
way to the hospital. "You could have been killed—for
the second time this week. Have you no fear? Didn't you
see that I had been shot? Which reminds me, I got shot.
I've been a police officer for half my life—never been

shot—until I met you. Sometimes I can't decide if God sent you my way or the other guy did."

He railed on. "You know what? You're going to follow the rules from now on, so we can be blessed. No touching, *Dr. Brown,* and definitely no kissing. I get kissed by you, and the next thing I know, I'm in love or have a bullet ripping through my thigh. It ain't right. You got me all messed up, Dr. Brown."

"Hey, Jazz."

"That's Lieutenant Brown to you. What is it, Dr. Brown?"

"You can call me Bell."

He stopped yelling and stared at me. "You just gotta win the argument, don't you?" he said.

"Yep," I said.

He smiled that wonderful, beautiful smile. "What am I gonna do with you, woman?"

"You'll think of something." I held his hand.

"No touching," he said.

But I held it anyway. Right now he was my friend. Later we'd figure out the rest.

Pocket Readers
Group Guide
discussion questions

1. The Lord's Prayer is prominently featured in this book. Is your experience with this prayer similar to Bell's—rote memory? How do you interact with this classic prayer?

2. Bell and Carly have very different lifestyles. How do you deal with other Christians who may not have the same values you have?

3. Bell is Evangelical and Jazz is Catholic, yet they have a strong friendship. Do you have friends who are of different religions and denominations? How do you deal with your differences?

4. The attraction between Bell and Jazz is undeniable. Do you think they deal with their feelings appropriately? What would you do if you were in their situation?

5. Jazz's conflict about remarriage after divorce keeps him from pursuing a deeper relationship with Bell. What is your opinion of divorce and remarriage? Do you think Jazz should move on or remain single?

6. Bell says that at her church, the Rock House, God is like a pal. Do you think this attitude is too casual? Why do you think Bell would choose a church like this after her experience with Adam? What is your idea of a healthy church?

7. When Bell goes to Gabriel's house to find Susan, she experiences a painful consequence. Should she have gone? What should she have done differently?

8. Bell experiences several traumatic life lessons, yet she continues to have faith. What helps you hold on to God, even in times of suffering?

9. Bell never grieved the loss of her daughter. What would you do to begin to heal from a profound loss? What support do you think you would need?

10. In the end, Bell discovers her anger is deeper than she realized. Her rage could have led her to make the worst possible decision. How could she have handled her feelings differently when she confronted Gabriel?

bell brown's
five ways to know if your boyfriend is a nutjob

1. Instead of asking you to be his girlfriend, he asks you to be his disciple.

2. His term of endearment for you is "sweetheart." He likes it when you call him "master."

3. His idea of a romantic date is taking you home and showing you his collection of guns and explosives.

4. Over a candlelit dinner, he takes your hand, looks deeply into your eyes, and asks you to be one of his wives.

5. Instead of Neighborhood Watch keeping an eye on his place, it's watched by ATF.

author interview
a chat with claudia mair burney

Your book is dedicated to your great-grandmother, Amanda Bell Brown. Why did you name your heroine after her?

My first memories of grace and holiness are mostly of my maternal great-grandmother. Ma Brown, like many old black women, was quite the mystic. She was wise, profound, and very kind to me. I remember so clearly the sound of her ambling down the hallway with her walker. Thump, shoosh, thump, shoosh. She'd be humming a hymn or praying. If she stumbled, her favorite expletive—which I won't say—would come tearing out of her mouth. She was just like the saints: holy, and quirky, too! She lived in a time when there were so few opportunities for women of color. She couldn't make her own dreams come true in the way I can, so I loaned her a bit of mine. I also wanted to keep her name in this world a little bit longer and to share, through a very thin veil of fiction, some of my memories.

How did Bell's story come to you?

Quickly, and after a publisher asked me what I had! It's true. But I always wanted to write a mystery, and I wanted it to be fun. I also wanted it to feature characters like me: flawed. I wrote the kind of book I wanted to read, with a heroine like me.

How did you become a writer?

I was in the fifth grade and found a scrap of a play on the floor in the hallway at school. It was love at first scene. I started writing plays and performing them in front of my teachers. After that I told stories to my girlfriends. Poor Keysha! I'd bend her ear for hours, spinning novels right out of my mouth. I learned later how to write things down. I still can't believe I get money for this.

Who inspires you?

That's an easy one. I actually wear a ring that says, "I am my beloved's; my beloved is mine." That would be Jesus, lover of my soul. Ken, my husband and best friend, is a close second. My family and my writer girlfriends—published and unpublished—are amazing, too.

What's your favorite book?

My fiction pick is Ron Hansen's Mariette in Ecstasy. *Nonfiction is without a doubt Eugene Peterson's* The Message.

If you weren't a writer, what would you be doing?

I don't understand the question. Is there something else I can do?

Famous last words?

"Pray diligently. Stay alert, with your eyes wide open in gratitude" (Colossians 4:2, The Message). *The Lord's Prayer is also a great option.*

Death, Deceit & some smooth jazz

an amanda bell brown mystery
book two

I HAD TO GIVE UP JAZZ. Not the music; the man.

Now I had Amos, and we were going to "bond." I stood in the middle of my living room holding him. I'd put on my favorite pajamas—the midnight blue pair Carly had gotten for me from Victoria's Secret. They were modest, even if they did have the VS logo on the breast pocket. Cut in the style of men's pajamas and a size too big, they had the effect of looking charmingly baggy on me. I didn't even need a robe with them. Perfect for bonding with the one you love. I could tell Amos liked them.

Amos is my new sugar glider.

I know, nobody knows what a sugar glider is. When the woman at the pet store first mentioned one, I thought she was talking about a kitchen accessory. I hadn't wanted to let her in on my woeful ignorance of household utensils, so I told her a sugar glider sounded intriguing. And intriguing he was.

When she led me over to his cage, I first noticed his peepers. He had big, black, round eyes that reminded me of my pastor and ex-boyfriend Rocky's "I can make you do anything with these" puppy eyes. Don't judge me. Not for that. Having a pastor who is your ex-boyfriend sounds a lot worse than it is. Besides, I've got plenty of *real* issues for you to choose from.

Amos was roughly the size of a Beanie Baby and looked like a cross between a tiny gray squirrel, a skunk, and a kangaroo—with the face of a bat. Kinda.

I never would have gotten a pet if my mentor and spiritual father, Dr. Mason May, hadn't recommended it. I'd gone to see him earlier that day, whining endlessly about being manless, being childless, having endometriosis, and about my grief over my eggs, which were aging faster than my mother said *I* was. I got frustrated while venting to Dr. May and threatened to have an intrauterine insemination procedure done with some stranger-donor's little soldiers. But Dr. May—Pop, as I called him—stopped me right there and told me I should pray about the matter some more and buy a pet. That's how I ended up at the exotic pet store near my house, feeling guilty about my baby lust and purchasing something that looked like one of the Crocodile Hunter's furry friends. And we had to bond.

How pathetic am I?

Amos didn't seem very prickly. A little standoffish, yes, but nothing that should have stood in the way of us getting cozy with each other. My initial mistake: I should have put together his cage first. But no, being a psychologist, I wanted to get straight to the attachment process. That's important. I reached into his little Exotic Petz cardboard box—the kind with the round peepholes—and picked him up. I could feel him freeze, and I do know body language. I figured it was just nerves bothering him, so I pressed on with the bonding process. Amos didn't complain.

We crossed to my couch. Jazz once described my apartment as "shabby chic meets Africa." Fair enough, I suppose. The ambience I'd created with my eccentric flea-market finds gave my home a comfy, livable feel. I'd often paint my treasures in hues with whimsical-sounding names like old lace, seafoam, and dusty rose. The walls were a sunny buttercup—I'd called it ocher just months ago, but that was when I'd felt more earthy and African-inspired. Something had happened in my soul, and I'd begun to feel more romantic and feminine. I think it was falling in love with Jazz. Since then I'd given away most of the masks that used to dot the walls and most of my Nigerian baskets. I was trying to make room for Addie Lee Brown paintings and sculptures. But I'd kept a few wood pieces I loved, and I still had all of my textiles—bright, colorful Kente cloth and a few mud-cloth pieces—to add warmth and texture. Candles cast a soft glow in the rooms and sweetened the air with rose, vanilla, and jasmine.

I took a seat on the couch and propped my feet on the coffee table, with Amos perched somewhat stiffly on my lap. I thought I'd better tell him a little bit about myself.

"I'm your new mom, Amanda Bell Brown. I'm named after my paternal great-grandmother and favorite diva in the whole wide world. Most people call me Amanda, and some even call me Dr. Brown, but you can call me Bell. That's reserved for the people who love me best."

Amos didn't say anything. I figured sugar gliders weren't very talkative. No problem. I'd fill the silence between us.

"I got you because I need someone to love. I hate to sound like one of those thirty-five-year-old career women who realize too late that they forgot to get pregnant. It wasn't really like that. I had a lot of hurts, but I don't want to talk about that. The point is"—I stroked his short fur, which made him recoil—"it seems the only prospect I have for marriage is my pastor, Rocky. That would be too weird; you'll see what I mean if you ever meet him. And then there's Jazz . . ."

Just saying his name gave me chills. How fine was he? Too fine. Fine like God didn't make him out of the dust of the earth that the rest of us mere mortals were made of. Jazz was made of something sparkly and inspiring. He intoxicated me. No, he made me feel, as Aretha Franklin sang, like a natural woman. But it could never work. He had issues. He kept using the word "unavailable." Not that he had a woman, mind you. Just an ex and a belief that he couldn't remarry. And God bless him, he had too much integrity to lead a woman on. Unfortunately for me, I didn't want anyone but him. And he'd never want me. Not really.

Even Amos didn't seem to be into me. I thought for a moment that, instead of Amos, I should have gotten a rocking chair and a pair of Birkenstocks and resigned myself to a depressed, childless spinsterhood. I told Amos, "I stopped seeing Jazz one month, two days, and three hours ago. I miss him. Now Christmas is coming."

I looked around my place, void of any yuletide cheer. *Well, Bell, that was smart, thinking of Christmas.* All I needed was to get some poisoned eggnog and put myself out of my misery. I rubbed the top of Amos's head. "I guess it's just you and me."

Either that head rub didn't please Amos, or he didn't like Christmas. He made a hissing sound like he was exhaling smoke from Hades.

The saleswoman hadn't said anything about evil hissing, and I hadn't read the manual.

Then he added to the hissing a raised paw—a gesture that did not look loving at all. I didn't have to be an astute observer of body language to see that I had myself a little problem.

I was on the couch, so I didn't have the luxury of backing away slowly. I hoped if I cooed and touched him affectionately, he'd relax and see that I was a "good touch" person. But when I gave his silken gray fur, with an adorable black stripe right down his back, just a tiny stroke, the rotten little stinker jumped on my sleeve and tried to kill me.

Our bonding session turned straightaway into *When Sugar Gliders Attack*.

The saleslady hadn't mentioned anything about aggression.

Amos scratched, bit, and clawed my pajamas like a veritable Tasmanian devil. I screamed. My pathetic manless life flashed before my eyes. I could just see my mother at my funeral, talking smack about me because I'd purchased, of all things, a *sugar glider*. "I always knew that child didn't have good sense," she'd lament.

Someone pounded on the door.

I leaped from the couch, still screeching, Amos still clinging and assaulting. While the vicious creature shredded my jammies and skin, I managed to unbolt my locks—a dead bolt and a spare, thanks to Jazz—and snatched my door open. I didn't bother to ask, "Who is it?"

There stood none other than the man my heart beat

for, Lieutenant Jazz Brown, homicide detective. He had his pistol drawn, ready to protect my honor. I noticed, after swiftly taking in his general gorgeousness, four fresh, angry slashes on his face.

In an instant he took in my situational challenge, grabbed the arm that was being attacked, and started pumping it like he was trying to milk me.

I screamed louder.

"Stop all that noise!"

"What? Are you going to arrest me for disturbing the peace?" I yanked my arm away from him as hard as I could, which had the effect of hurling poor Amos across the living room. He landed with a thud on the couch, right in the middle of the cushions.

I hurried over to the couch with Jazz on my heels. My arm ached and throbbed from the battery it had taken.

Amos was as still as a stone.

"Oh, no," I wailed. "I think I killed him."

"Good." Jazz put his gun back in his shoulder holster. He walked to my door and locked it. "You shouldn't open the door like that, Bell," he barked. "I could have been anybody."

"It's *not* good if I killed him. I'm supposed to love, nurture, and protect him." I touched one of many tender spots on my arm. My motherly instincts hadn't kicked in all the way. I glared at Amos. "The little beast."

"Are you okay?" Jazz took my arm in his hands. He shot a look at Amos and shook his head. "I can't believe you chose this thing for a pet." He gently pulled back the wreckage that was my sleeve.

I ignored his comment and took in his perfect beauty, his sculpted and slender body. He was wearing one of his trademark suits—the brown one—and the effect of the color, contrasted with his creamy skin tone, made him look as good as a Hershey's Hug. He wore no overcoat, which was odd for a cold December night, but so was the fact that he was wearing his suit so late into the night. I didn't ponder it too much. Except for the ugly scratches and pinched expression, his white-chocolate face was as fine as ever. Yum. *Lord, have mercy on my Jazz-starved soul.*

I felt awful for poor Amos. What kind of mother was I, ogling Jazz while my baby could be lying there dead? I wondered if Jazz would arrest me for cruelty to animals. Looking at his relieved expression, I figured not. Still . . . I glanced at my fallen furry friend. "Jazz! He's so still."

"I'd be still, too, if you threw me across the room," Jazz said. "We need to take care of your arm, Bell."

But my parental guilt was growing like mold on a loaf of bread in summer. I started wringing my hands, like my mother did whenever I cut my hair. "Amos is hurt the worst. What kind of mom would I be if I tended to my wounds without making sure Amos is taken care of?"

"Bell, you're not his mom, and he's probably dead. Now, let's get some antibiotic ointment on you before you get an infection."

I had images of Amos on life support. *Beep, beep, beep*. "Maybe it's not too late. *Do* something, Jazzy. He could be getting brain damage."

Jazz looked at me like he *didn't* actually get paid to protect and serve. "What am I supposed to do?"

"Do CPR on him or something." Honestly, I was becoming more histrionic by the moment.

He laughed right in my face. "Now you're trippin'."

My maternal hysterics compelled me to yank on the sleeve of his suit jacket. "He's unconscious. You have to help him."

"I'm a homicide detective, not a vet. I can, however, shoot him in the head."

"Please, please, puh-leeeze, Jazz."

"You're crazy."

When begging failed, I progressed to physical assault. I started hitting him with limp-wristed girl slaps all over his chest while shouting in a staccato rhythm with the blows, "How. Can. You. Be. So. Cruel?"

Jazz tried to stop my flurry of blows to his torso. "Bell, stop it."

I didn't stop.

"Woman, I said . . ."

I kept it up.

"*Okay,*" he bellowed, with a few added expletives. "What is up with all the violent women tonight?"

So it was a woman who'd scratched him? Interesting.

Jazz shot a very dirty look in my direction and dropped to his knees. He reached out his hand and gingerly shook Amos. . . .

Claudia Mair Burney